RAVEN
AND THE BOOK OF KNOWLEDGE

By

Rachel McJury

conFAB Books
Scotland

Printed in UK

First Printing, 2021

ISBN: 978-1-8382052-3-2

conFAB Books
Glasgow, Scotland

Cover Design by: Danielle Banks
www.daniellebanks.co.uk

Printed by: Mixam, Watford, WD25 7GS UK

www.confab.org.uk

Grateful acknowledgement to
Dee, Mary and Alison

Chapter One

I awake to her scent, laden with our love-making, rich with sun and sand, tinged with traces of the oil she uses to soften and moisten. For a moment, I surrender to it, am inside it and there is nothing else. Then I catch myself and it is gone. I tumble into unease and discomfort and, before I know it, I am peeling my flesh away from hers, softly, so as not to disturb her slumbers, but with a subtle urgency. I will not allow myself such peace. I grab a light silk shawl and throw it over me in a careless attempt to hide my modesty. Sabby, my ever-faithful wolf companion, lifts one lazy eye as she watches me tread lightly over the rugs and cushions to the entrance of the Bedouin tent.

There is nothing but golden sand in every direction for as far as the eye can see. A light breeze makes the all-consuming heat a fraction more bearable. I watch the surface of the sand dance with the wind. It is a comfort when there is little in the way of solace in these barren lands. Farah knows only this space, so it is comfort for her, but inside me is a yearning to be with trees, to hear water flow, smell rain seduce the land. Being here is a suspension, a place to pause, not to live, but live we do.

At first Sabby grew sick. The heat consumed all of her vivacity. I could not see a solution, I was so consumed by guilt and fear; to have brought her to the land of sky and sun when she was built to survive the longest, harshest winter not the longest hottest summer. I was afeared I had risked her life, again. How could I treat one I loved so dearly this way? Yet the elders knew exactly what to do. They cut her coat accordingly and she looks fine and handsome with her fur trimmed close to her skin. In the day she seeks shade and sleep. At night we take to the dunes. I shift and wolf and raven, the forever friends, roam the emptiness. It is strange to find your way and your path in a landscape that is constantly changing, yet all alike, to find anchor points that are felt and not seen, sensed and not set.

Each night is a rediscovery, but we are yet to find ourselves lost. We find little in the way of sustenance, but it feeds our souls to feel our bodies part the air in the vast

emptiness. Our wanderings are what I live for, what makes sense of everything. The sky is so big and so full we are on intimate terms with the stars. The night creatures of the desert have grown accustomed to us and accepted us into their lands. It is an honour I recognise but cannot yet feel.

Her breath against my neck recalls me from my reflections.

'Do you see beauty yet?' she asks

It is almost a daily question so that it has become an affectionate joke between us. Always my answer is no and, despite my expectations, it's an answer that comforts her. I smile and shake my head and she wraps her arms around my waist and folds her head into my neck. It is always on the edge of my lips to ask her her meaning, but her contentment and relief in my answer always inspires my silence; I desire to share her peace more than to disturb it. We stand as one, gazing into and at nothing. I am not sure how long we are there but eventually we hear the sound of fires being lit and pots and pans clanging. The temperature has begun to drop and soon Sabby has risen from her slumbers to join us.

It is Farah that breaks our repose as she leaves to join the rest of her tribe in the preparation of the evening meal. Out of the scarcest, simplest ingredients she will create a sumptuous feast and we will join the others in the nightly ritual of a shared meal with all the tribe, after which Sabby and I shall take to our wanderings. We will miss the stories and the songs of the people that have welcomed us as part of their family, but I am not ready to receive such gifts. It is true I speak none of their language, but it is not that that hinders my understanding. When the stars speak, I shall hear, until then I tell myself it is good for Farah to have time with her people without me.

I watch from the entrance to the tent as she dresses. The light catching her skin is a joy I had never imagined. She dresses simply but with the confidence that she needs little to augment her beauty. Sometimes it is as if she is the only thing that makes any sense in the world, as if she is the only thing that has ever made any sense; the dark tan of her skin, the thick blackness of her hair and the endless depths of her deep brown

eyes. She has a grace about her that imbibes everything she does as if nothing can ever cause her any disturbance. But, despite this, she cannot replace what has been lost, and this thought causes a shadow to fall across my being.

For distraction I turn and begin to dress too. I take up my bandages and begin to bind. Here there seems little point such is the dress; my lack of facial hair is more of an issue. Yet binding connects me to all that once was and despite myself I find I still have a need of that. She stops in the doorway, supplies in hand, and observes me wrapping and adjusting, wrapping and adjusting.

'It will be more comfortable without,' she says. I look up and smile at her.

'It is not comfort that is at stake.'

'Here, there is no need to hide.'

I turn away and into myself and in doing so erect an impenetrable wall between us. How can she expect openness when I all I know is secrecy? Why should she want from me what I cannot give? She turns away and I sense her sadness. She will not challenge me. Yet sometimes I seek her anger, seek her frustration. Where is her passion? My irritation affects my binding, it is uneven and uncomfortable. I unbind hastily and unkindly to my own body and throw the bandages into the far corner of the tent. If she so wishes I shall not bind tonight. Tonight, I shall not eat. Tonight, as soon as the sun drops from the sky we shall take to our wanderings. Naked, I sit with Sabby at the entrance to the tent, waiting.

The sun falls quickly from the sky here and many a night I have yearned for the hours of twilight, the in-between time of gentle transition, but tonight I am happy for its speed. As soon as the sun meets the horizon, before the stars have taken on their full glory, we take to the open spaces. I think I am the first Raven to fly the skies of the desert and whilst I sense my raven family in other parts of this land I do not seek them out. Rather I relish my solitude and indulge in my isolation. The moon rises full and fat. Tonight, it fills me, sates me; other nights I resent its permanency, resent it shining on me and all those that have betrayed, all those that have passed. How can it

be so indiscriminate? Does everyone deserve the blessing of the moon?

Tonight, we travel fast, the air is cool and the breeze behind us. We do not consider our distance or direction but follow the pull of the Earth - less trusting in and more not caring where we go. It is the same whichever way we turn so what use choice? Soon we reach a flat plateau I do not recognise. The land is dry and cracked, a river bed with no river.

I sweep down and perch on Sabby's back. I feel a loneliness in the earth, an all-consuming, overriding sense of desolation. It feels as though we are uninvited, unwelcome. This is unhospitable land, but we have been guided here, drawn; what does it want from us? The absolute stillness and quiet is oppressive, yet despite this I find myself shifting back to human form and we walk out into the flat, cracked, bed. It feels like each step on the solid, compact sand rips and tears at my feet. Yet when I look at my soles there is no blood; the skin is intact. I look at Sabby; she is peaceful, but she too takes care when placing her feet. I close my eyes; I want to sing, to shout, anything to break this interminable silence, yet I do not know the sound that can match it. With each step the fire in my belly grows. Why bother taking any steps? Are we going anywhere or is this wandering as aimless as it feels? I can see only flames in my eyes and begin to stumble, to trip. Then I fall to my knees, hitting the merciless earth hard, as I fall into the past.

I hit the deck of the ship with a thud, first onto my knees then, unable to maintain my position, I topple face first onto the unforgiving boards. I awake to find I have been moved to the hold and Sabby and I lie amongst the beasts, for where else would we be? My head is sensitive to sound and movement, my body a quivering jelly inside its skin. I remember little of the night before. I remember ale and fat fists around full tankards, boisterous joking and songs of the sea, but little else. I know little of how we came upon this ship, of why we are here. Then a cold fear washes through my body. Have we been pressganged? Yet why then are we with the beasts and not the

other men? I look about the hold; it is familiar. There is some movement, but it is hard to say if we are at sea.

I motion for Sabby, for her stealth. If this is the ship I think it is then it will take all our skills to escape as soon as we can. I could shift; become a fly on the wall to establish our circumstances, yet since shifting saved me from the gallows I have vowed to only use the gift when there is absolutely no other way. Together we tread gently towards the door. We listen and hear no sound. I try the handle - they have not locked us in. Gently I open the door and before me is the staircase I feared I would find. We are on the Black Gladfly and I fight every memory that rushes to the surface - once we were honoured guests aboard this ship and now we are but prisoners.

There is no sign of anyone; a little gentle laughter and snoring comes from the sailors' mess but otherwise our route is clear. Silently we tread up the stairs; the hatch to the deck is open and sunlight streams down the passage. Still no sound. Tentatively we approach the hatch. I raise my head above; in front of me are two fat, worn boots. I follow their line up to two strong, square legs and a body to meet the smiling eyes of Captain Langan.

'Master Raven, it is well to welcome you aboard our little dinghy once more,' and he offers me his hand to help pull me up out of the hatch. I take a step up, ignoring his words and his gesture. I can see just over the side of the ship. We are far out to sea. I look to Sabby who holds back, no enthusiasm for a reunion. I look to the captain and smile. I reach out to take his hand, then I wrench it back and place it over my mouth. Feigning sickness, I apologise with my eyes and we quickly descend the stairs

In the hold we seek safety with the beasts. I want to run as fast and as far as I can. We have tried so hard to avoid them, to escape their influence. It is weeks now since the hanging, since the rope tightened around my neck. We may not have had a clear plan or any means of delivering a plan, but we did have one very clear intention, to get away, to leave behind all that we knew, all that knew us. To be somewhere else, where the world would be something other than before. In the desperation of our defeat I consider the albatross; could I carry Sabby in my claws long enough for us to reach land? I consider the dolphin; could Sabby ride upon my back long enough? I consider the dragon; I could set fire to the ship as we leave but a fire breathing, flying dragon is not easy to conceal and hard to hide in open view, even though we have lived as a secret all our lives and stealth is our friend. Still, this is not a time that calls for shifting.

I am rendered motionless as the wall I have maintained between myself and my memory comes crashing down. The smells of the ship, the sensation of the rise and fall of the waves, transport me back to a happier time. That first night on the Gladfly and I am ashamed of my innocence. I thought then the world made sense. In my own way I was carrying on my grandmother, the healer's, ways. Working as an agent for the "Society of Historical Spiritual Studies". I laugh at the name, a Society that has such a lofty title, such ambitious aims as to protect and preserve the ways of the earth when the crown seeks to destroy and eradicate all connection with it. I thought myself the hero, part of something important, a spy for the Society that had finally found a place for my gift as shifter. A gift I had been forced to hide all my life.

That first night on the ship, the stars danced in the waves and the beauty of the earth sang to my soul. How I had wanted to share that moment with all who had brought me to that point, with all who I loved. Mary, my first love, Grace and Mother Gray who introduced me to two of my great passions; reading and marchpane. Grandmother, whose endless and unquestioned love guided me through life and through myself better than any mother could have done. Happy times swirl through me, I hear Mary's laughter, smell the comfort of Mother Gray's baking, the feel of books and pages from Grace's library in my fingers, See the look on her face when she showed me the Book of Knowledge, see the smiling face of Grandmother as she admonished Constantine. All before that first night on the Gladfly, all before Stephen and Ben.

It was Constantine, the always adventurer with his irresistible charm, that made the introductions. First myself to myself with my first blood so came his teachings how to inhabit the clothes of man and be safe. For I had never worn a women's dress, and all knew me as boy. Then Jet to myself, the most beautiful black colt who rode with us for but short time but was with us that first night on the Gladfly. Always a man to be first, it was Constantine that introduced us to the Society. We hear the door to the hold open and I curl into Sabby, feigning sleep.

Captain Langan throws down my black leather doublet, fresh linens and hose.

'Do not ask how I manged to retrieve those. It cost a lot and I do not wish to revisit it,' he says, taking a seat on some nearby boxes.

I would stretch and awaken, thank him for their return, but the sight of them stirs inside me a pain, a pain that, for the last two weeks, I have either fought on a minute by minute basis to supress and bury deep within me, or have drowned out with ale and wine. I feel deep sobs erupt inside me and it is all I can do to keep them silenced. Sabby sits up and stretches, then sits clearly and firmly between me and the captain.

'Alright, if it's time you need,' he says, and gets to his feet. At the door he turns back

'It is best to stay on your feet. If you lie down you may not stand again,' and he closes the door behind him.

As soon as he has gone, I sit up and reach for my doublet. I hold it close; it feels as it ever did. I run my hand along the inside; it is there, the coin my grandmother sewed into the lining. This feels more reassuring than I could have imagined. It feels like a tiny piece of permanency in an otherwise fluctuating world, a thread linking me to the past. I hold the doublet to my face and breath in its smells. They are there, a faint trace of Grandmother, a strong flavour of Jet and the undeniable fragrance of Mary all around the collar.

It was on that first quest that I was given the doublet by my mother, not that I knew she was when she gave it or that she has been any kind of mother to me. Yet as soon as I put it on my shoulders, I feel so complete, as if I had never really stood up before. It's rich black leather - the garb of sailors - and it has certainly seen me through some very rough seas, more figurative than actual.

The next night I boarded the Back Gladfly for the first time. I was such a naive fool then, to have trusted without question the guidance of Captain Langan. I thought him so worldly wise and, despite his rugged seafaring manner, understood him to be a man of integrity dedicated to protecting the ways of the earth. Yet he turned out to be just like all the others in the Society, corrupted by his own sense of importance, there not to protect the gifted ones such as I but to exploit us for their own ends. No matter how much they protest their innocence and accuse us of lack of vision, for not understanding the bigger picture, I understand the bigger picture and just how they sit alongside the likes of Stephen and Ben.

Stephen's face, as his pleasure climaxed at my expense, looms large above me and I cower to escape it, the king's man sent to reform and regenerate our little backwater. In the week I had been away on my quest he had claimed the castle as his own, requited my childhood rival Ben Lovell as his right-hand man and condemned Ben's mother. She may have been a nag and a scold, but she did not deserve the degradation, humiliation and brutality she endured at his command. It was but a matter of time before Grace and Mother Gray were ran out of the village, my grandmother hanged for witchcraft and I exposed for the woman in man's clothing that I am. If it were not for my gift I would now be nothing but a rotting body blowing in the wind, left as a reminder to all women what their place should be - three steps behind their husband.

I do not know it, but all the time silent tears have been falling from my eyes. I hold the doublet close to me, curling up into a ball, letting my body wrench and heave with weeping that is muffled by the cloth. I fear the tears will not stop, fear they will fall forever more, but somehow and at some point, there are no more tears to fall, although the pain still lingers. We lie a long time in the stillness, my head empty of thought and feeling. Then, as nightfall withdraws the tiny bit of light in the hold, I rise to my feet and, borrowing water from the beasts, I wash from top to bottom.

Fresh bandages are amongst the linens. It is a bitter sweet pleasure to bind with memories of doing the same in Mary's room, of binding for the first time with Grace, of Constantine's instruction on deportment and speech, as if these memories are being woven into the cloth, a protective layer between me and the world. It is good to feel fresh, clean linen and hose next to my skin. I stand, half my old self, half not. The doublet feels heavy and weighted and I fear I will collapse under its weight as I place it on my shoulders, yet as the leather touches my skin, I feel a part of myself return and, for the first time in a long while, I remember how to smile. I had known it was possible but had forgotten how. I look to Sabby and she is already waiting at the door.

I find the old swagger in my step has returned as we make our way along the passage and up the stairs. I fling open the hatch and we are greeted by a thousand stars and a moon that almost fills the sky. Again, I remember our first time on this ship, our first time at sea, and scorn the innocence and naivety we had then. Still, now I can recognise that familiarity gives us a sense of confidence and experience.

The deck is quiet, just the captain at the wheel whistling quietly to himself. It is a tune I remember, and I fight the anger that rises inside me. How dare he sing such a beautiful tune? It is one of Billy Bird the minstrel's finest and to hear him sing it is to hear your soul sing to your heart. Captain Langan can only slaughter the song as he slaughtered my trust in him. Billy would have a clever quip to bring Captain Langan to his knees, silencing his din, and I recognise, in the chaos of emotions that rage inside me, a yearning for my friend and guide. We knew each other but days, meeting on that first quest but there shall always be a place in my heart for Billy and his incorrigible ways. At least I have found some comfort in memory.

The sails are set, and we make good speed, cutting through the dark, gentle waves. We take our time approaching the wheel, taking in the view, the sea at night both terrifying and comforting in its dark eternity. We reach the wheel and with an exchange of nods we come to stand by the captain. We stand in companionable silence; I feel no companionship with him, but hope I can pretend enough. After a while he offers me the wheel. I look him in the eyes for the first time and smile.

'Thank you, Captain, it is an honour, yet how am I to direct the ship when I know not what direction we travel in?' He looks me in the eye unflinchingly, yet I can see a small glimmer of a smile in his eyes.

'Just hold her steady; to know more would cause unnecessary risk.'

'For you perhaps; still, what you do not tell me the stars will,' I say.

'Then you have no need to ask.'

It is my turn to smile and it is the first shared smile for a long time. He is right, but my knowledge of the stars is limited and not enough to plot our course from our position in relation to them, although I can tell we are heading towards the Africas.

'And am I being rescued or removed?'

'Amounts to the same, does it not?'

'Do both curtail my liberty?'

'We are bound by an agreement with your grandmother; we promised to protect you.'

'And when I no longer need your protection?'

'You cannot ask us to break an agreement.'

'But I can release you from it.'

'And where would you go? There is not a shire in England that is safe, your infamy being as it is. There have already been "sightings" of you all over Europa and the king's men, under Stephen's orders have been dispatched to investigate. We take you to a place where there is enough space and distance in all and every direction, so you may hide in plain sight to your hearts content.'

'And where the crown has no reach?' I say.

'But please release us from the pact we made with your grandmother and we shall withdraw our protection, shall be easier for us.'

'It is a fair night,' I say, and he knows for now I do not have an answer. I do not fear the crown, or my European neighbours but if I release the Society from the pact I become prey for them too. We are in no position to make that choice.

He whistles, and the ship's boy is at his heels in seconds.

'Take our guests to my cabin.'

He turns to us. 'You must be famished, food and drink aplenty await you.'

I bow my head in acceptance and we follow the ship's boy.

Inside the cabin, the maps and charts are laid in clear view, yet the ship's boy does not leave our side, placing himself between us and the plans. The captain has laid on a feast and we devour it all. It's the first decent meal we have had in weeks and our bodies speak louder than our minds. All the time though, there is torment in the background, when the answers to our questions lie so near. After eating we fall into a comfortable lull; the secrets of the charts can wait. We return to the hold and the comfort of sleeping with beasts.

It feels as if my kneecaps have splintered into tiny pieces and the hard desert earth cares little for my pain. I kneel on all fours, the sand as cold and hard as I am hot; I am filled with flame. I hear a rustling and look forward, into the eyes of a Death Stalker scorpion. I sense Sabby beside me, taut and ready to pounce. I freeze; it is as if everything I know about the earth and the beasts has been lost. I am trapped; to move would be fatal. Interminable moments pass, then the scorpion begins to gently move one back leg, then the other, until its whole body is dancing, and I realise he is courting us.

At first there is relief and we drop our guard. It is such a joyful, playful dance, we begin to laugh. Once we have begun, we cannot stop. I do not know when the scorpion leaves us, for soon I am rolling about the earth, holding my sides. Then a cramp in my belly and the tears of joy falling from my eyes turn to tears of pain and I lie prostrate, face down on the ground, my tears flowing into the earth.

I cannot stop; it feels as if I have wept a river, and soon I feel a dampness around me. I look up and a small patch of green has grown where my tears have fallen. I sit up and look around. From beneath the ground water begins to bubble up, underground springs reaching the surface. Soon the water is knee high and I scramble to my feet. Sabby will soon have to swim, so we turn and run, splashing and laughing through the growing river. We reach the bank as the river's depths grow. Instantly plants sprout, and animals appear as if they knew this was going to happen all along. They drink long and deep from the growing waters.

Suddenly there is life where there was none before. It is an unexpected re-introduction to joy. Soon it will be light, and I know, in the cool, before the sun claims the sky, I will lead the tribe to this place of abundance. For all the long nights of our wanderings never before have I thought they could be of use to any but ourselves. It has been a long time since I have felt the pleasure of giving to a people.

The next morning I awake with a start. In my dreams I have resolved to travel on the ship in peace. There is not much to be gained from creating discontent when there is no escape to be made. Still, Africa is a large place and why not there? It is surely a place to be lost and never found in; surely a place to hide in open view. We have no place to go, so why not let them pay for our transportation and then lose them once on dry land. It is a simple plan but one that will serve us. The ship's bell sounds, and we make our way to the deck to join the crew for breakfast.

It is a clear blue sky and the air is fresh. It takes little time to settle back into the camaraderie of the crew. Whilst I retain a level of distrust towards them, their company is still a pleasure. Soon the sailors put down their rest and take up their tasks and we are left alone on deck.

We go to the side of the ship and take in the wide expanse. If the wind stays in our favour it will take at least a week with nothing but the sea and ourselves. I am filled with dread. Inside me is a war of conflicting and contradicting emotions, energies and maladies that I seek to escape. My grandmother would tell me to look to the beasts, seek their guidance and wisdom, yet what use explanations? They do not release my torment. We should put ourselves to use, but to serve ourselves, not our fellow travellers, who in all but name are our gaolers. We turn from the deck and step below to the captain's cabin.

We knock on his door.

'Wait,' he calls. We hear papers being shuffled, instruments arranged then,

'Come in.'

We open the door to find him feet up at his table, facing the window, tankard in hand.

'Raven, come take a seat.'

'Thank you, but it is not leisure we seek, Captain, rather gainful employment.' He sits up straight, places his tankard down.

'You would rather sweep floors than pass the time with an old friend?' he asks. I would like to tear out his tongue for daring to use the word friend, but all I say is, 'Captain.'

'Why so formal? Have you not a multitude of questions? Grace and Mother Gray are...'

'I wish them well, Captain, but all life needs purpose and we are better made use of than pampered.' I shall not hear tell of Grace and Mother Gray from his lips.

He sighs. 'If you so wish. It is a lonely life, the captain of ship, but no use friendship if it is not willingly given.'

He stands, 'There is no shortage of work at sea.' We stand aside as he approaches. 'Follow me,' he says, and, with no further words, he leads us on deck and to the bow of the ship. There, in a tangled heap, is a pile of forgotten and abandoned fishing nets. It is not hard to see they are in a poor state of repair. Surely it would be of more service to dispose of them.

'You'll find all you need in that box there. It will be a good job done, if you can,' he says, and leaves us to it.

I stare at the nets. I have never used a net to fish, only invited fish into my hands. I have never sewn or weaved or knitted; how am I to repair these enormous beasts? Where do we even begin? What point is there in this? Sabby looks at me with an expression of exasperation. We have been landed with an impossible task and I asked for it; somehow that feels familiar. I think she would rather we declared defeat and that I ask for a return to our leisure but so little of what I do seems to matter now, why not spend days on a fruitless task in the blistering heat under an unrelenting sky?

I open the box There is some dried out thread and some rusty tools, their purpose I do not even know. I yearn for my dagger and feel its place at the bottom of my lower back, bare and exposed. I stare at the nets and Sabby takes a resigned seat. I think that if I can untangle them first I can study their shape and work out what to do from there. I lift up the top netting, and with it the rest, releasing the most putrid smell imaginable. I quickly drop it and run to the side of the boat and empty my breakfast into the sea. Sabby howls and cowers, turning away from the nets. The sun is high, and the heat splinters the putrid air, so it is hard to see, but I do not seek the shelter of the hold, but rather wipe my lips dry and return for more, propelled by what I am not sure.

This time I brace myself. Sabby is clearly unwilling to help, so I clasp hold of the top net again. Again, the smell is released, and, for all its rancid intensity, there is something familiar about it, something I recognise in it. I turn my face away from the smell and hold in my retching. After a few moments the sea air begins to mingle and dissipate the stench, enough, at least, for me to seek the source of the smell.

I fold back the net and there in the centre of the tangled mess is the carcass of a cormorant, its neck snapped and trapped in the net, its feathers matted in blood and rotting intestines. I peer in further and am assaulted by a swarm of flies. I pause and wait for them to pass. I am transfixed by the horror of the rotten carcass; in its form I recognise myself. Looking further I see the maggots feast, what has been consumed, what is left to be consumed, what shall be left to the elements to consume. For a moment I think everything is of use to something, but it is fleeting and still it does not provide the comfort that is intended.

I crouch down by the bird's body. The cormorant, the raven of the sea. It is myself I smell in its rotting, decaying flesh. When I move it, it will break into tiny pieces. Despite myself, yet in respect to my grandmother and all the wisdom I have from living with beasts, I wish the bird's spirit a fortuitous onward journey and thank it for its life. It's the very least I can do. Then I reach into the corpse and take a handful; as expected it crumbles in my hand, but I keep hold of what I can and throw it over the edge of the ship. I lose count of how many trips it takes to clear it. After the last handful I watch as, out of nowhere, through the clear waters, I see schools of fish feeding on the remains as they sink towards the bottom of the sea.

I have worked alone and thought Sabby to be keeping a safe distance, yet when I look down, I see she has brought us a pail and rope. I let down the pail and wash my hands in the salt water. I think salt will help sterilise the netting, and I lower the pail again, then throw the water onto the netting. It takes many turns before I can brush the muck and salt and remaining entrails away, the water drying fast in the heat and the salt falling from the netting in crystals that take with them a fraction of the filth. Then it is time to separate and untangle. There is a mesh of webbing, but gradually it is clear there are three separate nets entangled.

I begin to pull and tug, Sabby sees a game, and soon we are deep into a tug of war. Bits of netting snap or release and we tumble and fall. I'm not sure we make much advancement, but it is the most joy we have had for months. We are reminded of how to play and I find there is genuine laughter, genuine glee, inside me. In the end we collapse in a heap on the pile of barely untangled nets. It would make sense for us to rest now, take shelter from the unforgiving sun and relentless blue sky, yet I am driven by a defiance inside my soul and cannot rest. Soon I sit up, determined to continue my task. Sabby sighs and takes shelter, watching from the shade.

The moon is high by the time I complete just the first step and have untangled the nets from each other. Two are worth saving but the third is beyond repair, but I can use it to mend the others, so nothing is of waste. The skin on my face and hands feels sun soaked, brittle and sore. The heat inside my doublet has been beyond any furnace I know of, yet I dare not take it off. I think everything has changed for me, yet it appears some things have not.

I sit down on the now neatly folded nets and would sleep there and then, yet Sabby appears again; this time the pail is full of fresh, clear water and we both drink our fill. We lie back on our bed of nets and gaze at the stars. We can hear the laughter and singing of the crew and for a moment we have peace, yet as soon as I realise, it is gone. How can there be peace when Grandmother is no more, when Mary can be no more? When all of what I thought I knew was not what I knew at all?

I am filled with the need to move, to run, and it is only that my body is unwilling that I lie still, yet whilst I make no outward movement, internally I run in every direction, and in every direction, I hit a blank wall. Sabby places her paw on my forehead to still my thoughts but I bat it away. I cannot bear to be touched, to be reminded I have form. She rolls over to sleep, whilst I stare without seeing at the stars. I find the comfort of emptiness take hold and let my eyes soften. I am about to drift off to sleep when I see her face, in the constellation of the stars - my grandmother's face. I sit bolt upright, certain that now I have seen it, it shall go, yet it does not. I blink, shake my eyes, my face, and still in the sky I see her smiling down at us with love in her starry eyes.

I know it is supposed to be a comfort. I know this is supposed to be our eternal connection, that she is in spirit, not lost to us, but reached another way, yet I do not find it so. If they, the normal people, can live without our gifts, if they can say they do not need the spirits of our ancestors and all of their wisdom, then I do not need it either. I roll over with my back to Sabby, close my eyes and block everything out. Eventually sleep will come.

I awake with the first sun's rays and begin the task of mending. Now the nets are untangled, the rusted tools make sense. I will begin by mending weakened lines and from that discover how to build the mesh, yet I need a knife for all these tasks. I decide to join the others for breakfast and seek one out.

The sailors take their turn at jibes and jokes at our expense. They think our task a fruitless one and take great pleasure in teasing us. I play my part and hold our ground. What do they know of our path? They mean us no harm. Throughout, I keep a keen eye; the first knife I see unattended I intend to hide in my doublet, yet ship's biscuits require little carving. Gradually the sailors return to their work, or sleep if they have worked through the night. Still no knife is in sight. I think we shall have to find the kitchen and ingratiate ourselves with the cook when my old knife slides across the floor to me. I look up and the captain stands towering above.

'We did not abandon you,' he says, and turns and walks away.

I wait until he has gone below before I snatch up my knife. It feels like I have been reunited with an old friend and a little of my spirit returns, although I chose to deny it. Rather, I focus on the task at hand, happy to be able to lose myself in work.

Hours pass, the sun gets hotter and the work is painstaking. I may not move from one spot, yet it is arduous work. At first, I am slow because I don't understand; it takes time for me to learn the ways of thread, how to bend it, mould it, fasten it, how to treat it so it and I are happy with the results.

I try my hardest to leave behind the ways of the earth, to adopt "their" ways of dominance. I try to forget all that I know about the meeting of consciousnesses and working in union with the world around me but when I try to dominate, I find it less effective and really only begin to make progress when I put myself aside and allow myself to be led by the task. Then I fall into a steady rhythm. I do not notice the passing of the sun, only that I need a lamp to continue. I do not notice the hunger in my belly, or my thirst, but Sabby provides gifts to sate both. I do not sleep, it does not occur to me to do so. I feel the skin on my face turn to leather, my lips crack and split apart, my fingers blister and swell, but all feels such a long way away it does not disrupt my flow.

For three days and three nights all I know, all that is, is the thread, the weave and myself. No person comes near, but many pass me by fulfilling their duties, some just come to stare at the spectacle. I chose to take this as encouragement, although I am only half aware of them. When I am finished, I have two perfect nets with all the thread from the third used in the repairs. I fold them, close the box of tools, now made fresh with use, stand up, walk past the crew, down the hatch and into the hold. I lie down in the soft hay with the beasts and fall instantly into a deep, dead sleep whilst Sabby keeps watch.

My eyes snap open, alerted by the ceasing of movement. Sabby is anxious, pacing and circling, approaching the door, then retreating. Why have we stopped? I hear shouting from the crew, urgent thundering across the ship. I am on my feet and by Sabby's side immediately. Fear would grip me, but feeling is not something I have. Tentatively I ease open the door; the ship's boy runs past.

'Ahoy, what is the commotion?'

He stops, 'Pirates,' he says, before continuing on.

'From where?' I ask.

'Spain,' he shouts as he disappears into the depths of the ship. The Gibraltar Straits then; it is Morocco we head towards.

From what I have seen of the ship and the crew, we are not made for fighting, yet the Spanish pirates have an undisputed reputation for ruthlessness and brutality. I think this could be our escape – what better occupation than to sail the seas without the rule of the law? It is another form of family and one that shall ask no questions. We are bound to be captured – it will not take much to defect to their side. Maybe this will be our future. Slipping between the shadows, we make our way to the deck.

Co-ordinated confusion reigns. The only two canons that we have, that have never seen fire, are wheeled into place. Slipping through the chaos, we make our way towards the bow where, in the distance, we see the pirate ship, much larger and well-equipped than our own. A wall of cannons points towards us. Every member of our crew has been equipped with a weapon - even the captain sports a pistol. A few with rifles have taken up position in the masts and rigging, the ship's boy keeping watch in the crow's nest. I do not think our cargo is worth much, which means we may pay with our lives instead. The captain stands at the wheel, issuing commands that no one seems to be listening to. We find a spot in the shadows, by the nets, where we can see and not be seen.

It takes minutes until all are ready and in position, then an eerie stillness descends. We can hear our breath in the silence that grips all. We watch as the pirate ship sails into firing range. Will they fire or approach first? We sail without a flag, so they may think us friend rather than foe. We see them dip their ensign, a show of honour and to signal peaceful intent, but that may be a ruse to secure our confidence, giving them the advantage of surprise. I watch the captain and see he has the same thoughts. Still he signals for the crew to be at ease and reluctantly they comply. The pirate ship is now in shooting distance and our ship's boy sounds the bugle. They salute back as the ships come into alignment. They keep just enough of a safe distance to render pistols and rifles useless.

'Hola, mi amigos,' shouts the pirate captain.

From our vantage point we see a huge scar from forehead to chin running down his left side, cutting through the eye which is now covered by a patch. He does not disappoint, his build rugged and solid, yet agile, his looks fading but still he sports handsome, brutish features. He is everything I had hoped a pirate would be; he even sports gold, gypsy earrings.

'Hola amigos, como estas?' returns our captain.

'Ah English,' says the pirate captain. 'What brings you to these parts?'

'We travel light, en route to Tangiers.'

'Why, captain, I had hoped for more co-operation. Your cargo is, without question, precious beyond price.'

'We carry no goods.'

'It is not goods we are interested in.'

Captain Langan looks me in the eyes. I thought he had not noticed or considered us amongst the confusion. It is both a comfort and a concern that he has kept such a close eye on our movements. He turns back to the pirate.

'We wish you good day, sir. We know not of what you refer and simply wish to travel in peace,' and he signals for the crew to begin to set sail.

'Not so fast, captain. A shifter is of more value to us than you,' and he signals to his men.

From behind sails, from behind masks, at least twenty men swing in unison, flying through the air on ropes that easily reach our ship. It is a beautiful spectacle, one that should terrify, such is their skill, accuracy and speed, yet I simply feel disgust. They have come for me. It is why they have not fired a cannon or shot a pistol. They want to take me alive. What I thought was a route to freedom was anything but. Should I be proud that my infamy has travelled so far?

Within seconds the deck is assaulted by pirates. We sink further into the shadows. Let them kill themselves over me; their concern is for themselves not us, what should we care of the outcome? Man takes on man, sword hits sword, fist hits flesh. We hear cries of pain and cries of triumph, wince at the thud of bone on bone, at the crack of broken bone, at the crack of broken ship. It's impressive, yet I care little for who wins. Does it matter whose property I am?

Then we hear them approaching with stealth over the bow whilst the frontal attack has consumed us; they have sent men around to attack from the rear. I hear them climb the ship's sides, advancing from their rowing boat. Then it is beyond my reason, my body acts of its own will. Even though I think myself helpless, a blameless victim, I cannot concede to my capture when it is so closely presented.

I change position slightly; they will try to spread out, come one by one to avoid detection, but the fighting has spread across the deck and there is no way to pass and nowhere to pass too. They will think me held in the hold or down below for safety, so we wait until all are on board. They crouch low and spread themselves as best they can. Just as they are about to join the attack, I leap out of the shadows and on to the bow. They stop, frozen for a moment, unsure of what to do.

It is just long enough for us to cast one of our nets and, with one flowing, sweeping throw, we secure all under the net.

They struggle and resist, arms and legs reaching in all directions, bodies writhing and squirming, yet it takes moments for us to pull the net tight and secure it to the rigging, so they are suspended; to cut themselves free would be to break their necks in the fall. Then I turn to face the brawl.

'Hey, hey, catch me if you can,' I shout, and the fighting stops as all turn to face me.

I glance at Captain Langan, who reads my plan and subtly signals to his crew to hold back as the pirates charge towards me. As the first hand reaches to grab me, I rise up as Albatross, taking the net with me. The shift is swift, yet even so the sense of fluidity is a pleasure, a joy I am now sure I should not feel. I sweep above their heads and, when I am sure, drop the net, securing the pirates in a single tangled mess. I let the crew do the rest to secure them and perch upon the crow's nest. I watch and feel I should have some sense of triumph, yet I am filled with shame and disappointment that again I resort to my "gift" for answers when I am told the ways of the earth are worth less than nothing.

It does not take long to throw the pirates overboard and set sail as fast as we can. They will work themselves free, but it will be enough time for us to make our escape. I fly down from the crow's nest; Sabby has my clothes and we go down into the hold where I shift back and dress, sure I will never be able to face the crew or the captain again.

I sit in the hold, bathing in the darkness. How is the world to ever be a safe place again when even the pirates of the Spanish Sea have heard tell of my "gift" and seek to possess it and myself in turn? We have not been pursued by the authorities so they either do not believe the stories that are told about me or they have been misinformed and seek me elsewhere, but the underground have heard tell, believe and seek possession. I see no future for me, but a short-lived one.

I do not know my safest choice. Do I escape, try to spend the rest of my days in hiding, undiscovered in the back streets of Tangiers? I cannot return home, to do so would be certain death, and I cannot risk Mary's life. I have caused her too much pain. I seek no comfort from anyone in the Society, yet I risk their lives too. It's fairer to them for me to comply with their plan. I think either way my life shall be short. Survival in the backstreets of a port, or in the service of those that betray, and do nothing for the people captured and tortured in their name cannot be for long.

The door opens and the captain approaches with a lamp and a plate of food. He sets them down and perches on the crates.

'You have not lost it then,' he says. I do not respond but take up the food and begin to eat, as does Sabby.

'It will not be long now. By morning we should be docked in port.' Still I do not respond.

'We did our best but word travels fast and you are a lot to talk about.'

At this I glance at him with accusing eyes. To blame me when they should have protected? He should choose his words more carefully. As I look at him, his outline begins to blur. I blink but it is only worse. Then my limbs cease to hold firm and I find myself falling back into the hay.

'It is for your own safety,' he says, and then everything is black.

Chapter Two

I awake with a jolt, my body bangs against a tight wooden box. I smell Sabby in the darkness and feel her restlessness and her weight against my body. I feel us rock to the rhythm of her heart. I smell heat and sand and the stench of men not often washed. A little light creeps through the cracks in the lid. I think we are in some sort of coffin or disguised as goods in a crate. I try to think, to form a plan of action, but my mind is foggy, and the deep darkness of the sleeping draught claims my consciousness again.

Bright splintering light assaults my senses. I cannot help but my arm swings to protect my eyes; in doing so I barely miss hitting the face that peers at me from above. She is a smiling vision of beauty, dark hair and eyes, dusky complexion. I feel a connection to her that is inexplicable. Slowly I lower my arm. Sabby rises to her feet and stretches as I cautiously sit up. The sky is an enormous expanse of blue, it is mostly sky, the land flat and stretching forever, in every direction. We are in a box on a heavily loaded cart.

A man covered from head to toe in white cloth unhitches the donkey from the harness. A crowd of small children have gathered around us and the air is filled with laughter and tears and excitement. Sabby jumps down from the cart and the children scatter, squealing with joy and fear, only to return, one by one, their curiosity conquering their fear. In seconds Sabby has charmed them all; I find her confidence reassuring.

I bend my knees, noting their stiffness as an indication of how long I have been so disposed. The woman offers me her hand. I smile at her but place my hands on the side of the box and, in one continuous movement, I stand and then jump from the cart to land before her. I bow, a grand ostentatious bow, weakened in gesture purely by lack of hat. Otherwise all is intact - binding, linens and knife.

'Good day, Master Raven, it is our greatest pleasure to welcome you to our tribe,' the woman says and holds out her hand. I take it and smile.

'Thank you, it is a wonder to be here,' I say. 'Who do I address?' Looking into her eyes I feel a falling; it is a feeling I quickly dismiss.

'Please forgive my ignorance. Farah Nassar at your service,' she curtsies and I am charmed.

'Farah, what a beautiful name, and so excellently spoken in English,' I say and kiss her hand.

'Oh, we are a trading tribe,' she says and welcomes me in Arabic, Spanish, French and Hebrew. I cannot help but laugh and release her hand. I am humbled and in such a graceful way.

'Come,' she says, 'you will require sustenance after such confinement and for so long.'

She leads us to a large tent, the first in the camp. A fire is set outside, and the sides are open. Underneath the canopy, rugs and carpets line the ground while silk cushions provide comfort. She sits me down, seeing to my every need. It is a joyous game and I am surprised how quickly I forget the most recent events. Sabby seeks the coolest spot she can find; despite her calm I feel her panting is too much, yet it is not long before she is asleep

Once we are settled, Farah claps her hands and a young girl appears with a tray and two cups. Farah thanks the girl in Arabic and sends her away. Then she pours a steaming hot brown liquid into the cups. She hands me one and takes one herself.

'How do you say? Cheers?' and she clinks my cup.

'Cheers,' I reply. What has she given me? The only time I have drunk hot liquid was a soup or an herbal infusion made by Grandmother. I take the tiniest sip, expecting a savoury flavour, yet a bitter sweetness ignites my mouth with an explosion of flavours. Instantly I take another sip. I cannot hide my expression of wonderment and curiosity.

She laughs, 'Good, no?'

'I have never tasted such before. What is it?'

Again, she laughs, 'It is a tradition with our people that dates back as far as anyone can remember. We call it tea, Bedouin tea, extra sweet.'

'It's good,' I say. 'And its effects?'

'It's effects? Why, it enlivens the spirit,' I think she does not know my meaning but there seems little point in pursuing further. I shall find out soon enough.

'You must have many questions,' she says. I do, but they are questions I do not think she can answer.

'Perhaps,' I say, 'it has been a long journey.'

'You would rather rest, settle in. Let me take you to your tent.' She rises to her feet in one swift graceful move whilst I clamber inelegantly to my feet.

Sabby walks slowly, following and not leading, listless in the heat. Farah notices my concern but doesn't say anything. She shows us to a small corner of a large communal tent where some bedding has been laid. Across it are a fresh set of linens and a set of the long gowns and a headdress worn by the male members of the tribe. I look at her; am I expected to wear the linens or the gowns?

'It is at your discretion,' she says. 'At night fall we shall gather to eat, and I shall introduce you. You shall know when to join us. Till then I bid you welcome and peace.' She steps away, bowing her head slightly.

My concern is for Sabby. She is listless and weak. My skin has already begun to brown but she is not meant for this land, this heat. I sit beside her as she cowers in the shade. It would be wise for me to take some time to learn the layout of the camp. Apart from the children, no one has yet approached us, and all fall silent on our advance. I must assume there is no harm meant to us, that we have been sent to a safe place of hiding, yet apart from Farah's welcome there is not much to suggest that. Still, I will not leave Sabby's side.

Then approaching from the far side of the camp are three men. They chat and joke as they walk but fall into a serious silence as the reach the tent. They walk directly at us with certain purpose. I am on my feet between Sabby and them, ready to reach for my knife. They consider me and say some words in Arabic I do not understand. Then one of them steps forward and slowly approaches us. He speaks in a soothing tone, but I do not understand his words. It is just a muddle of harsh and aggressive sounds and although his face is one of tenderness all I see is threat.

He keeps advancing so I pull out my knife. It stops him in his tracks but not for long; keeping his eyes on me he makes a comment to the other men and all laugh. Now they humiliate us too. I am ready to fight for our lives. I circle round Sabby with the knife, keeping all at bay. One steps closer and I am ready, but inches from his features, and he backs away holding his hands up but more amused than afeared.

I think this is some sort of game to them. So this is how it will be. The Society has moved me to a place of "safety", away from all those that have heard of my gift and want to exploit it for its own uses to a place where I shall be exploited for other gifts. As a foreign woman I am little more than a whore to them. Every part of me seeks to shift, to protect us, but I will not do it, I will not resort to the ways of the earth. It seems I fight an internal and external battle.

Sensing my distraction is all they need and in one swift move, one of them has me by the throat, holding me from behind, one holds Sabby and the other reaches inside his thobe. I struggle with all my might and I can tell it takes all the strength my captor has to hold me. They shout, this time at each other; there is some urgency to their tone, especially from my captor as I wildly thrash and twist and turn as much as I can. Then from out of his thobe the man produces a large pair of shears like those used for sheep.

The other men hold Sabby's body and both Sabby and I are still. They leave enough fur, so she is protected from the sun but released of most of her layers. Her relief is palpable and therefore mine also. I would like to say I showed gratitude, that I begged for forgiveness, that I fell at their feet in thanks and relief, but I did not. At least I gather up Sabby's fur, a valuable commodity, and give it to them; at least we reciprocate in some way.

They take the fur and bow their heads in thanks, but I get the impression that they intended to take it whether we gave it or not, that that has been the motivation all along. Laughing, they trundle away with little regard for me or Sabby. I lie down next to her and let the expanse of our surroundings settle in whilst I try to block out my feelings of shame and calm my nerves as they rattle around my being.

We must drift off because we are awoken by the drop- n temperature. We are in a land of extremes, the heat of the day stifling, the night fresh and cold. Yet we know this temperature and know how to be in it. We get up and stretch. We can hear a fire crackle and laughter, conversation, and our gaze follows the fragrant smells of cooking. The camp is made up of a number of tents, varying in size, and, it appears, in no particular order although they are roughly located around a central area that hosts the fire. Each has a smaller local fire to source the constant cups of tea they drink.

Whole families have gathered around the central fire. Children run and play, babies cry, the men take the prime positions whilst the women work, preparing the night's meal. Maybe this world is more familiar than on first sight. There are looks when we arrive, but no one stops what they are doing, neither welcoming nor rejecting. I do not know what to do and stand hovering by the fire, yet it is the hot fire of my humiliation that rises from my boots that I feel and not the fire's flames. Maybe this is their way of hostility and we have transgressed without intent to do so. Then I spot Farah deep in conversation and food preparation.

Her fellow cooks notice me watching and nudge her. She looks over and her face lights up. She is quick to her feet and, with a spring in her step, she comes to greet us.

'You are more comfortable now it is the cool of night, I see,' she says, and I laugh.

'It is that obvious?'

'Oh no, not at all.'

'There is no need to spare my feelings,' I say, and she laughs.

'Well, a little obvious, yes,' and she smiles coyly, tucking a stray hair back under her scarf.

'Later I will get you a jubble, a coat, you shall need it.' I find that hard to believe but thank her anyway. 'Please join me by the fire. I have a spot for you.'

'I don't wish to intrude,' I say.

'And you shall not. Do not mind the others just now. We transport many different cargos across the desert. I am afraid to them you are just another piece of such. It will be easier after the sheik officially welcomes you later.' I nod and turn my attention to the flames of the fire. We are little more than freight and I find I am happy to be just that.

As I sit quietly by the flames, Sabby finds much joy in playing with the children. She makes great headway in winning the hearts of the entire tribe. I am grateful for her charm and their reception of it will make it easier for all. It is good to have space to watch the harmony between the people, the simple understanding they have of each other. Despite their differences, there is an acceptance of everyone for who they are. They are self-contained within the comfort of their own creation. It is a bond between people I have not seen before but one I recognise like a forgotten memory.

There are clear rituals to the night's proceedings with each having their part, each appreciated for their contribution. Rich herbs and spices, that at home are only the choice of the wealthy, enrich every dish. Large round flat breads that I have never seen before tease and entice the senses. I cannot remember the last actual meal we have had, and every part of my being begins to yearn for what is about to come.

When the women are happy with their efforts, they approach a large, older man who all evening has held court at the head of the fire. The chief sheik, he has had a constant stream of visitors, some with questions, some with gifts, some with information. He has settled disputes and shared his wisdom. Prompted by the women, he calls order with two clear hand claps. In moments the company is gathered and around thirty families take their places about the fire. We sit on intricately woven rugs and I am transported to Grace's house and feel a confirmation that I am in the place I am meant to be, yet I do not understand how this can be so and resist its comfort with all that I have.

Once seated, the women lay out the dishes, breads and fruits, something that looks a lot like pottage, which I later find is called tagine. A feast is laid before us, and a blessing begins, led by the chief sheik. I do not understand the words but the song ripples through my body, awakening sensations I didn't know I had. It is at once familiar and alien. I feel dislocated but do not dwell on my discomfort such is the urgency of my hunger. The blessing seems to take far too long but in the presence of such a feast it is fitting.

Once concluded, a ritual of serving out the food begins. I am at a loss to follow protocol, but Farah comes and sits next to me.

She hands me more tea and says, 'I shall be your guide.' My gratitude is obvious.

Plates are passed and order observed and finally I take my first bite - a chunk of bread laden with rich tagine and my mouth explodes with flavour. I do not know how long I will travel with these people, but I know I will always carry this food with me. It is a joy that stands out in the bleakness of my soul.

After many more helpings and endless tea the dishes are cleared, and everyone settles down. Some kind of meeting is held, announcements are made, and there are discussions, sometimes spoken with a passion no one in England would ever dare to express. Then all eyes fall on me.

Farah takes to her feet, the only woman who has been allowed to speak directly to the crowd all night. I do not know what is said but I can tell there has been a prior agreement for my passage with them and this is some sort of formal welcome. The words repeat, and it sounds like some sort of blessing. At the end I am invited to my feet and led to a flat clearing by the fire and encircled by all. I begin to fear that it is another sort of ritual - one that leads to me being tomorrow's feast. Then I am filled with shame for thinking so when I have read so much of others' cultures. How base my reaction; it seems there is nothing between me and the establishment after all.

At Farah's lead all burst into song and they take up a few simple steps side to side, fist one way, then the other. I am overwhelmed; it is as though I am being sung into being. The melody is so different to what I understand as a tune, yet it is a song nonetheless. Sabby has joined me and I cannot help the tear that escapes my eye. It is the first since the execution. I had expected anything other than this welcome. They know not of me, of my past or of my value yet their generosity of spirit is not limited by such things. I feel a guest that is part of the family. It will be sometime before I come to terms with such an unfamiliar and unexpected sensation.

Afterwards we return to the fire, more songs are sung, stories told, and it matters not that I do not understand the words - the meanings are clear. They resonate so deeply with my grandmother's teachings it is almost an injury to hear them. The night does get colder and Farah gives me a beautifully embroidered jabber. I wish I had had one of these before, it makes the warmth of a cloak look like an insult. Eventually children fall asleep and we are lulled into a natural peace. Gradually adults take to sleeping, some where they are sitting, some seek the shelter of their tents. We remain until the chief sheik has taken to his bed.

Farah rises slowly to her feet. We had fallen into an easy quiet watching the flames dance.

'Do you seek sleep?' she asks. I look at Sabby, who is exhausted by her games.

'I think that would be well,' I say and, smiling, get lazily to my feet. I begin to make my way back to the tent where we spent the afternoon.

'Not that way,' she says. I stop and look quizzically at her.

'This afternoon you were guest, now you have been admitted into our tribe and you shall sleep beside me.'

Instantly I am afeared. What does this mean? Does she know I am not a "usual man"? Does she mean simply to lay beside me or has she different designs?

'Come, do not look so afraid. What do you think I shall do?'

I do not answer, simply smile and shrug my shoulders as if I am playing the fool. She smiles in return and turns, walking toward the tent where we received our first sip of tea. She does not look back so certain she is that we shall follow and follow we do.

Yet terror rages inside me. To be brought to safety only to be discovered and die amongst the sand dunes. How are we to escape this time? I do not know the ways of this earth and we have no idea where we actually are or how long we would need to go without water should we follow the stars. When she reaches the tent she stops and turns, smiling a welcome to me. A gentle breeze catches her gown and the moonlight glints in her eyes. I have never wanted to be man but tonight I see its advantages. She ducks her head and goes beneath the canopy. I look at Sabby - are we ready for our life to be cut so short?

Then I think of all that we have lived so far. My grandmother's rearing and teachings of the ways of the earth. A childhood of playful shifting, service to the Society, the love of Mary, of our friends, our guides. Of the brutality of the new establishment and of our near death at their hands. I think it is not such a short life. If it is time for its ending, then I shall do nothing to stop it. I duck my head and follow her under cover. Whilst the tents provide shelter and shade from the sun their open sides do not provide much discretion. There is not much room for secrets here.

A small lamp illuminates the inside, casting delicate shadows across the space. I cannot help but notice the rugs and blankets are of a high quality, finely embroidered and woven. She has made a bed of silk. I look at Sabby, but she has found herself a comfortable spot and is already snoring. How can she leave me to negotiate this alone? I think I shall claim exhaustion and see if it gains us a night of life. I stretch and yawn.

'I knew sleep was calling for you,' she says.

She has removed all her outer garments and, without looking at me, she lies down on the silken bed and pulls a finely woven woollen blanket over her.

'Do not take so long - first light is not so far away,' and she turns on her side and closes her eyes. I stand at a loss as to know what to do.

'You may lie beside me; my smell is good and it is our way.'

I had hoped she had fallen into an instant sleep and I could lie with Sabby.

I have not lain next to a woman since the Inn in London and I am not sure I want to. Yet there is no choice - I am a guest and must follow custom no matter the cost. I take off my boots and jabba and lie down with my back to her curled in a tight ball. I cannot imagine either of us is comfortable.

Although she is right - her smell is good, it will take me all my strength not to breathe her in. My eyes are fixed open and I think one of us should extinguish the lamp when I see in the far corner a store of jars, of measures, of pestles and mortars. I recognise their shape, their form and suddenly sleep is no more.

As gently as I can, when I feel such urgency, I lift up the lamp and go to the store. I pick up an earthenware jar; can they have these too? I bring the lamp in close for I am certain I recognise this particular pot and there it is, Grandmother's handwriting - 'Hawthorn for the heart' and I remember the day we picked for this particular remedy. It is as if I am back in the woods adjacent to our cottage. I hear the birds, smell the grass, feel the sun on my back and hear the happy chatter of Grandmother as she instructs me on harnessing intuition with plants. I feel myself in two dimensions at once and it stirs a rage in me. I have vowed to leave all that behind - why must it persist so?

'How do you have this?' I turn and accuse with my words, but she has already risen and walks calmly towards me.

'Import and export,' she says 'We have things you want that you cannot source. So why would it be different for us?' The obvious simplicity of her answer stalls my rage.

Then she says, 'Your grandmother's fame was worldwide - her passing was mourned in all corners of the world.' Then she knows. How much does she know?

'As you have read about me in books, so I have heard tales of your ways.'

'What have I read of you in books?' I say. How can she know so much when secrecy is our creed?

'The third sex, the Shamans of the third sex, at your service,' she says and bows ostentatiously.

Yet I see nothing that is of humour. I have longed to meet others such as I, but never dreamed I would ever meet a genuine Shaman, let alone share their bed and travel in their company and protection. Yet that was then and it was not like this. Not dreamed of in these circumstances.

We are over a moon's cycle from our home, in a land some people at home do not even believe exists, and I am confronted by all that I seek to leave behind. I look at Sabby; she is alert, yet composed, and this only heightens my distress. How can she be so accepting of such outrageous fortune? I want to escape, to be free; I do not know how to be in this place, how to be in this moment, and before I know what I am doing I feel myself changing. I feel the fluidity, I feel the wings, and I am Raven, and I am flying through the empty desert skies with Sabby following in fast pursuit on the ground. Yet the only thing we hunt for tonight is a remembrance of a peace I never expect to find again.

Chapter Three

I do not know how far we fly. How can you measure distance when each grain of sand is like the next? I simply feel the wind in my wings and never want to stop. I never want to feel the earth between my feet again. Sabby grows tired; she barks and howls, calling me back, calling me to human form. Yet why should I heed her when no one heeds me? When things that were once beautiful dreams become soured horrors that torment and traumatise?

I discover my plan is to fly until I can fly no more, until I fall from the sky and let the dunes devour me. The sun kisses the horizon and still I do not stop. I have grown slower, Sabby is ready to drop, yet still she follows. I am comforted that this torment I enforce her to endure shall soon be over. My death shall set her free and she shall be the guide for who she chooses. I am beyond all understanding of exhaustion and still I fly. The sun is high, the heat blistering and suffocating when, like Icarus, I fall.

As I hit the ground, I take human form and lie naked on the blistering heat of the sand, yet I do not pause, do not feel the exhaustion and fatigue that must be rampant throughout my being. Rather I scramble to my feet and begin to walk. I do not look as to which direction to travel, do not make a choice; it is as if I have lost all my senses. I feel no heat, although it is hotter than a furnace. I do not look, although I can see, there is nothing to smell, but the heat of the sand and my own stench, nothing to hear but the sound of my laboured breathing.

I think I stumble, trip and stagger, but I cannot feel my body. It is as if I am driven by something other than myself. Yet there is nothing but me for miles around. I can tell Sabby is following, but she hangs back, keeping a distance. I must have a furious thirst. My skin, that has mostly never seen the sun, is now completely exposed to a sun that peels the skin and leaves the insides bare. If I could think I would fear for Sabby and make her health and safety my priority, but there is no activity in my mind, only the endless drive for motion. It is as if it is all that is, all that has ever been, and all that will be; it is as endless as the landscape that surrounds us.

It is this way for three days, no sleeping, no resting, no stopping, just this steady trance-like state. I do not know if I encounter other beings, for I am not in that consciousness, but as night falls on the third day and the sun sinks towards the horizon, I take a step and stand on something harsh and jagged. It is the first sensation I have had for three days and it jolts me out of my trance and back into the world.

I look down and, as surprised as I am, it is a small desert hedgehog, who takes one look at me, curls into a tight ball and rolls down the sand dune as if it are a dust ball driven by an unfelt wind. I am curious and astonished, a hedgehog in the desert? If it can adapt, then can I? I look at my feet to check for damage and discover hardened skin, burnt and leathered. It's as if I have trodden the sand into my skin. I look up and around me. The sun is caressing the earth, casting shadows and creating colour on the monotony of the sand dunes. The air is cooling, and I sense the indestructible peace that is in all things. It's as if I have seen beauty for the first time. It is sublime, yet somehow known and obvious; it is not a discovery but a retuning.

I look behind me as Sabby approaches. Her smell triggers life inside me and I feel complete and unobstructed love for her. I drop to my knees and our reunion releases an ecstasy of joy inside me. Then I see how frail she is, how much it has cost her to hold me in her sights, how much I have asked of her devotion. Then I look to my own body. I am covered in blisters from head to toe, my skin reflecting the broken and cracked landscape around me. Then it hits me; the pain is insufferable. There is not a part of my body that does not hurt. I would hold Sabby close for comfort but there is not a part of my skin that can bear touch. Together we howl - it is the only release. We howl until we can howl no more. I am about to fall into unconsciousness when on the horizon I see a camel approaching at a gallop.

When I awake, I feel soft silk on my leathered skin. The air in the tent is cool and I can see in the distance the sun begin to creep into the sky. My first thought is for Sabby. I turn my head and meet her eyes. She is panting contentedly although I can see she is still frail and weak. I lift my head and hunch up on to my elbows, scared to move for the memory of the pain that was my last waking moment. My body is inside a tent of its own and I can smell a nutty, citrus oil. I lift the flap of my body tent and see my naked body, calmed of red fury and closing its cracks, covered and coated in oil. I wiggle my toes and have movement; tentatively I attempt to move my legs, and it is possible but only with the utmost care. I sink down carefully on to my back and gently let my head fall into the pillow.

It will be sometime before I can escape or even move with ease. Sabby looks the same, her coat think with oil. A tear rolls down my cheek and I care not to wipe it away. It is bad enough to be a captive, to make one of oneself seems foolish to an extreme degree, yet I have little time to wallow in pity as I am gripped by a thirst that threatens to drive me to insanity. I begin to struggle when Farah walks in carrying a large gourd.

'Cease, be still, it shall only hinder you longer.' I submit as she sits down next to me. She pours some water from the gourd into a small cup and holds it to my lips. I want to seize the gourd and drink all the water down in one, but I accept my limits and greedily sip all that I can. After a few cups I understand her caution, for one more and I would be sick.

'Give your body time. You have asked a lot from it and it has served you, now you must serve it,' she says as I lie back on the pillow.

'Thank you,' I say but only courtesy makes me say it.

'It is not needed,' she says.

'Sabby?' I ask.

'She is stronger than you and shall recover faster.' I close my eyes and fall into a deep, sound sleep

I do not know how many days I drift in and out of sleep, taking small amounts of food and water, but gradually I regain strength and movement. Soon I am able to sit up and am given a seat at the mouth of the tent, in the shade, but with clear view of the tribe in its daily routines.

Farah tends to me with patience and tenderness whilst maintaining her other responsibilities. The endless succession of folk with one malady or another reminds me of Grandmother, and Farah has the same knack with people. They arrive in distress and leave with comfort and hopeful of solution. When Farah is not in the tent they either about turn or sit and wait but at a respectful distance so as not to warrant contact with us.

It is such a time, and as Farah confers with the sheik, we doze in the searing heat. I can still move little and have learnt in this heat stillness is an advantage. Rushing up to the tent is a young woman, carrying in her arms a young boy, but one or two years of age, screaming in pain. She clasps hold of his wound, a deep cut to his hand, but still the blood is pouring. There is not much time before a wound that can easily be healed becomes a wound that endangers his life. She is frantic and after glancing quickly around is about to take off in search of Farah but there is no time for that.

'Stop,' I say in a firm loud voice as she is about to leave. She stops in her tracks and he is silenced. I know they do not understand the word, but they understand my tone.

'Sabby, bring me the peat moss,' and in a gentler tone I say, 'Come, come,' and hold out my hands so she can see I mean to help; there is a moment of hesitation but we both look at the blood and she is by my side. I use what drinking water I have and the peat moss to clean the wound and stop the bleeding.

'Sabby, my linens,' and I use them to bandage up the wound. By the time Farah returns both the boy and his mother are smiling. The woman rushes over to Farah and they talk excitedly as I finish off the binding.

'Sabby, take him, it is time for you to play,' and Sabby and the boy run happily out of the tent as if nothing has happened.

'She can't thank you enough,' says Farah

'We should all thank my grandmother,' I say, unhappy to receive any glory for what anyone else would do.

'Without you he -'

'It is what anyone would do,' I say.

'She wants to thank you.'

'It is not necessary.' But before I can protest further she is at my side, her hands in prayer position, her head nodding profusely. I reach out to touch her, to quite her but she pulls away from touch.

'You cannot touch her,' says Farah, ushering her away and calming her in Arabic.

'She is her husbands' property and as such cannot be touched by you or any other.' The mother bows one last time before hurrying away to find her son.

'Has it always been so?' I ask

'Not always,' she says, and I lay my head down on the pillow, defeated, even here we do not escape the rule of domination. I choose sleep whilst Sabby chooses to play.

She finds herself no end of friends in the people of the tribe. Soon I think she will be invited to help herd the cattle and sheep. There is a rhythm to the days, full of rituals that all play a part in sustaining the life they have created. They do not need laws, so tightly woven are they. They live without supervision, their only master the earth. I watch as they live in happy harmony with its ways. I think this is how things can be, all with a place, all needed, all respected as they respect the earth. I think this is how it can be, this is how it must have been before the words of the Pope.

Soon the seasons begin to change, and it is time for the tribe to flow with the earth and follow the rains and grass for grazing their herds. I am not yet well enough to travel, and it is decided Farah, Sabby and I shall wait a few days before we catch the others up. Their route is well established, and Farah will have no trouble finding them.

I am unable to help with their preparations and it negates all that I think I am. I hope the Society has rewarded them well for I have been a demanding cargo. Reciprocity is such a primary value to me and I do not know how I shall ever repay them. Sabby does her best to assist and when she cannot fetch and carry, she provides light relief amongst the back-breaking tasks. Yet everything has a well-practised pattern and the entire camp is packed up and away within hours and, before the sun has kissed the sky, they set off.

They are already behind and will need to travel by morning and night, instead of just in the cool of the night. They take all provisions they need with them, water, firewood, food until they reach their destination. It is no small task and I am fascinated to see that to live in flow with the earth takes such effort, yet there is something about it that is worth it. Despite my resolve to leave behind the ways of magik, I feel a deep understanding and respect for this life and it is as if all I have ever known and been taught has been validated.

Farah has packed away most of her medicines and tools to go ahead with the caravan. We are alone with the provisions we need, a camel for our journey and a donkey to carry our camp. Sabby is bereft to be left behind; as a pack animal it is the pack she seeks, yet I see the love in her eyes for me and know that she will never leave me. Again, I call on her patience, which seems to be inexhaustible.

I have spent many days observing the desolate landscape and discovered the hidden subtilties; the life that lies in the desert is less bold, less obvious but there nonetheless. Now I do not see emptiness and only sand but the wealth of life that happens out of the bright glare of the sun. I feel and sense and smell the extraordinary ability of beasts that have ancestors in my home, who have their own particular approach to their environs. Despite the circumstances, I consider that a blessing, yet now the tribe have departed I feel that same sense of desolation and loneliness.

Farah has shown me nothing but understanding, yet still I do not trust. Her beauty is undeniable, and I think must be a frustration to the men in the tribe as she does not seek their favours. I do not understand how or why she should care for me. What have the Society offered or given her for such attention? Why, when she is so free, does she heed them?

As the sun rises she takes herself off into the dunes, as is her common practice, at sunrise and sunset. Sometimes she is visible, sometimes not, as each time she finds a different spot for her mediations. It is not a practice I know, and I am intrigued by its purpose. Today we see her silhouette on the horizon facing away from the direction the tribe have taken. She looks a picture of peace.

After she returns, she prepares food and today is no different, yet there is a sadness to her movements.

'How long afore you allow me to travel?' I ask. It is meant kindly but sounds like an accusation.

'It is not up to me,' she responds.

'You could have left me. It would have made more sense.'

'It would but that is not what matters.'

'What is it that does?'

'That you are well and restored to health.'

'Do you not receive payment if your cargo is not delivered in good condition?' She puts down her pots and pans and looks at me.

'It is your choice not to love yourself, but do not sully my love with your shadows.'

'Your love?' How can she claim love? How dare she claim love?

'Yes, my love. For someone who has seen so much of life you seem so ignorant of it.'

'I have not asked for your love,' I say, fury filling my being; it is the most energy I have had since the night we fled.

'You cannot ask for love of someone. It is either there or not and I have loved you a long time.'

'How so, how can you love what you have not met?'

'Yet I have met you, I have known you of old.'

'What riddle is this you speak?'

'No riddle, what do you think my gift is?' I do not know how to respond, she is healer, but I had not considered more.

'What do you think I do each day at sunrise and set?' Again I know not what to say. 'I listen.' What is she listening to? There is so little to hear out here.

'To what?'

'To the past, to the present, to the future.' I am not sure I understand and look at her so.

'How else did you think I knew you were coming? How else did I know how to find you when you were lost to yourself? How else did you think I know to seek your grandmother's medicine?'

'The Society?' I ask, the fury shifting to another sort of fire.

'Oh the Society, the Society! They are but buffoons, necessary but mostly ineffective.'

'What have they told you? What do you know?'

'I know the sound you made when your grandmother found you in a basket on her stoop. I know for you shifting is all but breathing'

'How dare you accuse so?'

'I know the soundlessness of the peace you grew in, know the letters you sounded out in your lessons with Grace and Mother Gray.'

'How can you know all this?'

'I know the sound of your laughter with your found brother Constantine. I know the sounds of the pleasure you shared with Mary.'

'Stop,' I shout and raise my hand to slap her silent, yet she stays my hand without even pausing for breath.

'I know the sound of your fear when you retrieved the notebook from the cardinal.' I snatch my hand free and turn my back on her. I cannot hear my past spoken so, cannot bear all inside that it stirs.

'You turn away from me, yet how do I turn away from the sound of your tears when you see your grandmother hung as witch?'

'Enough,' I cry and go to leave the tent, yet she blocks my route.

'I know the sound of your partner, the colt, Jet when you set him free. I know the sound of your soul when it is torn apart by Stephen, Ben and the others as they each took their pleasure of you.' I try to push past her, but she grabs hold of me and will not let go no matter how I struggle.

'I know the sound of your heart breaking when your birth mother does nothing to save you from the gallows.' And at that I am stilled.

'I know the sound of your spirit rising when as Raven you cheat death.' My tears begin to fall silently.

'How could they tell me that? How could they tell me of the soft spots of your heart, your soul, wherein lies such beauty? Raven, I have always known of your coming, long before the Society even knew of my existence. Raven, shifting for you is breath to others, you cannot be otherwise.'

Then I know there are no need for words. What use words when she knows all of me and still has love for me? What use words when she is right there? I look her in the eyes, take her face in my palms and our lips meet.

It is as if my blood is of gunpowder and she has set it alight. I think I shall be gentle, shall be full of tenderness, yet it is an eruption of passion, an upsurge of desire. We tear and grasp at each other's clothing, our flesh desperate to be joined. Her smell relieves me of my senses as my tongue tastes her flesh, my mouth her breasts, my hand, her cunt. There is not a part of her body I do not explore, do not delight in. There is not a part of my body that she does not awaken.

Her touch sends me into a frenzy, alighting parts of me that I did not know I had. There is no thought, just complete abandonment. To surrender suddenly makes sense as we give ourselves to the moment, the sensation, our bodies. Then it is as if we leave our bodies behind and become flowing, expanding energy. We leave matter behind as our energies combine in one glorious explosion of consciousness.

Afterwards I think that had it been night our light would have challenged that of the moon and the stars. We dedicate the day to further discovery of our love, our lust insatiable, our desire greedy and our bodies willing. Sabby takes solace in the shadows outside the tent as we break the silence of the desert with our ecstatic cries of pleasure. As the sun begins to fall from the sky we finally lie in peace, in each other's arms.

'Should I ask our fate, oh wise one?' I tease.

'To know the future is to know the past and to understand the present. It is not a gift that many have the stomach for.' And she sighs a heavy sigh.

'Then I shall take each day with you as the gift it is meant to be and ask nothing more,' I say and seal my promise with a kiss.

Then she releases her hold and rises from our bed. I know it is sundown and she shall go to listen. I do not try to stop her but watch her dress and compose herself; as she is about to leave the tent, she turns back to me and smiles. It is the most vulnerable I have ever seen her, and I know this love is eternal.

After she is gone, I lie still for a few moments luxuriating in the sense of satiation. I feel my spirit renewed and regain a sense of my place upon the earth, yet I am too invigorated to lie still and so I get up. I walk to the mouth of the tent. I watch her sitting in the dying glow of the sun; tonight she has not gone far, tonight she has not hidden from sight. I feel her peace and it is a calling.

I stretch, call Sabby and begin to shift, this time as a choice. Raven and Wolf go hunting once more. I know Farah will understand, know that she already knows this will take place. I circle overhead and cry a greeting but do not wait for an answer. The cool air through my wings fills me with joy and for the first time I am able to recognise location, not through stars or what can be seen but something inside that is more certain than either. That night we return with two desert hares and we feast and grow heady on sweet tea and lovemaking.

Chapter Four

For three days we indulge in this blissful life of fresh and eager love. The freedom to be together and not be afeard of discovery is intoxicating. I cannot quite accept it and shadows of fear sweep across me at the most beautiful moments which we both choose to ignore. It is a fear we shall need at other times, after all. After the third day we pack up camp, to wait longer would make re-joining the tribe almost impossible and our love has restored my health and my spirit. We wait until after Farah's evening commune and then head out into the cool darkness of night.

The moon caresses our skin and we travel in comfortable quiet, taking turns to walk and then ride the camel. We wait until the sun is high and set up a temporary shelter to protect us all from the midday heat. We eat and rest until the sun begins to drop and we begin our travels again. It is a joy how easily we fall into a pattern, at ease with each other's rhythm, ebbing and flowing, a happy tide and shore. We each are both at sea and land. Sabby leads the way, contented and satisfied by this temporary tribe.

It is at the end of the second day that we see the tribe far in the distance. They have settled by a dry oasis that should have offered them the paradise of water. A salvation in the dry, waterless expanse, yet has just offered them disappointment. Neither of us says but we know this shall put a strain on supplies and survival. The sun is high, our usual stopping point. We are still out of their sights and, without conversation, we stop and set up our usual temporary shelter.

We set a fire, drink tea and warm the last of our flat breads on the flames, yet both taste bland and lack the richness they had yesterday. I do not question it, I have already begun preparations to draw a veil over my feelings.

'They shall not expect us to hide,' she says, and I know I shall never win an argument against one who hears the future.

'They think me a man?'

'They think us beyond such distinctions.'

I look at her with questions in my eyes. This is a possibility I had never even conceived of.

'To them we are manifestation of spirit on earth. We are allowed our own laws.' Still I do not believe. 'They do not fear us, we are for their service.' I do not trust this logic; it is the world inside out. I cannot fathom such freedom, such autonomy and yet such obligation.

'You do not need to comprehend, just accept,' she says. I laugh. I have long since understood I comprehend almost nothing and soon, we are both laughing, laughing till it hurts. The release is glorious.

We take a pause to lie in each other's arms and breathe in the moment. Soon the sun will begin to drop, and we shall take the last steps towards re-joining the company of others.

'How much do they know?' I ask.

'As little as possible.'

'Which is?'

'That they have been paid handsomely for your safe passage across the desert. It is a request that is often made and often granted,' and we both smile as happy conspirators.

'If you'd like to soften your place in the tribe you could take the cloth of the men,' and she indicates the thobe she has carried with us.

I do not even consider it. For all that it may be practical, for all that it may ingratiate me into acceptance, it is too like a dress. Why does everyone keep trying to make me wear cloth that is not for me? I smile wryly at her. She knows I shall not accept.

As I mount the camel, I ask, 'You do all the negotiations?'

'It is I that have the languages.'

'How is it that you have studied so many?'

'I have not,' she says, 'I listen, remember?' We both laugh in recognition and set off towards the camp.

Sabby is greeted by a welcoming party of children led by the young boy who has since shed his bandages as he has healed, and they are deep in play by sunset. The adults pay us gentle but distant respect just as before, yet they have kept a spot for our tent and our camp is soon established with the help of the hands that come to join us without being asked.

They are respectful of Farah but also at ease; she is not to be feared. She provides a maternal love that transcends the body she is in and they cannot help but feel loved. For this they will accept her wisdom and guidance. I feel such an imposter, it is hard for me to stay in their company, but I too cannot resist the sensation of her love and shall suffer indignity to be part of it.

Soon we are settled, the sun falls, and Farah takes to the dunes before she shall join the other women in the preparation of the meal. Sabby joins me in the tent and we observe. The desire to shift is overwhelming and I fear I shall not be able to resist. When I did it last, in the company of the tribe, it was dark, and all were asleep. How do I do it now? I am stifled, trapped between a need to fly and a fear that to do so will cost our lives or the life of Farah. We are trapped with or without my gift.

Instantly I am so uncomfortable in my skin that every part of me begins to squirm and it is then I hear them, I hear their call in the fading light. It is not exactly the same as mine, but I recognise it all the same. They form a band in the sky and circle the tent. It is all I need, and within seconds I have joined my cousins, the Brown Ravens of the desert. Sabby follows as we swoop and dive, embracing and playing as the whole tribe stop to witness the wonder. Some fall to the ground in gratitude, some seek to join in, some simply to enjoy. We circle one last time before taking noisily to the open skies, busy singing our own praises. Sabby follows and we are complete.

When we return, Farah is waiting for us in our tent. She watches with peaceful pride as I shift back. Ready with scented water to wash me, as she binds my breasts, she hums a tune of love and satisfaction. She has brushed down my clothes and paid special attention to her own dress. I sense we shall be presented. Even Sabby has been provided with a bowl and scented water to wash away the dust from her coat, a luxury she is happy to indulge in and one in which she makes much noise and merriment. I am perplexed, to use such a scarce resource at such a time, to waste it on us, but I do not question when there is so much pride and satisfaction for Farah.

When she is happy with our appearance, we head down towards the fire and join the others. As we approach, they take to their feet, and each and every one bows their head as we pass, my discomfort increasing with each bow. Farah leads us to the head sheik who drops to his knees and clasps my hands and kisses each in turn. I am mortified and embarrassed into silence. Why am I being treated so? I pull him to his feet. I think he sees this as indication of my humility or grace, yet it is simply that I cannot receive his offering. Why does he offer it to me? He rises and lifts his arms with a great joyous howl and the celebration begins. Grey wine is poured, food is served and there is much joyous chatter. Farah leans in close.

'Now they understand why you are such precious cargo.' I look at her. 'It is an honour beyond their imagining to travel with one who has your gifts.'

I cannot help but brim with tears. To be accepted or even tolerated despite my gift has been the extent of my ambition; to be honoured for it is beyond my comprehension. The only way I can understand it is to deny it. How can I take this seriously? That night there is much dancing, singing and drinking in which I indulge to the fullest. It is the only thing that makes sense.

We fall into a regular routine of early evening shifting. I do not know what compels it, but each night is a returning and each night the tribe observe the to-ing and fro-ing of raven and wolf. It never ceases to amaze them, and they never ask anything more of us, although their reverence does not sit easily with me. I am not sure what I should do with it, how I should respond or receive it, so I do nothing and hope it is enough. I would rather simple acceptance, to be one of not the only one, yet each day I await eagerly for the feel of the air on my wings. It is a conformation, I do not know of what, yet it is a freedom that I have not had before, and I cannot help but indulge in it.

At first our days are filled with each other. I hear Farah's tales of growing up. How she was held by her tribe when her parents were killed in a bloody battle with another Bedouin tribe.

'I was so young and understood so little. The stories of great battles were common but in practice we all knew each other's routes and knew how to avoid them. Why foster destruction when all any want is to live freely? Yet the earth can be unkind as well as bountiful and when the belly speaks there is little room for ethics. I can still smell the blood as it fell from my father into the sand and my mother's wails before she too was silenced. I believe our tribe were the "victors" but there can be no victors in war only survivors.

'After that I didn't speak for a long time. I was not present for a long time. Although my body continued regardless I was someplace else. Yet they were good to me, no one asked anything of me, but all played a part in keeping me fed and safe. I became a child of the tribe rather than of any one parent. I would spend whole days on my own in sight of the tribe but as far apart as I dared, just sitting. It was then I learned to listen and the more I listened the more I heard. The more I heard the more I understood; the more I understood the more I healed. Then I did not know how to stop.'

'I know the feeling,' I say and ruffle my arms and shoulders as if I have wings and she smiles. It is a tender moment but inside I shrink away, unable to understand it.

'At first it was little things; I could predict a simple insect bite or the birth of a son. But it was when I heard of another battle that things changed. So distraught was I that I ran screaming and crying down the dunes. It would have been easy to ignore me, to disregard the hysterical ramblings of a child but he did not. It was the sheik I ran to, breaking all the etiquette we have, I ran straight up to him. Flung myself on his legs and begged him to change course, to take a different route. I do not know what compelled him, maybe it was pity, maybe he thought it a game to entertain our fate with the wishes of a small girl, maybe it was just as easy for us to take a different route. Maybe because it was the first time I had spoken. Either way he heard my request and we took a different route.

'Later we heard that another tribe had gone the way we had originally planned the day after us. They were attacked by bandits and only one lived to tell the tale. After that the head sheik took me from my daily chores and told me to develop my gift. I have made it my life's work.'

For all the beauty in her story I cannot help but feel the chill of jealousy run through my blood; to have grown up endorsed by all instead of hidden from all. Still I hope I hide it well from her but mostly from myself.

She knows she has a blessed life. She hears the changes happening across the world. Knows the ways of the earth are under threat everywhere. Knows even here in the remoteness of the desert their traditional way of life shall come to an end. She says even when you know what shall fall it is still a surprise, the feelings the same, yet to live with such vast connection in all directions overwhelms me. I cannot fathom how she holds such eternity inside herself. She says she doesn't have to, it simply is.

I tell her of my life, even though she has heard it all before. Still there is something in the telling that binds us, something that adds more shape and texture to what she already knows and understands. It is a beautiful time that we both know shall not last. We need to find water and soon.

Before first light everyone is awake, packing up in the cool of the moon. At first light we will be ready to set off. Although everyone has their tasks and role it is as if we are one unit working as a whole. No one is ready to go until we are all ready to go. There is much banter and complaining but no harm is meant, and it helps ease the boredom of the tasks. Once we are all assembled, the caravan sets off. The cattle lead and the domestic follow.

It's not long before, through the dust, Sabby and I spot a stray calf lost and left behind; without pausing we break our rank and quickly we guide the calf back to the herd and the anxious mother. Yet as we watch the happy reunion the lead herds man approaches at some speed. I fear reprimand, fear beating, fear we have overstepped but as he gets closer I see a broad smile on his face and he shakes my hand, talking non-stop in Arabic.

I smile back and nod even though I do not understand a word he says. Then finally when he has finished speaking and we just stand there grinning he gestures for us to join the men as they heard and then I really grin and nod my head eagerly as we happily take up a new role. I know from the looks between the tribe's people that they think it is an act of humbleness on our part, yet it is really a relief to step down from our elevated position.

We set up camp just as the sun becomes high in the sky. This has been the first morning I have spent away from Farah's side since our arrival and my hunger for her is ravenous. As soon as we have established camp we take to our bed, our lovemaking feverish and rapacious. Afterwards, we fall into a deep sleep.

I awake first and rise to take in the late afternoon sun. As I look out at the beauty and peace that holds us, I am filled with fear. I do not trust such happiness. What is my place here? How can these connections be made when I shall soon be deposited at my destination, a destination not of my choosing.

Farah awakes and comes up to stand behind me, embracing me with her love. Yet I cannot receive this love when it shall come to an end. Why does she play with me so? Unwanted images and sensations of hot greedy breath against my cheek, of faces taking their pleasure at my expense, erupt to the surface. I do not know what to do with them. I turn to get dressed and Farah offers me the thobe again.

Every day, since my gift has been acknowledged and welcomed by the tribe, she has offered me the thobe. I know she thinks I no longer need to bind, that I am accepted so no longer need a disguise. I do not appreciate her insistence, albeit well meaning. Today it is too much, and I take to the skies. It is that night I discover the oasis and the use of our wanderings for the tribe, who, at least for a while, are our family.

Chapter Five

The next day Sabby and I take the lead. We estimate the oasis to be a day and a night's travel and we are certain of the route, mostly passing through a large flat open plain filled with heat. There is no breeze and although there is nothing around for as far as the eye can see, it feels suffocating and claustrophobic. This is not their usual route and there is hesitancy in some people's eyes, yet they would not question me, and, although I am certain of our choice, I would welcome challenge to ascertain the strength of my conviction. Farah, forever forgiving, supports me in our direction and that it is all the corroboration they need.

At least we are protected from other tribes. There is no one who would approach when they would be seen from such a distance. When we set up camp for the afternoon it feels as if we have travelled no distance at all, so similar is the view. We rest and, at dusk, as others eat and prepare to travel through the night, I take to the skies and Sabby and I travel ahead to be sure of our route.

When we approach the oasis, we sense a change in energy. It is not the peaceful, welcoming place we first discovered. We slow down and proceed with caution. Then we see smoke drifting out of the dunes around the oasis. They are not in full view but rather have chosen the shadows, out of sight. I signal to Sabby to hold back whilst I fly high and circle above, out of range of arrows or pistols.

They are a significant number, but their camp is roughly made and lacks the abundance of our own. They have taken what they need from the oasis, water, wood and food, yet they have not received or embraced it. It makes little sense to me why they have chosen ascetic over comfort and by their manner and expression it makes little sense to them either. Their head sheik is set apart from them and any that approach him do so fearfully and with shame. Their route and direction are unclear; it is good to know of their presence, yet it does not bode well. I return to Sabby and we head back to the tribe.

After the meal I sit with Farah and Sabby, drinking in the brilliance of the stars before we set off for the night's travel.

'You did not speak of them. Do we not meet them?' I ask.

'You have lived with secrets,' she replies, 'you know their ways.'

I want to ask why it is a secret and not information that will allow us to prepare, but it is time for us to set off. We shall be at the oasis by the time the sun is high in the sky, alone or with company. I take the lead again, this time with some apprehension. I feel something is approaching but do not know what. Still the moon is bright, and it is hard to believe in tragedy when the stars are so brilliantly beautiful.

It is just first light as we approach the dunes. I think we are safe; if the other tribe were traveling in our direction, we would have met by now. Although, to myself, I try to deny a presence that is not benign. I glance back at the caravan and can tell it is not only me that feels it. All have shrunk a little in their stature.

We reach a circle of flat land amongst the dunes which reach up high all around. It would be a perfect spot for a ceremony or celebration, yet it is a danger spot for those passing through. Still I am sure any threat to us must have passed in the opposite direction. The feelings of foreboding I have belong to the ways of the earth, and, although I have made peace with shifting, or believe I have, I shall not follow the ways of the earth, not when they have failed me so. There is no reason to fear, so I shall not believe in my feeling of fear.

I reach the other edge of the circle as the last of the caravan enter it. We are not far from the oasis, but then we see them blocking our way. They sit on their camels with spears and scimitars at the ready. We halt, I look behind and it is the same. I hear Raven's cry and look up as one by one those not riding beast take to their feet. The sun creates black looming silhouettes, casting long shadows down the dunes. They have the high ground and we are surrounded.

I signal for all to stay still and a piercing silence pervades. They do not move and make no attempt to approach.

Are they simply toying with us? They do not need to do anything, such is their advantage. I am incapable of action. Both reason and intuition have failed me; I have led us all to certain death, for such a desperate tribe will have no cause to spare us anything, especially our lives. Shifting will serve no purpose; there is not a beast large enough to protect so many. We are barely armed and at such disadvantage, I can barely recognise it, for it shall prove me the fool I believe myself to be. Another solution must be found.

A piercing cry shatters the tension as a Short-toed Snake Eagle circles above. Does it not feel the tension, does it not feel the inappropriateness of its arrival? Part of me wants to laugh, to welcome the intruder; surely it is a sign we should be friends with our attackers and not foe? I gaze as it circles; I know of the beauty of that sensation, know the peace of the hunt. Then it is as if it happens in slow motion. I see an arrow pierce the eagle's heart, watch it writhe, trying to free itself as it falls, but the arrow is deeply embedded. I am jolted back in to quick time as the bird falls dead in front of us.

My rage is such that had I not had a whole tribe to consider I would have shifted to bear right there and then. I'd have torn apart and disembowelled all I could. Instead I slowly dismount and, with hands clearly in view, clearly without weapon, I walk towards the head sheik of the other tribe. Instantly a spear lands in the ground just in front of me, blocking my path. I cannot tell from where it has been thrown and I cannot look to see. Gently I go to step around the spear. Instantly twenty spears slice the air apart and pierce the ground. I am surrounded by spears, a perfect circle that allows no escape. So tightly packed are the spears I can hardly see between them. I fear our tribe will seek to retaliate, yet all is still, the tension palpable as it ripples amongst us.

I listen intently to see if now they shall approach, for surely now their massacre shall begin, but all I hear is the song of the sand shifting in the heat of the sun. Then it is clear. I close my eyes, take a deep breath and let the song of the sands sing through me. It is a sound I did not know I could make. I did not know I had this voice. I sing, I sing, and with each breath I sing louder and stronger, with each breath I open up more, with each breath I let the sound have more of me.

Farah must have understood my meaning, for soon the whole tribe is joining me. I cannot tell what sound we make so inside it I am; I have become it. It is a wonderous sensation. I lose sense of my bones and muscles being fixed, being solid, as the sound supports all. It's a vibration, the vibration of life. The sound transforms us all, yet is created by us all. We have become one beauteous point of focus, and, shining out of us is the song we make yet it is the song that binds us, that makes us. It is all one, no before or after, no chicken or egg, just all at once. There is not a hesitation, no choice even, just an absolute surrender to the moment, so much so that I fear I shall not remember this when it has passed, think it shall be lost to my consciousness, yet somehow part of it.

There is no separation, yet it is made of all separateness. We are at once completely free of the earth and yet completely and utterly part of it. We are of it and not of it at the same time and it is not long before I feel the earth respond. It is as if we have awoken the dunes and I can feel the earth's energy rising and shifting. I feel the movement of the earth as the dunes begin to fall towards us. Then, through the crescendo of our song, I hear our attackers turn, I feel them run, their horses scrambling for footing, their feet for footholds. I hear them trying to out run the shift of the sands. I sense their confusion, their fear as the earth is no longer stable, as what they thought they knew, what they thought they could depend on takes on a form not of their choosing, takes on a form that does not serve them. Never shall they approach their problems with violence again, not when the earth has taught them so.

Then it is us that are on the move - as the dunes are released so the sand approaches us. Farah tears away the spears and grabs my hand, pulling me forward.

'Quick, come, there is no time,' she says

'Was it as you heard?' I ask, resisting her pull.

'Better,' she says, and we scramble upwards as the sand falls downwards.

The others haul us to safety as the last of the dunes fills the circle, blocking the pass, making the site unsuitable for capture and torture for ever more. Our spirits high we sing, this time well-known ballads; we sing our way to the oasis and set up camp.

The fire roars and the grey wine flows. Everyone has a poem or a song or a dance. We sit with the sheik and, as all enjoy the festivities, we are presented with gifts. One by one each member of the tribe approaches, each waiting their turn, some offer gold, some food, some beautifully hand-crafted trinkets, some merely their thanks and to prove it they lay prostrate on the ground in front of me. I would like to be able to receive their gifts with appropriate grace, but each gift just serves to make me more ashamed. How can they thank me when it is I that led them to an almost certain death?

In the end I turn to Farah. 'Can you not make them stop?'

'Why, when infamy of their triumph shall travel far and wide and for many years?'

'Is that all that counts?'

'Sometimes.'

'I do not even have the words to thank them for the gifts.'

'شكرا – Shukra'.

'Shukra,' and she nods conformation of my pronunciation. I stand and the sheik calls all to silence with a small and simple gesture of his hand. All eyes turn to me and I am glad I cannot speak Arabic for a speech is surely called for. Instead I take my time to take in each and every face, acknowledging with love and gratitude in my eyes, each and every one in turn, even the sheik, so there may be no doubt that I speak to all.

'Shukra,' I say as loudly and as clearly as I can and bow deeply. I am met with rapturous applause. I had intended a humbling not a crowning still it seems to fulfil a need they have so I smile and applaud them back. Farah signals for the music to start up again and the celebrations begin in earnest.

There is much to celebrate yet I am not with them, not lost in glory. When they are so engrossed as to not notice, I take myself away and find a quite spot by the water's edge. It is a pleasure to hear their merriment but inside me is a storm of confusion. I do not understand what or how we were triumphant.

I think the sound must have dislodged the sand. It's a reasonable explanation, or an explanation at least that does not depend on the ways of the earth or magik. Yet where did the song come from? Part of me knows the answers yet I reject them for they cannot make sense. They cannot be when I have watched my grandmother hung before me. When I have been so brutally treated. When I only just escaped with my life.

That day we did not stop. That was the day I escaped with my life. I flew and Sabby followed until we could travel no further. I had no destination in mind, no place to aim for. We did not even pass our home. We did not stop to pick up supplies, to pick up memories. My only desire was to get as far away as possible. The feel of the executioner's rope was imprinted on my neck. I could not fly fast enough or far enough. Eventually we flew into a storm; rain lashing through the sky, lightning threatening our safety, thunder resounding all around me. I am pulled down to the earth. I hit the ground as raven and it is the last I remember till I awake.

I am naked and wrapped around Sabby for warmth. She has found a sheltered spot at the foot of a bank of granite. The moss is thick beneath us and a fine layer of dew blankets us all. I am too frightened to rise, frightened to raise my head and look about me, frightened to face where I am, yet Sabby senses my wakefulness and she has no such fear, only joy at reunion. To greet her, to receive and reciprocate her love is life afresh. Our re-joining makes everything possible. We indulge ourselves in our affection until I recall my duty to her and it becomes of the utmost importance to feed her, to tend to her.

She has found a good spot for us, a fast-flowing river is nearby. We are surrounded by trees and there is no sign of other humans. I stand and feel the earth between my toes and the fresh morning air caress my body. It is late morning by the place of the sun and I want nothing more than to wash away the scent of the gaol from my skin.

I race Sabby down to the river, and, of course, she wins. I dive into the fast-running water and the shock ignites my senses. It is as if I have been purged of all that was before, and a piercing clarity fills my mind. I scramble to the shore; I shall collect firewood whilst Sabby fishes. I watch her choose her spot and gather her energies ready for when opportunity presents.

Despite the storm the night before, I find plenty of crisp dry wood and leaves under the shelter of the trees. I return to our camp, set and light the fire using granite stone for a spark. The fire is roaring before I think to fear that the smoke shall signal our existence. I am about to put it out when Sabby arrives with two large trout in her mouth. My hunger is such that I would rather be captured with a full belly than be free without. With the aid of stick and stone the fish is soon gutted and cooking over the fire.

I have never been more grateful to another living being for the gift of their life, so fine tastes the trout's flesh, so eagerly my body feels its restoration. There is not a speck of meat or skin remaining. We leave the innards of my fish for the woodland beasts and lie back in the midday sun, unable to move such is the fullness of our bellies. Yet the sun's warmth on my skin reminds me of my nakedness.

I consider staying forever in this spot; there is abundance all around and it would not take long to set up shelter and live in quite comfort away from the world, a naked hermit amongst the trees with nothing, not even clothes, between myself and the earth, yet I do not believe I would be so undiscovered when word of my escape and its manner must be spoken across the land by now.

To stay here would be to become my own gaoler. Forever hiding, forever looking over my shoulder, there would be no way to hide in open view, and I cannot ask that of all that surrounds me, the trees, the river, plants and beasts, it is not their purpose. We must move on. I sit up and look around me. I must find some clothes, establish our whereabouts. I breathe in deep, filled with resolve and the heavy scent of flower, river, and earth boosts my spirit and is my inspiration. We shall travel to the stench that fills the lungs with dread. We shall go where they expect to find us. We shall hide in plain view and live only as a true recluse can, in the depths of London Town surrounded by people.

I stand, and we put out the fire and leave no trace of its existence or our own. When I look back, I can see no suggestion of our visit, yet I shall remember this place of shelter and carry it with me for when I will need to call on its memory. I let Sabby take the lead. She found this place, she shall know the next direction. We have barely walked three yards when we reach a path. I duck behind a bush. Why has she brought us such when I could be discovered so easily.

Then I hear them, their chatter and laughter preceding them. I sink further into the undergrowth, not caring how much my skin complains about the tears and scratches. Then they come into full view. Five women varying in size, shape and age - all maids or mothers, one younger, maybe a daughter or young bride. They carry large woven baskets filled to the brim with dirty laundry. They must be making their way to the river.

A young farmer's lad, carrying a weight of corn, approaches from the opposite direction and they fall into a demure silence. He doffs his hat and greets them respectfully as he passes. We all notice a shy smile stolen between him and the young woman. Once they consider him out of earshot, they explode into laughter and excited merriment. He is traveling towards and they are traveling away. We must be very near a town or village. I am shocked that what I thought, just minutes ago, was a rich endless wilderness is just directly near a settlement of people. How easy it is to be deceived.

Sabby begins to follow the women, moving silently amongst the undergrowth. She keeps a safe distance yet one in which they are never out of sight. I follow, yet much slower as it is not as easy for me to travel soundlessly and my feet are yet unhardened and unused to walking without boots. Many a time I stifle and swallow a cry of pain.

The sound of women's voices increases as we approach the river. Sabby has taken up position and is surveying the scene with keen intent, her body poised and ready to pounce. Her focus is on a shallow part of the river. Large flat stones lie under the water's surface and create the perfect conditions for laundry, and it must be laundry day as up to twenty women of all ages have gathered with bundles and baskets of clothes.

They chat and joke, someone starts a song and their joyous voices fill the air. They have found a way to make a pleasure out of a boring, demanding chore and I am envious of their camaraderie, jealous of the apparent simplicity of their lives where they are not different, where being part of a community is not questioned. The trees and bushes swell with freshly washed clothes. There are all shapes, sizes and forms of costume. I sense Sabby's plan and begin to pull back, ready to follow her lead.

We sit sometime waiting for just the right moment. Then Sabby leaps into action before I have even understood what has happened. Diving from a nearby tree, on the other side of the river, is a large magpie. Attracted by a cluster of pins catching the sunlight, he sweeps in to claim his share and the instant the women's attention is taken up with chasing the magpie, Sabby responds.

She is so quick that she has selected linens, doublet and hose and disappeared back into the thicket before any of the women have noticed. When they have made sure the magpie shall take none of their valuables they return to their tasks. It will be sometime before they realise their actual loss, not till they come to collect their freshly-dried clothes will they wonder at their disappearance. The whole thing has taken minutes and I have a full set of clothes. It is now my turn to move with undiscovered stealth through the undergrowth to Sabby and my new wardrobe.

I find her not far from where we first met the path. The undergrowth is dense here and a large yew tree creates a clearing and coverage. Quickly I dress, keeping some linen for binding when I have more time. She has chosen for me a simple attire. The cloth is still damp, but shall soon air out in the sun. My wardrobe is complete with a worn and shabby hat. At first it is a disappointment to have such a basic accessory, but then I place it on my head and the brim flops down covering my eyes. Then I understand her logic. We shall travel as paupers, beggars even, our adopted shame our disguise.

There is comfort in being washed and dressed, yet a loss too that I must separate my body from the earth. Sabby barks her approval and we walk boldly onto the path. I look down at my bare feet; although dressed in dirt they still look fresh and unused to exposure. I rub dirt into them. Then I consider my clothes and think that although not unique, their freshness is inappropriate, and I take dirt and daub it where it would gather naturally. As we set off to the town there is a simple clarity, our only need to live from one moment to the next. It's as if all that has happened has not, as if, for a short while, I walk with no shadow.

I think we shall walk humbly through the town gates, pleading protection and offering our services in return for shelter and food, yet as we approach, as we begin to take in the comings and goings, Sabby takes us to the left and we begin to travel round the town's wall. Sabby sinks back into the undergrowth so I follow. The river will flow through the town and I think she will take us to where the river meets the wall. It will be guarded but also busy, an easy entry point.

The wall creates a bridge over the river high enough for small boats and wherries to pass unhindered but low enough to defend the town if need be. It is indeed busy, a constant flow of traffic in both directions. Jovial mockery mixed with riled tempers lubricate the interactions of the sailors. A large round man with a smile as broad as his belly is in charge of the water gate. There is not a sailor who would cross him, so I think there is more behind his smile than first appears. He is joined by a small wiry man and, although they are discreet, I notice in their greeting an exchange. I am not sure of what, but it is enough to fit unnoticed into the gate keeper's doublet unseen or ignored. The smaller man waves on his wherry; as it approaches, the skipper cries out, 'I pray, my good man this is a raven-free town,' and all three howl loudly.

'What use have we of ravens when we are besieged by Robin Hood?' retorts the gatekeeper. Again they laugh as if they are far superior men of reason and intellect to be fooled by such gossip and foolish folklore. I am at once relieved and insulted.

So it is Nottingham and Sherwood Forest that has proved our sanctuary. We have our whereabouts, we have conformation of our infamy, we need little else from the town. We know the ways of the earth and we can make our way to London finding food and shelter as we go. The forest shall be our guide and our protection. I look at Sabby, the wag of her tail indicates she concurs. We are about to turn and crawl deeper into the undergrowth when we hear screams. They are piercing and clear, not a scream of distress but a call for help. We stop. I do not wish to look behind. I do not want to see her suffering. Our only intent is to get to safety; it is not our concern, it is not our battle.

She cries again and in her call I recognise part of myself and it is as if she reaches out to that which I seek to ignore as I continue on my way. Sabby has moved ahead, keen that we do not risk ourselves for a stranger, yet how can I have lived through all I have and not help another in need? Her screams have silenced the frivolity of the sailors, although their silence is not of shame or remorse but of justification and a sense of necessity. Sabby creeps ahead.

The woman screams again, this time in pain, this time in despair. I try to follow Sabby, resolve to keep my resolve. I have been clear and focused on my intent but now I feel a million walls begin to crumble inside me and I cannot move, no matter what I tell my body it does not respond. Sabby too has stopped. We hear a wailing this time and jeers of laughter, of a crowd, and there is no longer any hesitation. We both turn back but I am determined no magik shall be used. My "gift" shall not endanger anyone else again. Yet the truth is I am far too afeared to use it, far too afraid to trust it, far too confused to understand what I have always known. We shall help and it shall be on their terms.

To enter the town will be no easy task. We have nothing to sell, no money to buy anything and I am wearing clothes that could easily be recognised by their owner. Vagrancy is against the law and if we are seen as such we shall be in the stocks, or worse, we could be recognised for who we are. Now I wish for my doublet and the hidden golden piece. It would make all this so much easier. Then it comes to me. We creep back to the Watergate. It will be easy enough.

I wait until the to-ing and fro-ing of boats returns to a steady and regular pace. I stand and brush myself down, Sabby shakes herself presentable. I grab a handful of granite stones and calmly we walk up to the gate keeper.

'It's a fine day,' I say.

He barely looks at me and keeps a still eye on the boats. The woman screams again, and I wince.

'It is a frightful noise she makes. Someone should cut out her tongue,' I say, and he looks me square in the eyes. I do not flinch.

'Whatever it is she has done her punishment shall not be enough,' I say and slowly he smiles a broad and satisfied grin, yet still he turns his gaze back to the boats. I go to pass him into the town and he steps to face me blocking my route.

'Do you stop a prospector stating his claim?' I ask. He looks at me and sniggers. I hold out my hand and show him the rocks.

'I came in search of the famed hidden gold of Robin,' still he does not respond, 'and I have found it under yonder river bed,' and I beam a happy innocent smile. He studies me hard, then laughs.

'You take me for a fool,' he says.

'I take you for an honest man who would not rob an innocent of his fortune.'

He laughs. 'You jest with me. If gold it was in that river bed we'd know by now.'

'And the lords and ladies would have kept all for themselves.'

He nods his head in recognition.

'Look,' I say and make a show of scraping mud from one of the stones. 'See this vein here,' and I make sure the stone catches the light. 'When this is polished off it will be pure, beautiful, gleaming. A nugget of pure gold.'

He regards me suspiciously but with interest.

'I knew I could trust you,' I say. 'I knew you would not spread word until I had chance to stake my claim. Here, take it, I shall have plenty more where that came from.'

He takes the stone.

'Just at the river there?'

'Just past the white water where the women do the laundry. Where the sediment is still and deep,' I say, beaming with satisfaction and accomplishment. Sabby has already gone past him unnoticed. The woman lets out a loud moan and I see Sabby's urgency. I edge past the gatekeeper as he studies the stone.

'Thank you for keeping our secret,' I say, and he looks up as we slip into the crowds and out of sight.

The town is busy, still we are unknown faces and I do my best to stand out and be visible, so no one shall question us, so no one thinks us out of place. We have barely made our way to the market place before we hear the rumours that gold has been found in the river. There is a healthy disbelief but also enough keen interest, such is the way with people now and I do not understand it. I do not understand how normal people have chosen to abandon the earth in favour of the treasures of the earth, that a tiny fraction of the earth has become more important to them than all its wealth, the wealth of wisdom, of sensations, of experiences. How can a coin replace the soul? It shall not be long before there is a crowd waist deep in the water and muck. Internally I apologise to the river for this intrusion and thank it for its assistance. Twice it has given us life today - what more wealth is there?

By the time we reach the square we are walking against the tide of people rushing towards the river. Then we spot her, bound by chains to a stage, wearing a scold's bridle. Blood runs from her mouth and she is growing faint. I think she has a powerful will to remain standing till I see she cannot fall to her knees; the bridal is chained to a scaffold above her.

Soon the square is deserted; even the stall holders have abandoned their wares such is the exodus. I consider our options. Do I take a saw to free her? Do I cut through chains? Then I think what Constantine would do and it is not long before I have the very tool I need. I find a stall selling hats and collect a selection of pins. She would wince and retreat from my advance if she could, her eyes wild with fear.

'Be still,' I say in the softest voice I can. 'I come to release you, be still, it shall take but seconds.'

She stands still, and I bend down to release her legs. Her feet are soft and petite, not the feet of one who has worked the fields. I release the ankle cuffs, still she does not move. I reach above her head to release the chain that holds her, the smell of fear outweighing the smell of rose perfumes that she has used to augment her beauty. Still she does not move, I almost fear she has turned to stone so petrified she is.

The scold's bridle is harder; if I dislodge it, if she moves, the spike that sits above her tongue shall end her life. It has already drawn blood. She knows the danger too and holds her perfect stillness. With the utmost tenderness I ease the lock, find just the right angle and then gently release the hold. It's like I am handling the finest crystal. I gently but surely release the back of the bridle and then, with even more care, I release the front. Scraps of flesh and blood hang from the plate and spike. We are too late.

Once released she does not collapse, she does not fall into my arms. She does not pause but turns and runs. In seconds she is out of sight and we are left holding the scold's bridle. Such are the times that women who talk "too much" are placed in murderous traps of metal. We would take after her, yet it is fear that is fuelling her, and she shall not run for long before she breathes her last. At least she will die a free woman. At least we were able to give her that.

We do not have long to ponder our fate. We can hear that the scene at the river bed has descended into riot as, without any cause, they turn against each other. I seize some supplies, a cloak, some boots, wine and bread, a knife, even a little money to help establish ourselves in London. There are horses aplenty, but it will be easier for us to hide on foot and we have a lifetime ahead of us and no one to answer to. I glance once more around the square. There is no sign of her.

Despite the danger we cannot help but enjoy the chaos we have caused. Keeping deep within the trees we approach the river. It is hard to see for the crowd that has amassed, yet we can make out a full-blown skirmish amongst the men of the town, the gate keeper in the thick of it, the women cheering and egging on their own. It is not long before they too are throwing punches and pulling hair. I take the rest of the handful of stones, thank them for their service and return them to the earth. I think what sport it would be to leave them to it. There is satisfaction in seeing their greed destroy themselves. How good it feels not to be part of it.

We think that she has had enough time now to have either died in freedom or sought sanctuary. I make sure I am unseen by climbing a large oak tree, Sabby hides in the undergrowth. We are out of sight and out of the way.

From high up in the canopy I throw my voice into the crowd, 'Come quick, thieves, quick thieves.' It is the stall holders that hear first.

'Thieves in the square.' It starts the second stampede of the day. It's all I can do to stop myself from laughing out loud. What power a few well-chosen words can have. Soon all is deserted.

I scramble down from the tree. We will not have long before a search party is sent for her and her saviour. We head south, deep into the forest. Alive and joyous, for the first time in a long while, there is pleasure in being apart. We may have lost everything and everyone but there is a heady freedom that comes with the loss. We have no one, yet we have no one to answer to. I am drunk on the notion. Still all that has gone before is distant and unfelt.

That night we find shelter deep amongst the trees, far from human contact. I make a fire and Sabby catches a rabbit. The air is still and the moon high in a cloudless sky. I make a bed from my cloak, sip the wine, and soak in the tranquillity of the night. We are suspended, held in the moment. There has been no past, there will be no future, only the moment. It is a state I wish to stay in, yet one I know will pass all too soon.

Chapter Six

We awake kissed by the dew as first light caresses the horizon. We should rise and make an early start before prying eyes have also risen. Yet we have no one to answer to and nowhere to be so we sit in the peace and absorb the beauty. The certainty of the cycle, day following night following day, it is the only thing of any value, the only thing we need. How have normal folk chosen to forget this? What illusion have they chosen instead? Why wasn't the connection to all that nourishes and feeds us good enough?

Eventually hunger inspires action and I take some wine and bread. I wonder how the townsfolk of Nottingham have made sense of yesterday's events and which way they sent the search party, if they have realised it is I that they seek. It is best we pack up and move on, yet that is the only reason to do so. We know the earth and could live happily with it for the rest of our days. It is this moment I will return to often in years to come. What if we had stayed? What if we had chosen the honest integrity of a life lived in harmony with the earth? Yet at the time I did not consider it an option or at least not an achievable one, more of an ideal I was not worthy of. The sun is high by the time I check that we leave no trace and set off towards London Town.

We have no map, no compass, just a direction and an intention. The weather is fair and our route lush and wealthy with plant and beast. It is easy to believe we travel for leisure, yet I pay attention to all that is around and the sense of direction inside. It is not long before we reach the edge of the forest. We wait, the road seems clear, yet we shall not follow it. I wish to see no one; our route shall be longer but less risky. Then we hear it. It is a joyful tune and one we recognise. My heart leaps to my throat and I expect my body to leap into action and run eagerly with open arms to greet him, yet I do not move, not even flinch, even though the impetus is there.

We watch from the shelter of the trees as he turns the corner and into full view. Constantine and Blossom, idling along without a care in the world, whistling a merry tune. Inside me I alight, everything wants to run to the safety and comfort of his masculine embrace and cutting humour. Everything I have been taught says it is a sign, it is a gift that I should receive with all my heart, yet still I do not move, still no sound escapes my lips. I simply watch him pass. Part of me hopes his own sensibilities will feel my presence and seek me out or that he shall fall from Blossom and need our assistance or that Blossom herself will feel us and find us, yet none of that happens, they merely continue on their way. Sabby looks at me but she remains still and silent. It is then I know I have turned my back on the past.

There is still no sensation of the past, no memory that fills my mind, just a knowledge that it has happened; more a sense of safety in the present and the promise of a different life in the future. We continue following the route of the road, but from a safe distance. Sometimes the undergrowth is dense, and progress is slow, but we are happy in our task, taking the time to admire the butterflies and bumble bees busy in their work, thinking ourselves lucky not to have any. It's no wonder they have made laws against the wandering ways, no wonder they have turned nomads into vagabonds. Who would they find to do the jobs they don't want to do otherwise? I think how even now I am against the law. Even now, when I seek to be an upstanding subject to do so means working against the law. It is well I have grown with secrets and learnt how to keep them. I do not dwell on thoughts for long; they threaten to break the serenity I am happy within.

We stop for lunch next to a babbling brook which provides beauty and comfort with no painful associations. It is late afternoon and we doze in the sun, Sabby resting at my side. There is nothing and nobody I want for. Something inside me says this cannot be so but I do not pay it any heed. I simply pack up and move on whenever this happy place is challenged.

At late evening we can hear and smell a town ahead. From our vantage we can see the town walls below, hear the clatter of human life, see the fires burning. It is a picturesque scene and one travellers should welcome for the comfort and security it offers, yet we do not need or want it. We descend to a spot well-sheltered and where we cannot see or be seen. In the morning we shall rise before first light to put the town behind us well in advance of the traffic of the day. It is barely a conscious thought, but I know we have taken a route that has given us a wide margin between us and our home town.

We travel three days as such, feasting on the gifts of the earth - nuts, mushrooms, flowers and roots, whatever Sabby catches and whatever has been left behind. We want for nothing. Each day my excitement grows a little more at the anticipation of a new life. To be someone and something different fills me with a joy I did not know I lacked. Things will be different in the city. I consider taking a new name. It would be wise after all and I while away an hour trying on different names to see if they stick. None do, and I think maybe I could have a new name every day to suit my humour. Gradually London becomes a place of opportunity. I consider myself world wise as I am not so stupid to believe the streets are paved with gold. I know it will be hard at first, yet I have charm and looks on my side. I am a quick study, and no one will know me. I shall be free, freer than I have ever been before.

It is night fall on the third day when we first smell it, the stench of the city announcing its approach. We decide to take one last night in the arms of Mother Earth. She has held us on our journey, sheltered and fed us. If it was the old ways I would sing and make a ceremony of thanks. Yet it is not the old ways and I shall not, although inside I cannot help but thank her. It is a small weakness when the next day promises so much. That night I sleep a fretful, splintered sleep and Sabby watches over, not resting herself at all. Before I would have understood this as portents, and I am glad in the fresh morning light that I no longer have to consider things so. There is a happy release to this, followed by a doubt that I choose to ignore.

It is not until we reach the city gates that it hits me. What shall I do now that I am here? Where shall we find food? Where shall we find shelter? I have the money taken from the market but no idea how to obtain more or how much I shall need to obtain. How shall we feed ourselves without the earth's assistance? Yet we are not given long to consider our fate. The flow of traffic in and out of the city walls is constant and we are carried along by its current. We are part of something but disconnected. The magnitude of people is such that it is impossible to connect with all and this seems to mean no one connects with anyone. It's perfect for our needs. Such is the indifference amongst people that even if we are recognised no one will care, unless there is a bounty on our heads. Yet I doubt there is; there is not a man amongst them that would admit defeat by a woman or a witch.

Where there should be trees there are buildings. The earth beneath our feet is laden with waste from man and beast. The only green is seen in cloth and paint. The sounds envelope everything as if we are in the thick of a murder of crows, all screeching at once. It is not alien exactly, but overwhelming. Nonetheless, our last visit to the city was just that, a visit, and on horseback all looked different. This time we plan to stay and all that seemed play before now becomes our life. It now has a different flavour, yet being able to walk freely amongst people is intoxicating. Anyone can belong here because no one belongs here. We feel opportunity surround us - even though we do not yet know how to access it, we cannot help but be seduced by the notion of it.

Following the flow of people as we would follow the flow of a river, we soon reach streets full of shops and stalls. It feels like the whole world is laid at our feet for display. Some things I recognise from books, some things I cannot imagine what they can be used for, some that are familiar. I ask the price of some trinkets and find it three times what it would be at home. Our money shall not go far. We spend most of the day wandering the labyrinth of streets, trying to make sense of their route, but so much looks alike it is easy to lose a sense of direction. Eventually all routes lead to the river, its hustle and bustle, its dense aroma announcing its presence. It is hard to see water, so densely packed are the boats and gangways and people, yet we feel it there, and its presence is a comfort that I deny myself.

Such has been our consumption of the myriad of entertainments of the day we have not eaten or drank. I check Sabby and, whilst she does all she can to maintain her enthusiasm, I feel her need. It will cost us nearly all we have but

I buy us two steaming hot meat pies and we retire to an alley a little back from the docks to feast in peace. We find an almost dry and clear bit of ground and sit together as we eat. The pie looks so much better than it tastes, the meat is of the poorest cut and is laden with gristle. It promised so much more, yet our hunger prevails.

As we eat I become aware of people in the shadows, at first shy, or at least unwilling to be identified. Gradually though, women of all shades and ages step out. Their dresses are tattered and faded, their faces hidden by rouge. There is something missing in their eyes, as if they have long ago vacated their bodies, yet they turn their gaze upon us nonetheless. We are about to leave when a closed carriage pulls up and blocks the entrance to the passage. A hand appears out of the curtained window and points to one of the oldest, roundest women who trots eagerly and gratefully to the carriage. The door is opened, and she steps inside. The other women look on with a contempt that hides their disappointment. We have chosen the street of brothels to picnic. The carriage door closes and the horses speed away.

I am filled with shame and embarrassment. I stand and hope to leave without further notice when the youngest of the women approaches. She studies me up and down. 'New to town?'

'I, yes,' I say, although, all parts of me inside denounce honesty on this occasion.

'You'll have better luck over there,' and she looks down the road indicting an alley with an inn on its corner. Outside the inn lounge a few young men. I turn back to thank her, but she has already stepped back into the shadows.

We turn and walk in the opposite direction. How can we earn our keep that way, when on the outside I am man and on the inside a woman? It has not occurred to me yet that that is exactly what some would seek. Besides there will be river rats to eat before I let anyone near my body again.

We are about to begin to find a place to sleep for the night when we see him. A large crowd has gathered as he slides the cups around the board, a common ancient game of magic seen in every market place. Still he is one of the best we have seen at cups and ball, his sleight of hand precise and ruthless. The fascination for such a game has always perplexed me. Why waste time and money on certain loss? We watch the bets get higher as each one knows better than the last. When the pot is as full as I think it can be, I speak out.

'I'll wager this penny for all you have if I guess correct,' I say.

The crowd fall silent, all eyes turn to me, to set such terms is bold. The boy studies me. He must be no older than twelve, but his life has afforded him wisdom beyond his years. He smiles broadly; he is confident that I am a simple country bumpkin who does not understand city ways.

'Lay your penny down, master,' he says, and I do.

All is quiet except the scraping of cup on wood. He stops, and I choose. I am correct, a raven's eye is hard to fool and when you have magik it is easy to see how magic works. The crowd watch expectant. He locks eyes with me now, yet still he sees his own glory reflected.

'Best one of three?' he says.

I nod, and he works the cups again, again I pick correct. A frozen moment suspends us all. I have broken the spell. He studies me again, then smiles.

'The fates are in your favour, sir. One more for luck?'

Again I agree and prepare to chase for surely now he shall grab his winnings and make a run for it, yet such is his confidence in his own skill, he goes again, again I pick correct. This time there are gasps from the crowd, some of wonderment, some of jealousy, some of defeat. I see him calculate and compare his options. Eventually his face softens and a warm smile spreads across his face.

'Sir, you have the eyes of a hawk; it's a pleasure to have you sharpen my game. Come, let us take your winnings and toast your success.' As he has spoken, he has packed up his belongings and he holds my winnings in one hand and offers me the other.

'Master, you are an expert in your craft, it has been a joy to play you. Pass me my winnings and it will be an honour to feast with you.' And I hold out my hand, making it clear we shall not shake until I have my winnings.

The tension rises; I have won my takings fair and square, to deny me risks the wrath of the crowd. He would have to be a certain runner to make a dash for it. Slowly and reluctantly he hands me the coins and it is my turn to run. He will not be working alone. If I take these coins, I shall not be allowed to keep them, yet we have no choice. I hold out my hand and he lets the coins fall in. As the last one drops we about turn; the crowd parts for us as we take to our heels as fast as we can.

I let Sabby lead the way and we weave in and around people, crates and beasts. I look back. The boy has taken a few steps in our direction and it is then I see he has a club foot. He did not run because he could not run. I would feel more shame but for the pursuit of a large, heavyset man who pushes all and everything aside in his chase. Sabby takes us down some steps and we manage to hide under the gangway. We see his feet above us, pause, falter, then take the direction they came from. We wait a while, regaining our breath. I count our winnings. In my hand it feels substantial, yet I fear it is worth little in the long run. We pause to regain our breath and let night fall.

The dark offers us some protection, as it does for our foes; with caution we climb out of our hiding place. Sabby is alert and watchful and every part of my being is listening. The streets are no longer full of comforting indifference and wonderous opportunity. They are the streets I had hoped to leave behind, where every glance, every sound, every movement, every smell could be an attack. I want to run as far away as possible, yet there is nowhere to run. We make our way through the docks till we reach the edge of a cemetery. I am unsure if it is safer amongst people or apart, but the shelter of a large old yew is too much to reject. We crawl inside. I hold Sabby close, wrap the cloak around us and we blend into the shadows. A sickly fatigue sweeps over me as I close my eyes and seek the sanctuary of sleep, trying my best to ignore an overwhelming feeling of disappointment.

We awake to the sound of spade in earth and the tears of a mourner. Sabby investigates the scene whilst I come to my senses. I feel yesterday's takings heavy in my pocket and ponder its uses. I think Mary would know exactly what to do. If she were here we would have a plan in place with clear direction. It is the first I have allowed myself to think of her since our escape and it is as if I have pierced myself with a multitude of tiny knives. I think I shall cry, weep with heartbreak and loneliness, yet I am unable. There is only emptiness where I know there should be feeing.

I dismiss the thoughts by crawling out from under the yew and into the day. A lone woman kneels at a nearby grave. I am jealous of the tears that flow freely from her. I think she must be a young and new widow to feel such pain, such loss. The gravedigger cusses and blasphemes, his disregard for the Lord's name gives me a little cheer. I dust myself down and we head back towards the docks. There is such variety there our difference is lessened.

All is how it was yesterday; countless people, deafening noise, every bit of space filled with life. Yesterday it was intoxicating, today it is as if we are seeing a mirror image. Today we are not blinded by colour or transported by smells. Today we see the beggar children scavenging for whatever sustenance they can get. Today we see desperation eat at the souls of the sailors. Today we see man live off man and we do not comprehend it. I have no means to digest or negotiate this landscape. I have failed to protect all that I love, all who I love, and now I cannot fathom the alternative. A sense of uselessness washes through my entire being and I feel myself begin to disappear.

Sabby keeps alert, keeps leading us forward when I would carelessly sink to the ground. I care little for what people might think or say. What does it matter? Then we see them in almost the same spot as before. The boy is setting up and his keeper is keeping watch when he is approached by a sailor. I think I recognise the face but cannot place it. We duck out of sight and watch the sailor ask some questions. At the conclusion of the conversation the sailor hands the keeper some coins before slipping into the crowd. I have grown complacent in my curiosity and, without noticing, have stepped out of our hiding and into full view and the boy spots us.

Sabby is quick and clear with the route as we slip back into the crowd, moving as fast as we can without raising suspicion. The keeper does the same and we feel his pursuit. We are just passing the alleyway when we see up ahead the young bawd from yesterday slip into the inn she pointed out to us. Sabby has the same thought as I. We glance about, we see the keeper a short distance behind. A carriage approaches, between him and us. We stop and show ourselves in plain view; he sees us and the carriage cuts between as we slip unseen into the inn.

We burst through the doors and all stop to look at us. It is mostly empty but the woman from the alley sups ale and pottage. Some foppish men huddle together round a table, already drunk on wine and in high spirits. The look on my face says all and the young bawd indicates a booth and table tucked out of sight of the door. We take cover under the table just as the doors are flung open and the keeper steps into the doorway, blocking out the sunlight. The landlord steps forward, broad and rotund with hands that threaten a deadly punch.

'What ails you, master? Will libation be the cure of your malady?'

'A young boy and a dog are the only cure I require,' says the keeper and at that the whole inn erupts in laughter.

'You are not alone in that,' replies the landlord and gives him a wink. In exasperation or disgust the keeper turns and exits, slamming the door behind him. Everyone laughs.

The bawd bends down to us and offers me her hand and we crawl out from our hiding spot.

'Thank you,' I say. I am bashful, slightly embarrassed but mostly grateful. The landlord has joined her

'He's an innocent, ain't he?' they say to the bawd. They mean me, but I feel anything but innocent.

'Quiet and aw,' says the bawd.

'What can I do you for?' asks the landlord. My suspicion is such that this could be a genuine question and not a whimsical twist on a common saying. I hesitate to answer.

'Wine or beer?' asks the bawd and I smile.

'Do you have fire water?' I ask and there is surprise around the room, yet they are equally impressed.

'Only the best,' replies the landlord and goes behind the counter.

I place a crown upon the bar. 'All round,' I say, and it is met with approval by all. 'It's the least we can do.'

'Bottoms up,' says the bawd and we clink our tankards and down in one. We take a seat at the bar. I check Sabby and she is happily panting on the wooden floor.

'Come to seek your fortune?' the bawd asks.

'Something like that.'

'Have you found the golden paved streets?'

I laugh. 'Surely the gold is to be found inside?' And I signal the landlord to fill our tankards.

'That it is.' She smiles. When we clink tankards, I think I see a flicker of something soft and genuine behind her eyes.

'Still there is a fortune for your making if you choose it,' she says. I laugh and look at her with disbelief.

'There's many that would pay a pretty penny for what you offer.' Now I am confused and do not want to understand her meaning.

'It is safe here,' she says. Now I look at her with suspicion.

'Be still,' she says, 'takes one to know one,' and I look again around the room. The landlord has no beard or Adam's apple, they smile and wink at me. The men in the corner raise their tankards to me and I see they sit as couples. I glance at the other wenches, at their eyes for each other and my whole face alights.

'Welcome to the family,' the landlord says and offers me their hand. I shake it with vigour and relief.

'There's a small room in the attic, it is basic, but it will serve you well enough. You can earn your keep until you are ready for more lucrative employment,' and he exchanges glances with the bawd. I am about to protest when Sabby barks approval.

'Come, I'll show you to your lodging,' says the bawd.

'When you are settled there's a cellar that needs your attention,' says the landlord as we approach the stairs and it is as if we have lived here all our life. I am speechless with gratitude.

The attic room makes Mary's seem palatial. There is barely room to lie flat, and there is a basin and water jug, bed pan, and blankets to make a bed. Yet it is as if we have fallen from a great height and landed on our feet. Sabby has inspected every corner and lies spread out on the blankets.

'It's not much to look at but there is worse,' says the bawd, as I step inside. There is not room for two. 'I'll let you get settled.'

'Thank you,' I say, and she closes the door.

I lie on the blankets; they are rich with others smells and slightly damp, yet I care little. We have a start and it is with family. The execution, the rapes, my grandmother's death, Mary, all seem so far away it is as if they happened in another world to another person. I am sure it will all be left behind. Nobody shall have a past here and neither shall I. I shall be who I chose. I hear the cooing of a wild rock dove and look up. There is a space between the walls and the rafters and they have set up home there. If I still believed in signs, I would take this as a good omen, yet I do not so simply find comfort in their company. We may be in the heart of the city where people feed on people rather than the earth, yet we shall keep our connection to the earth through these, our roommates.

I am too energised to rest. We have no possessions so no settling to be done. I hide the rest of our coins deep inside the cloak and hide the cloak amongst the blankets and we head back downstairs. A bowl of pottage and a tankard of ale await us. It is near dinner time and the inn is filling up with all manner of folk, highbrow to lowbrow, sailor to judge. It is hard to be sure which sex accompanies which dress, but it is sure this inn is a refuge where masks that are worn outside are left at the door. Most of the wenches are not to be seen, instead the men at the corner table are doing a roaring trade. I realise it is now that the wenches take to the streets. I eat as fast as I can and, without prompting, help out behind the bar.

It takes little time to learn the prices; the selection is sufficient but not substantial and it is easy to find our place amongst the crew. By the time the afternoon slump arrives it is as if I have known no other life. I am exhilarated. I sit with the landlord at the bar, catching a pause.

'You have never served afor?' they ask. I nod. 'It is a gift you have then,' they say. The word gift stirs a feeling of repulsion in me.

'Perhaps,' I say. 'It was a pleasure.'

They laugh. 'Say that in a weeks' time and I'll believe you.'

'I'll set to work on the cellar, master,' I say, yet I wish to escape the feelings inside me and not their company.

'Fulke please, or Fulco to my friends.'

'Fulco,' I say.

'And yours?' they ask. I hesitate; it is as if I have forgotten my name, it sticks so in my throat. 'Do not bother if it is too soon,' they say.

'No, it is not that,' I say. 'Just I have not heard it spoken for a spell, Raven.'

'Raven,' they repeat, 'it fits you well.'

'Thank you, I'll get to work,' I say and leave before they ask more for I feel there is nothing more to tell. It doesn't occur to me that it was then I could have chosen a new name.

That night, after the regulars have left for their beds, the wenches return, full of complaints and stories. They comfort their weary bodies and flagging spirits with ale and ridicule the men that have taken their pleasure and left coppers in return. I have learnt the second floor of the inn is reserved for rooms of special interest, for acts best performed out of sight. In the early hours of the morning, when the customers have returned to the marital beds, the wenches take up residence and fill the rooms with sleep and dreams. It is an efficient use of capital. I sit with the bawd; she has not spoken since she has returned but sat apart from the others in a silence of her own. I do not speak but wait for her to offer conversation. In time she turns to me

'Raven, is it? It's a handsome name.'

'Thank you,' I say, 'and yours?'

'Felicia,' she says with a sardonic laugh. 'My parents wished luck for me.'

'Maybe it's catching, I feel lucky to have met you,' I say, and she looks at me.

She looks at me for the first time and actually sees me; it is as if I am without clothes. Not an entirely unpleasant sensation.

'Come, let me take you away from all this,' she says and slides off her perch.

She walks towards the stairs. I watch, unsure of what the offer is and if I want to take it. She stops at the first step and nonchalantly looks over her shoulder. Her eyes meet mine and her face folds into a softness that melts my heart. Without knowing what I am doing, I slide from my stool and follow.

Sabby calmly takes a seat outside the room as I step inside. It's a large room, the window covered with a painted cloth of a tranquil country scene. The bed is four posters with ostentatious and abundant lace decoration. There are large, comfortable, yet ornate chairs by the fireplace. She goes over to the table and pours us glasses of deep red wine. I stand uncertain in the middle of the room. It's as if I have never loved before. She hands me my glass, keeping eye contact the whole time, and we clink glasses. The moment is intimate, and I feel myself shrink inside and run from it. She smiles and flops down on to one of the chairs. She indicates for me to follow and I feel foolish I have not had more initiative.

'It has been a long day,' I say.

'It always is,' she says and is lost for a moment in a different dimension which does not look entirely pleasing.

'I know a trick that can help,' I say, eager to regain some self-respect.

I put down my glass and kneel at her feet. Gently I unlace her boots and ease them off her feet. She watches with mild amusement, used to others handling her body. Then with a firm but tender pressure, I begin to rub her feet. Instantly she sighs, sinking into the cushions, her eyes closing. It's not long before sleep calls her. I am mostly relieved; it is too soon to love another, even though my life that was but days ago, feels like a life time away. As gently and as elegantly as I can, I pick her up and carry her to the bed.

I slip off her outer garments and she falls back onto the bed. I pull the covers up, ready to tuck her in, but she stays my hand and pulls it toward her. I resist, but her grip is firm. I slip off my boots and hose. It is such a relief to know I do not need to hide what I do not have. I lie down next to her and she turns on her side, signalling for me to do the same. Lying as spoons we fall into a deep, comforted sleep. From that night on I never sleep alone, but we never ask more than spoons of each other. Ours is a friendship of mutual need and platonic comfort.

Life falls into a steady pattern. When I am not serving behind the bar, I clear out the cellar. It is a great satisfaction to pile and sort the debris. What is discarded I break down and burn on the fire. What is kept is revived or a different purpose found for it. Nothing goes to waste. I know this cannot last, know they have plans that will ask things of me I am not willing to give but we all enjoy this pause. Within a week so much familiarity has grown I feel as if I have never known otherwise. I luxuriate in this small enclosure of acceptance, ignoring the feelings of dread that underpin all I do, that haunt me at all times.

It has been a full week and to fall into a soft bed and curl round a warm body feels sublime. I am ready to drop into a deep, comforting sleep. I close my eyes, concentrating on all that is hopeful about our future at the inn. Felicia smells of stale perfume, ale and smoke. It has become one of my favourite smells. I cannot help but breathe her in.

'Was she your first?' Felicia asks, her voice an almost whisper.

'Hum...' I murmur not wanting to encourage conversation.

'Mary, was she your first?' My eyes snap open, all notion of sleep destroyed.

'You call to her in your sleep.'

I pull away from her and lie on my back, horrified to learn my slumber betrays me.

'It is with such tenderness. Is it that which brings you here? Heartbreak?'

'Something like that,' I say. 'We should sleep, it is already tomorrow.' And I roll back on my side to fit her frame.

'It is my dream, to one day be loved as you love Mary.'

She wants to talk and in the dead of night, for a short while, all is at peace and it feels safe to do so. I cannot close my eyes now anyway for all I see when I do is Mary's smiling face . Besides which this is the softest Felicia has been, her guard down, and I have so many questions.

'And to love yourself?' I ask, not moving.

'Oh, it is easy to love. Loving has never been the issue. It is the liking that is the problem. I do not think I shall ever really like anyone. There is so little to like in people.'

'Thanks,' I say, and she kicks my feet playfully.

'You know what I mean,' she says and in truth I do. If this did not bind us I would feel saddened by the weight of it.

'Has it always been so?' I ask.

'I don't know. There is so little I remember. Memory is not my friend. There was a time before, I think but I do not know how to reach it. I think it was happy.'

'Before?'

'Before the attention of the local priest. Sometimes I see little children of the same age as I was, six or seven, and I cannot fathom it. Cannot understand it. What was in his head, how did he live with himself?' For that I have no answer and simply squeeze her close. Yet she shrugs me off.

'Oh, I got him, got him good. I knew no one would believe me, knew most would not care if they did. It was not hard to lace the communion wine with chasteberry. It was not hard to leave evidence, so it could be found, once all the men of the town had gone soft. They thought him a religious zealot. He was lucky he escaped with his life and I am sorry that he did.'

'Chasteberry?' I ask

'Chasteberry,' and I cannot help but laugh, the stratagem so complete, so simple and so effective. Soon she is laughing too. I love this use of the ways of the earth and think briefly that maybe there is something to be salvaged from what I know. It takes some time but eventually we find our senses and composure.

'After that?' I ask.

'After that I had no taste for life in the country. I did not know city ways then, but I knew too well the ways of country folk. I could not wait to get away. I did not know what I was coming to, but I did know what I was choosing. The first time, the first time I took money for my sex. It is not the life of dreams, but dreams are just that. It is easy to make me a victim. Yet I shall not be a martyr for some pious sisters' pity. I know the value of my flesh and it shall earn me a pension when others shall still be scrabbling about in the dirt looking for potatoes.'

'And Fulco?'

'Oh, we go way back. We arrived in the city the same day. We spent our first night in the city huddled together for comfort.'

'And the inn?'

'When we couldn't find a home for folk such as ourselves we made our own. Fulco thinks they are ruthless, thinks they are worldly wise, but they are the softest person I know. Still they have built this place up from nothing.'

'And I am grateful to you both.'

'It was but a shell when we found it. At first it was just a place to sleep, a squat. They come from far and wide, rejected, beaten, shamed. Yet all are a beauty in their own right. One day there may not be a need for the sanctuary we provide. Till then, we shall ask no questions and -'

'Hide in plain sight,' I say.

'It is so. I like to think we are as colourful and as assorted as the dicks themselves. There are many that find us distasteful, but I have little time for virtue and the mockery it makes of honesty.'

'And yet you have no time for love?'

'Not in my spare time.' And we both laugh.

'Here,' she says pulling out a tiny silver flask from under her pillow.

'Bottoms up,' she says, and I take a quick swig. It has a sickly-sweet taste, a mixture of what I am not sure.

'Just a little night cap, shall help you sleep,' she says and takes a much longer swig herself.

'Come settle in,' she says, returning the flask and settling back down. I do not know what was in the flask, but I do know I drift off to sleep on a cloud, hoping my tongue remains silent.

We are a few days into the second week when I awake to the sound of Sabby scratching at the door She has never slept within, preferring to keep sentinel. Today she is anxious. I survey the hallway and stairs but find nothing to warrant such concern. Anyway, I have left ways of the earth behind and will no longer heed its messages. Instead I scold her for being so. Still she persists until I am forced to shut her in the cellar for fear she will wake the whole inn, yet still she whines without ceasing the entire day.

During the dinner rush I see Felicia and Fulke deep in conversation; they keep glancing my way. I fear I have overstayed my welcome, fear it is time for me to take residence in one of the rooms on the second floor. Eventually they call me over.

'You have worked well. It is time for you to rest, we may not observe the sabbath here, yet tonight you shall dine and drink at our expense. A small gesture of our gratitude,' says Fulke and so relieved am I, I do not think to question more.

After the diner rush, I wash and brush down my clothes, my hair. I release Sabby from the cellar but demand her silence and obedience, even though I can tell it pains her to stay still and to heel so. She would rather run but such is my trust I cannot see what it is we would be running from. That night I am given the best spot at the bar. The wine flows freely, my tankard never empty, roast meats and bread in constant supply. I feel it is my birthday and think I shall claim this date as such from now on.

I do not remember much of the night, just a haze of laughing, smiling faces. A song for my new birthday, handshakes and pats on the back. The one image I do have is the look on Felicia's face as they drag me from the inn, Sabby snapping and barking as they do. Felicia runs over, stops them as they are about to throw me in the carriage.

'I'm sorry. Poverty is a cruel master and the price they offered...' They throw me into the carriage. The last thing I remember is Captain Langan's boots as I fall into a stupor on the carriage floor.

Chapter Seven

In time Farah comes and sits beside us. At first, we do not speak, just watch our reflections in the water, the multitude of stars reflected within us. It is as if we are in two dimensions at once.

'Have you found the sense you seek,' she asks

'Do things ever make sense?'

'It's part of the fun, is it not? Part of the game? To find meaning when there appears none.'

I laugh. 'Then life is a game we are all poorly equipped to play.'

'But play we must,' she says. I do not answer; it feels more of a warning or a decree than a comfort. She reaches out and takes my hand, but the intimacy is an intrusion. She is not Mary and suddenly it is as if I am at sea with a thousand different tides pulling me in different directions.

'We should get back,' I say, standing, 'there is grey wine to be drunk.' She follows me to her feet.

'Are you dancing?' I ask and she takes my hand. That night I drink and dance all I can. I might not feel the joy of celebration, but it is a blessing to be lost to it.

We take a few days rest at the oasis, restocking our supplies and recuperating our energies. It is an easy peaceful time. Held in abundance the earth cossets us and lets us play. A time for me to take stock, as with the remembrance of the past comes the question of the future. Is it here with Farah? Do spiritual leaders of their tribes live happily in the ever after? Am I being invited to be that happily ever after? Do I have a choice even? We are travelling towards Marrakech to deliver the cattle and collect the new cargo for the return trip to Tangier. It is a life I could live with a degree of honesty and integrity. There is freedom and acceptance of what I am. Yet even here I do not know how long it will last. Even here they have chosen a jealous, greedy God over all that has got us this far.

Still there may be time enough for us to live out our lives before the ways of the nomads are no longer allowed. There has been no talk of the future. There has only been the present. Maybe I am simply cargo that shall be deposited with the cattle or there is a more obvious destiny that they have agreed upon and I am slow to catch on to it. I am not sure of our safety; after London, this is our way - the way of movement. Constantly moving on for fear of our fate and the fate we bestow on others by association. I find no answers to my ruminations; in the end I reconcile simply to ignore them and live by the moment.

The last night before we set off again, I am helping to tie bundles up and together, ready for loading in the morning. It is just three days' journey to Marrakech and I am expectant, eager to see and explore its offerings. Farah brings over more supplies to be bundled and sits down next to us while I work and Sabby pants approval. Farah's face is taut; she is not at ease, I have never seen her so.

'What is it that ails you?' I ask.

'Keep working,' she says; it is an instruction I feel compelled to follow so odd is her tone. I pick up the thread and continue to tie and wrap.

'There is something,' I say, not looking at her.

'It's not far to the city,' she says, 'travelling light it would take no time at all. It is such a big city it would be easy to hide in plain sight.' I cannot help but stop and look at her, yet she indicates with her eyes for me to continue; reluctantly I do.

'What say you?' I ask, not looking at her. 'Is this instruction?'

'It is observation.'

'Am I to meet you there?'

'You are free to do as you please, it is not for me to make demands.'

'We are more to each other than that, are we not?'

'There is no need of love to be obligation.'

Then I understand it is a test. 'I do not love lightly,' I say.

'I know, it is that I fear,' she says, and we look at each other.

I see only love in her eyes, a bottomless love that I would happily fall into, yet she drops her eyes as the head sheik calls her name. It is as if she is ashamed, yet what need of shame have we here? She rises to join the sheik but before she leaves, she smiles at me a smile that hides fear, yet is meant to quieten my own. I want to tell her my love for her cannot be questioned, that I shall not abandon her even though it is within my power to do so, that I am sincere and seek a future with her; yet how do you talk of tomorrows with someone who hears all time at once?

That night our lovemaking is a song from deep within and we are in perfect harmony. Afterwards I lie in her arms and I feel a release of the fear that has held back my emotions. The Society has unwittingly given me a new home. When they stole and banished me to a dry and barren land, that I had no connection to or understanding of, they sought a punishment when there has been a rebirth, a gift when they sought to deny me. I am resolved to be forever Bedouin. It is then that Sabby becomes restless, she whines and seeks attention. Only once before has she been so, yet again I shall not recognise her warning; this time I banish her from the tent, refusing to hear or heed her.

That night my dreams are full and busy. I cannot remember them even though I awake fatigued as if I have been engaged in passionate debate all night. I call Sabby back into the tent, yet she will not come. I would take more time to consider this, but it is first light and we must be quick. By now my skills have improved and it takes no time to pack up our tent. Sabby is listless and does not help as is her usual way. I place her on the cart. It's not long to Marrakech we shall have time then to discover her malady. Maybe the city shall awaken her spirit. I find it is easy to let her fall from my mind as I join the men in herding. Never before have I behaved such and at the time I hardly even notice.

The day is a haze of dust and cattle feet. When we pause at midday, Sabby will not eat or drink. I can see that she is sick but somehow it does not register. It is just a thought that echoes round my mind. Farah shows more concern, suggests that desert ways might not be her path, suggests we walk together in the moonlight, yet I do not hear. I have chosen this life; the ways of the past will no longer resonate. Sabby simply has had too much heat and needs to rest. She shall improve in the shelter of the city with all the fresh meat she can eat. Farah looks at me with resignation in her eyes but says nothing. It's as if she wants to tell me something but does not. I think maybe she is hiding her depth of love for me, for of that I am sure.

The next day and night pass the same. Sabby gets weaker as I get more excited in anticipation of the delights of the city. I expect colour and the non-stop noise of chatter of men and beast. I imagine fragrances I have never smelt before, tastes that awaken parts of my mouth never before blessed, teas that will set my being alight. I plan to break out the gold coin and buy Farah the most beautiful jewellery and silks. I know she is beyond such things, but I wish to spoil her, to demonstrate my thanks, my commitment to this new life. When we get to the city I will begin to learn her mother tongue so I may be of more use to my people, so I will never have to shift again.

On the third day the heat is insufferable, even before the sun has risen the air is full of intensity; it is almost palpable as if we have to cut through it to walk, as if cutting through a dense forest. Sabby is mostly unconscious which adds an additional need to reach the city as soon as possible. Although I ignore and bury the voices and fears that speak to me of Sabby's illness, I may refuse to hear them, but they inspire action anyway. It is midday when we see the city in the distance rising up out of the desert. It's tantalisingly close but the heat is too strong; to continue would be unnecessary foolishness when our deadline for delivery is flexible. We set up a few temporary shelters and take refuge in shade.

We drink sweet tea and study the city before us. Every now and again a scent is carried on the breeze or the sound of a rabab wafts over us. I am filled with energy despite the heat and find it hard to rest. Farah suggests I take Sabby for a walk, yet Sabby is not able to raise her head let alone walk. If I asked her, she would, and would that not be the utmost cruelty on my part? I do not understand Farah's suggestion; she says maybe Sabby is not cut out for life in the desert yet surely no one is?

She simply walks into the distance, sometimes she feels so far away. I think I shall remedy this with a gold ring.

As the sun drops so does the heat, it is as cold as it has been hot. I think this will help Sabby, but she seems worse than ever. Still there is not time and it simply increases the urgency of reaching the city. As I leave Sabby behind I join two of the herdsmen as we walk back to the herd. Without words we have worked well together, often as a team, and I have marvelled at how little words are needed. I am taken aback when from out of his throbe one of them produces a small gourd of grey wine and offers me first taste. I take it as a great compliment that I am worthy of their companionship and that I am offered first position. I can feel Farah watching as we go. I turn around to smile reassurance when I feel my knees buckle and fall away beneath me. I am out cold by the time I hit the ground. My last thought is that I should have heard Sabby.

I awake to feel my check flat against wooden board. With my eyes still closed, I can hear a cacophony of sound. Endless voices talking, shouting and laughing in a language I do not recognise. Music plays in the distance, carriages and beasts layer the sound. Without moving my body, which is splayed flat on the boards, I open my eyes. I see an iron bar directly in front of me, beyond that a large crowd. There is much shouting and waving of arms by men in kaftans and tunics. I see and hear no women.

Then I sense her, and it is as if I have been thrown a lifeline. She has sensed my alertness and I feel her breath on my check and her tongue in my ear. I scramble to sit upright, and clasp hold of her. My head spins and the crowd fall silent, yet I do not care; all that is of importance is Sabby is here, Sabby is here and she holds me no grudge. I do not truly understand how she can continue to love me, but I do not seek to question it in that moment; I just receive her love gratefully. She is still weak but healing. I know I should feel the deepest regret, know that I should be full of self-recrimination, know that I should consider myself the greatest living fool to have thought I did not need to heed her yet all I feel is relief. I would vow never to evade her wisdom again, but I do not have confidence in any promises I make and prefer not to add injury to insult with an empty pact.

I look around me; morning sun is casting shadows across the street. I am in a cage made of iron bars suspended in the air from an iron arm extending from a loading dock attached to a storehouse on the edge of a square. Standing on the dock below me is the chief sheik. He is delighted I have risen and begins talking very fast, waving his arms excitedly. The ropes and pullies that keep us in place are closely guarded. We are just out of reach, close enough to be inspected, yet with enough distance to ensure we are untouchable. We are clearly a thing of great value; people in the crowd seem to be making offers the sheik refuses. I had forgotten it is us that has been the cargo, it is us that has been the delivery all along.

Slowly I rise to my feet - the cage is stable enough. I step to the edge, hold on to the bars and peer down at the crowd. The cage wobbles just enough to silence them again. Their faces are full of greedy curiosity. My first instinct is to run; in a second, I could be raven, slip through these bars and be flying free in the wide-open skies of the desert. Yet to do so would leave Sabby behind and I will not and cannot do that. They know that, Farah knows that. It will be an eternal shame to me that I neglected Sabby so. It is a betrayal of all that we are. Now I understand I listened to the wrong voices. My desire spoke loudest, yet my desire had no foundations. A fever of rage soars through my body.

I consider a shift to a large bear or gorilla, something strong enough to bend these bars into an opening wide enough for both of us to escape, to terrorise the crowd into parting. Yet still I do not wish to shift and besides deserts surround the city for miles; alone we would not last long and we would be easy to find. I curse reason as a companion and slouch down next to Sabby. I stare at the rough-cut wood that makes the bottom of our cage and wish I could shut out everything in the world but Sabby and me.

The shouting and bartering continues but to no end or conclusion. I partly wish it would then at least this would be over. If we are to be seen only as an expensive commodity does it matter where we end up or who pays the highest price? Then it is clear there is a voice in the crowd who does not believe the sheik's promises; dissent speeds through the crowd, soon folk threaten to lose interest, to walk away. At the sheik's signal the ropes and pullies are instantly in motion and we are lowered so we are head height with the crowd. He snaps his fingers and Farah is pushed forward from inside the storehouse; she lacks her usual elegance and grace and looks down at the ground. She stops feet away from the cage. I am still sitting with Sabby, resolute in my refusal to engage. They push her again, this time she slams into the bars, sending us swaying from side to side. It is a small satisfaction to see the crowd scatter and duck.

When we have regained stillness Farah speaks, her head down, unable to look at us,

'Forgive me,' she says, 'they are my people. I had no choice.' I do not respond, rather take to petting Sabby. They shove her again.

'They want you to shift, to prove you are the prize they say you are.'

Still I do not respond, although it crosses my mind that with a tiger's claw I could at least take out an eye or two before they raised us out of reach. They shove her again and this time she falls to her knees; instinctively I want to rush to her aid, yet I continue to feign disinterest.

The sheik takes a long walking stick, wrapped in snakeskin, and begins to prod me, at first tentatively, then when I do not respond he becomes more confident and forceful in his strikes. I leap to my feet and for a short while we play prod and dodge. Then when it is clear this shall not work he turns to Sabby and I have grasp of the stick before it even touches her fur. I yank hard and the sheik slams against the bars of the cage. There is a moment's pause and we lock eyes; my mouth is parched but still I find the fluid to spit in his face and watch it slide down his checks as he drops to the floor.

Instantly we are raised back into the air, this time well above the crowd and out of reach. They pick up the sheik hurriedly, ushering him into the storehouse, dragging Farah in as they go. Gradually the crowd begin to disperse, satisfied they have seen some kind of beast in a cage, even if it is not as entertaining as they had hoped. Yet they have the satisfaction that their disbelief in a shifter, in magik, is justified. Sabby looks stronger by the minute, which is some comfort. I think when nightfall comes there will be a way to escape, and I fill the rest of the day with elaborate and fantastical plans of liberation.

As dusk falls Farah comes out of the building and the guards lower us to the ground. The streets are almost empty as the new God demands they pray. She has brought us bread, roast meats and tea. I do not look at her and will not take the food from her, but she passes it through the bars and leaves it for us. Then we do not hesitate to snatch the offerings and eagerly devour all. What use would be self-inflicted privation? She says nothing whilst we eat and, still, we do not make eye contact. She waits until there is nothing left, and we sit quietly with our backs to her.

'I heard this was a delicacy you enjoy,' she says, and I hear her open up tissue paper and place something on the floor behind us.

The smell is instantly recognisable, marchpane. It is a step too far. I swing round and before I know it, I have grabbed her tunic and pinned her to the bars. I stare into her eyes, ready to rip her soul from her being. I do not know what I expect but there is nothing there. It is as if I peer into two empty wells. In the end I drop my hold; to harm her would be a greater disservice to myself. I look down at the marchpane as they rise us up into the air again. For a moment it is as if I am in Grace and Mother Gray's kitchen so vivid is the memory. Yet we are not, and seeing a heart-shaped piece of marchpane on our cage floor is an insult to such love. I kick it out of the cage and it lands just in front of Farah. She does not pick it up, rather turns and walks back into the building. She does not look up.

The night temperature drops and Sabby cuddles in close as she drifts in and out of sleep as folk return from praying, light lamps, cook food and swap favours. It is the dead of night before peace has fallen over all. It's too cold to sleep, yet I hanker after the escape of dreams. If we cannot be free in our bodies, then at least we could be free in our minds. When we feel a jolt, it is gentle and silent yet we begin to descend. Sabby is silent, so with stealth I peer over the edge. There is a hooded figure lowering the rope. I see thick dark puddles next to the guards and understand their throats have been cut. I am elated. Farah has rescinded her decision and has come to release us. Come to start a new life with us. It will have been part of her plan all along and it is I who have been foolish to not understand this. She has better ears than me.

The cage is expertly and silently lowered. The figure turns to me, I cannot see their face, but they signal for us to remain silent and it is the least we can do. The figure skilfully picks the lock and gently prises open the gate. We step outside, they close the gate and relock it. Together we rise the cage into the air again. Still we have not seen her face and her smell is not her own, yet familiar. I wonder again at her skill to disguise herself so well that she thinks to alter the one thing that cannot be denied. She indicates for us to follow her.

Slipping from shadow to shadow we weave through a myriad of narrow alleyways, down and up stairways, crisscrossing tiny squares and courtyards. We duck under an archway and then through an arched wooden door into a cellar. Dim torches light the passageway down. We stop at the bottom of the steps and before she opens the door she turns to me. I am ready to plead forgiveness, to take her in my arms, to savour the kiss that will surely follow. Yet as she slips the hood from her head, I am greeted by a wide-open grin and a twinkle in the eyes. It is Constantine that is our rescuer. I am unable to move but he calmly clasps me close to his chest.

'Old friend, it has been too long.' And he releases me, opens the door and steps inside.

I am frozen to the spot. We have been released from one gaol to another. Sabby has gone ahead and is waiting expectantly, as is Constantine. I look at him in disbelief, not that he is here but that he can betray me so. He may work for the Society, but I also thought him my friend, thought our friendship would keep me from the clutches of the Society and it is surely the Society behind all this.

'Such accusation of the one who has saved your life?' he asks. I do not respond, I am unable to respond.

'Come,' he says and steps beside me. He reaches around my shoulders and guides me into the room.

Inside it is lit up with a million tiny candles in a million tiny lamps; rugs and cushions cover the floor. There are a group of men in a corner passing round a sebsi pipe. They pay us no heed.

'Take a seat,' he says and pushes me down onto a large pile of covered cushions.

Sabby sits happily panting at my feet. I do not understand her ease and feel abandoned by her too. Constantine settles himself and snaps his fingers. Almost immediately a young woman appears with steaming, sweet tea.

'Thank you,' he says and makes an elaborate show of pouring it into two small cups. He offers me one but still I do not respond so he places it on the rug within my reach.

'Sweet tea is good for the nerves,' he says and sips his own. We sit in silence for what feels like a long time. I cannot stop myself from glaring at him. He does not flinch from my gaze, but it causes him discomfort.

'It was not part of the plan,' he says eventually. 'They were paid to safely escort you here, not to sell you.' I snigger as if that makes anything any better. 'Are you not pleased to see me? Even a little? I have waited with eager anticipation for our reunion,' he says. Now he seeks camaraderie; it is a step too far

'What do you want with me?' I ask. If it is easily done I shall do it and find a way to be gone.

'So direct, do you not have time to pass the night with an old friend?'

'If I had one, I might be so inclined,' I say, looking him directly in the eyes.

'We cannot afford to be so divided, you and I, there are many, even Farah, who would happily stand against our creed.'

'And your assistance in our hour of need has been gratefully received.'

'And I shall carry the shame of my previous absences with me for all eternity such is my sorrow, my regret.' I cannot help but smile, he is always so dramatic and romantic.

'Sir, you offend my honour with your disbelief,' he says.

'It is not disbelief but recognition that alights my humour,' and we look each other in the eye and laugh. I feel something melt inside and despite myself I find it is a relief.

'It's quite a place you bring me to.'

His face brightens, 'Do you approve? It's a favourite haunt whenever I am in town.' I answer by raising my tea; we clink cups.

'Can I offer you the local delicacy?' he says, offering me a sebsi pipe.

I shake my head. 'I have been put to sleep enough,' I say, and he concedes.

'I know what will soothe you,' he says. Again he click his fingers and the wench appears. She bends down so he can speak in her ear and within minutes we are presented with fire water and simple oval-shaped pieces of marchpane.

'To absent friends,' he says, holding up his glass.

'To absent friends,' I say, all be it ingenuine. I have lost loved ones but right then I feel I have never had any real friends.

The fire water loosens our tongues and soon I am as enraptured by his tales as I ever was. To hear him is to believe his life is one long voyage of adventure and exploration. In my firewater haze I hope and desire he has come to seek me as a companion, an accomplice in his tours, that this is his plan no matter what the Society or the sheik have in mind. That he is in fact my true rescuer. Still we have not spoken of the plan, so it is that thought that fills my dreams that night as I slip against my will into a deep slumber.

I awake wrapped in silken quilts on a sea of cushions. It is only Sabby and I. Next to our bed is a bowl and scented water, fresh linens and hose, beside them a tankard and a jug of fresh cool water flavoured with rose. I have no sense of time yet in our sobriety I know we could make our escape. I consider the water, the linens, inside a voice says leave them, leave now while you can, yet it will be some time before we will feel refreshed and pampered again. I think the scented water will hide our smell as I had thought Farah had hidden hers and decide to take what is on offer while we can instead.

I wash quickly, and the rose water quenches my parchedness and eases the foul taste in my mouth. I dress and the feel of fresh, clean linens against my skin is a joy that should not matter so. I feel dapper and ready for our escape. The opportunity to join Constantine as his fellow adventurer now seems a silly fantasy that I am not sure I would wish for. We are capable of our own adventures. I check to see we have not left anything behind and that there is nothing for us to take that would aid us. Then I approach the walls where I remember the door was, yet it is hidden, the wall, flat and smooth. We are no strangers to hidden doors. A quick scan of the room offers no alternative route, so I feel around the walls for a lever or button.

'My company is so repellent to you?' he asks from behind me. Where has he come from? Slowly I turn my head, still subtly stroking the wall. Then I feel it, it is intended to seem like a fixture in the wall, yet I sense its purpose.

'You have not abandoned us then?' I say, 'as is your usual want.'

'Touché,' he says. 'I brought breakfast,' and he clicks his fingers and again the wench appears, this time with bread, pottage and, of course, tea.

They are distracted with the laying out and I press the button. Silently the door opens, and we edge towards it. We are about to turn and run when, without looking up, he says,

'Do you abandon Grace when she is in need of your help?' The utterance of Grace's name stops me in my tracks.

'It is why I am here. I have been sent to get you. It is only you that can help them now.' Mother Gray too?

I want to feel no obligation. I want to be able to walk away, yet my memory of them is untarnished by the failings of the Society. They too had to flee. Images flood my mind of books and laughter and love. I cannot walk away from that. I sigh and slump as I turn to face him.

'Breakfast,' he asks cheerfully. Sabby seems content to stay and I feel I am being called upon to do something I do not want to do but need to do. I take the cup of tea Constantine hands me and we sit down as our pottage is served; it is good pottage at least.

'Am I to know the cause of their need?' I ask, when he does not offer.

'Come now, you know how this works by now,' he replies.

'Then how am I to trust it is a genuine need?' I see a flicker of disappointment pass through his eyes as if I have betrayed him, but it is soon concealed with a laugh.

'She said you would ask that.'

'Who? Who said I would ask?'

'Mother Gray.'

'It is a rouse then; you seek to trap me and set me to work like all the rest.' And suddenly it makes sense. Farah's offer, before we reached the city, for us to take to the desert - it was not her fear, but her advice, a warning. I begin to scramble to my feet.

'She said to remember the spider to you.' Slowly I sit back down. I did not know that Mother Gray knew about the spider.

'What did she say? What spider?'

'The spider that taught you to read.'

Instantly I am transported back to Grace's room, the classroom of my childhood. The light that streamed through the window, the ornate chairs by the fireplace that never seemed to be used, the candlesticks that were really levers to open the secret door to the library. For a moment I am held in the softness of the memory and I remember what it is to love. That day I had been told words should not dance about the page, that they should be fixed. I did not understand why words could not dance about the page, we meant no harm. It was as if I had been told that everything about me was wrong. In my frustration and pain I turned away from Grace to stare at the tapestry on the wall. It was then that spider came to me. There was a beautifully woven spider in the tapestry that awoke and began to weave and through its weaving unwound my fury and confusion. Words have never really stopped dancing about the page, but we have reached an agreement that suits all. I have never told anyone else that story and I trust that they have not either.

'Is she in danger?'

'Mortal.'

'It will take weeks for us to reach her. How can we help?'

'Truth be told I know little more myself. It was always the plan that I was to meet you here and transport you to your next destination. The sheik's decision to sell you was opportunistic. He was paid handsomely for your transportation with the remainder paid on delivery but he…'

'Saw an opportunity and seized it.'

'He saw an opportunity to provide security and status for his tribe.'

'At my expense.'

'At your expense.'

'A short-term gain for a long-term loss. I could have, should have, been an asset to them.'

'Surplus to requirements, is Farah not their guide?' he asks. I am engulfed in a feeling of uselessness. I possess an extraordinary gift that no one is interested in, even myself.

'And the Society?'

'The plan was for me to take you to a safe house until they could find a more permanent solution. There is hope there are lands yet to be discovered where it will be safe to be who we are. This call is from Grace and Mother Gray directly.'

'Yet the Society assist?'

'I understand they have their own reasons for wanting your return. It will be your most direct route to helping Grace. They are all we have.' There is something in his tone that suggests apology and resignation. I look at Sabby, her eyes are certain; she fixes my gaze and it is then I know I have no choice.

'When do we leave?'

'Nightfall.'

'Of course.' Why did I even need to ask?

'Come, in the meantime there is something you need to see.' I am defeated, I am always defeated by his charm.

It will be like a holiday. It will be like we can suspend time, such is his magnetism, we shall be held in the moment with the past and the future far away. I expect to bargain in markets, visit mosques, drink endless tea and laugh like we did at my grandmother's. If he asks me, I will follow him without question, yet I know he never will, and it is part of his charm. Before we step out, he insists I throw a thaub over my doublet and hose and places a shora scarf upon my head, so my face is mostly hidden.

'I prefer to travel in plain sight,' I say.

'Today we will discover disguise, why have only one approach?' He winks, and I think life is but a game to him.

We step out into the street. I expect hustle and bustle, sun finding whatever way it can to reach the narrow streets and alleyways, sellers of all manner of trinkets and necessities lining the path, yet there is an eerie emptiness. No one is in sight, yet they have left behind traces of themselves, stalls left empty, yet erected, prime positions for begging or selling left abandoned. In the distance we can hear men's voices rise and fall in joy and dissent. As we look up and down the street, a woman in the dwelling opposite snaps the shutters closed. I look at Sabby; she is alert, her whole body attentive to every sound. I look at Constantine,

'Follow me, today silence is a virtue;' he whispers and places his fingers on my lips when I go to respond. I want to go back inside, to while away the day with naps and firewater. Every part of me shrinks and squirms, yet Constantine turns and walks swiftly towards the sound of the mob. Sabby follows, just as determined; I in turn reluctantly fall in line, yet everything smells wrong.

It takes no time to slip through the streets, all as empty as our own, all shutters closed. I would not know the route and do not know if it is different from the night before, yet we are soon at the square. No wonder I felt such resistance; why revisit our place of imprisonment?

At first all we can see is bodies, bodies of men pressed close and filing every available space in the square. Spirits are high and a feverish energy ripples constantly around the crowd. The men are joyous and bonded, unquestioning in their sense of power. Their collective smell grows stronger and bolder by the second. It is that smell that returns me to the night outside my grandmother's, the smell that takes me back to my face in the dirt and my body a vessel for other people's pleasure, this same pleasure that now surrounds me.

Instinctively I turn my body, now not under my control but taking protection into its own hands, yet Sabby and Constantine block my path. I glare at Constantine, unable to speak, for I am neither here nor back in the past but in both places at once. He takes hold of my shoulders and turns me round. He guides me to a spot where I get a better view and there in front of me raised just above the crowd is the cage; inside Farah sits cross-legged, eyes closed; she is oblivious to the jeers and insults that are thrown at her.

The head sheik of the tribe is deep into a crowd-pleasing speech and I do not need to understand his words to understand their meaning. Even here they are choosing to dismantle the equality once shared between the sexes. Women are to be put into an inferior place and kept there by force.

'They blame her for your escape,' Constantine whispers in my ear. 'They think it is she that slit the guards' throats.' I look at him, unable to speak. What should our course of action be? Surely, we cannot leave her so?

'There is nothing we can do,' he says, reading my eyes.

'But -'

'But nothing. Have you an army? Should you both lose your lives?'

How can he be so? Where is his heart? I cannot look at him and turn my body and face away. There must be something I can do. I look at Sabby; she is sunk low on her haunches, her eyes wild and full of fear. I look at Farah and expect to feel love, compassion, a need to protect and return her to safety, yet I do not. I do not even feel shame. More a deep satisfaction somewhat marred by her ability to be at ease, even now; even now she does not feel her torture. I discover I want her to feel pain, want her to know the humiliation, to feel the betrayal and heartbreak I have.

The more I look at her sanguine face, the more I see peace when there should be torment, the more enraged I become. Does not peace betray us all when it can behave so? When it can manifest even here, even now? Why is she not suffering, not broken by the betrayal of her tribe? I want to slap her, to shake her, to look into her eyes and see pain and sorrow, for her to beg for my forgiveness. Forgiveness that I would deny her. I look down at the ground; there are stones aplenty. If I but pick up one and throw it, it would start a deluge. There is not one man here who would not take it as a prompt.

'What shall they do with her?' I ask Constantine

'If she is lucky, beheaded with a sword.'

'And if she is unlucky?'

'They shall cut off her ears, maybe gouge out her eyes, then leave her to wander the desert alone.'

'Then either way she is saved,' I say. She does not hear with her ears or see with her eyes and death is just a continuation to her. 'I am parched. Is there not a tea house still open and serving?'

Constantine looks at me, unsure.

'As you say, there is nothing to be done here,' I say.

He nods his head. 'I know just the place,' he says, and we turn and walk away from the square.

Sabby is slow to follow and will not take my touch. Still it does little to sway my conviction. I feel nothing as I turn away. Part of me wants to see if she hears, wants to see if our exit rouses her from her peaceful meditation, causes her to cry out for us, yet she does not. I take one last look before we turn the corner, her face a picture of divine composure. It is Farah at her most beautiful and right then I hate her for it and hate that she will have already heard my hate, already she will be far in advance. I take what solace I can from each step that takes me away from her and with each step she is further from my mind, so it is as if the scene in the square is simply a mirage. Hot, sweet tea has never tasted so good. One day I may find disgust at my actions, dismay at my cold-heartedness, but right now and here all feels just.

Chapter Eight

Before nightfall, we return to the café to collect our meagre possessions, or, rather for Constantine to collect his. Once again, the only things we own are what we wear, yet Constantine has prepared a pack for us, a change of linens and bandages, a cloak of beautifully-woven black wool, a pouch for carrying water and a stash of marchpane for when times are hard, plus a knife that I carry tucked into my hose in the small of my back. His enthusiasm is infectious, and it feels more like we are setting out for a spring celebration than setting out on a journey that I do not wish to take, that will risk mine and others' lives, that has an unknown ending. I allow myself to be carried away, allow myself to escape.

'Ready?' he asks and pats me on the back.

'When you are,' I say and clap him back.

'No goodbyes to anyone? No farewell note or gift?' I have been so lost in the day, so eager to escape the moment by being in the moment, tis as if his question has cast a shadow across every smile and every laugh and every discovery of the day. I can barely think of her. I have an image of her face, smiling, full of love. It is the only memory I permit myself. What would I say to that face if it was before me? I think of the last time I saw that face pressed against the bars. It does not seem a fitting resolution to our love, yet I do not have words of forgiveness or understanding to offer her, and I am some way from acceptance.

'There's no need,' I say, for will she not have already heard?

A covered carriage is right in front of the door and we slip inside unseen, unnoticed. We begin our return as our arrival - deep in espionage. The familiarity is a comfort, but the repetition is waring. No one has anything to say. Constantine's giddy joviality has taken the shape of focused attention on our task; neither of us, it now appears, is happy or confident in it. Each of us is lost in our own private darkness. I try not to think; it is too painful to try to make sense of any of it. All that seems of import is to survive it. Sabby is calm and I sense she will be glad to leave this heat behind, as I shall too. Despite myself, one image keeps circling in my mind. It is the look on Grace's face when she showed me the Book of Knowledge, the open unmasked light that shone from her. Still, I fight it all I can; what use is memory when it is laden so with pain.

We reach the outskirts of the city and come to a stop. The shutters have been closed the whole time, so we have no indication of where we are except that the sounds of humans have given way to the sounds of persistent wind. The driver knocks on the roof of the carriage three times and it is as if Constantine has been brought back to life. His eyes open with a look of joy and readiness. Life is a game once more. He motions for us to remain silent as he gently opens the door. A gust of wind sweeps dust into the carriage and it is all we can do to contain our lungs. Blinking, we step out.

There is a caravan of camels, one with a covered seat, to hide us I presume. I look at the camels and the clear open sky full of a billion stars. I think of the nights Sabby and I took to these firmaments. I think I could reach Casablanca in no time if we were raven and wolf hunting. Then I think how shifting always seems to lead to tragedy and the connection is lost. We climb upon the camel and we make ourselves as comfortable and as out of sight as possible and eventually we fall into a slumber.

At first light we make camp, or rather we watch others make camp whilst we take in the flat dry river bad. Dunes surround us but far in the distance, as if sentinels of sand both protect and trap us. The sun shall be unforgiving in such an exposed spot. I think we are either led here by ignorance or necessity. Yet soon tea is being served and our company gathers for refreshments.

There is little chatter, just a subdued focus; it is as if all have had their tongues removed. Even Constantine's endless exuberance impacts them little. He sits next to us and I am grateful for his energy. We speak little more than pleasantries but that feels such a luxury in such harsh, barren surroundings. A glorious sunrise spreads across all, bathing us and colouring us in a rich red hue. It signals to our guides to take shelter and sleep. They crawl under their temporary shelters. In time, Constantine joins them, lying back in the shade whilst Sabby and I watch the day awaken.

It is a constant wonder to me that even here, where there is no obvious way to sustain life, we feel the earth awaken and the beasts that have made this their home go about their business. The space and peace begin to seep into our being. Sabby is at one with the world and I am filled with jealousy and envy whilst she luxuriates in this expanse; for me it serves to amplify all that is inside and all that seeks to have a voice. I look to sleep for escape but cannot close my eyes for the images that flash before me. There is no sound, bar the breathing of the sleeping men; the air is still yet it's like a cacophony of voices and places crash inside my ears so deaf am I to the peace. It is agony to wait it out till the worst of the sun has passed. Whilst my body has languished in the heat, my mind has run ragged and, as soon as my body permits, I take to my feet and walk.

In the emptiness, we are sure we cannot lose sight of or be lost sight of, so we walk without direction, simply following where my feet take us. It is not long before the rhythm eases my mind and confused thoughts of betrayal, of love offered with no regard to consequence loosen. How far into the future does her gift travel? When she took me in her arms, when her lips touched mine for the first time, did she know then our ending? If so, was her choice noble, to choose love knowing it would be lost or was it selfish to take what she wanted without thought for the one she took from? Was I in such need I saw and heard only what I needed and not what was in front of me? Yet with each step the thoughts fall from me, it is as if I am being emptied. I do not understand these shadows to be lost forever more, rather they are for a while suspended.

We come to a stop in the vast emptiness and stillness. The sun is beginning to wane, and the endless sky fills with an astonishing myriad of colours and shades. Clouds, the first we have seen for months, are gathering, creating shadows and form in the sky that tell of other worlds and other possibilities. Every part of me opens up to this beauty, the honesty of the moment. It will be the last desert sunset we shall see, and, in that moment, it is the saddest thing to receive, to know. Yet it is also the most joyous and wonderous thing to know such beauty exists and will continue to exist long after we have left. I drop to my knees and surrender.

Tears flow from my eyes but without distress; they are just a release of all emotion at once, joy and sorrow. I look down and watch as my tears fall onto the parched dry land. I watch the earth greedily drink them up. They are joined by more of my tears and then I am surrounded by tears. I look up as dark clouds block out the sun and lightning fills the sky. Heavy fat rain drops fall in vast unimaginable number. I stand and let the rain soak through my clothes, through my skin and into my being. I raise my hands high and open and twirl and play and dance in this cleansing. It is a joy we did not expect; it is a joy we shall carry with us.

Then we hear the shouts; we are called back to the camp as our guides quickly pack up. Yet we cannot run, we cannot dismiss this, so we saunter back, indulging in this luxury, and by the time we reach them all is packed up and we are ready to begin the night's travel.

'Here,' shouts Constantine from his mount and he tosses us a sort of pastilla, for the rain has forgone the chance of a proper farewell supper under a desert night sky; it is followed by an oilskin and we climb under cover. In the shelter we warm and dry each other, feasting on meaty Moroccan pie, content to be alone with that moment.

The rain persists all night; what was at first a beautiful gift soon becomes an endurance. Yet almost immediately, new life springs into being; the rain has lifted a veil on a reality the sun hides. Eager, hungry plants and beasts appear as if from nowhere such is the magik the rain has released. Whilst we have cowered, others have flourished. By the time we reach the city, our spirits have fallen from us, as the rain has fallen from the sky; we are a bedraggled and weary sight.

First light begins to show as we knock on the city gates.

'Stay back and out of sight,' says Constantine as we peep out from under the covers.

We are barely through the gates when he says, 'Captain Langan awaits, speed you well my brother, anon,' and before we can respond, he has turned down a narrow side street and is lost to us. His partings are always unexpected, always a disenchantment.

There is both jealousy and loss in my gaze as we pick our way through the empty streets; I have half a mind to make our own escape to be lost amongst the people and buildings, yet at every turn I see Grace's face filled with light and love and I know that I will do all I can for her, not for the Society, but for her I shall travel the oceans with those I detest.

We reach the docks and it is clear that they are usually a hive of activity yet today the shutters are down, and the covers are over the boats. All are hiding from the rain. We do not belong here, and it is obvious. I spot the Black Gladfly and pull our camel to a halt. The others stop too, there is some confusion. Why have we stopped now? Their voices are muffled so as not to raise suspicion but anxious none the less. We dismount our camel and, as a gesture of gratitude, we offer him the last of our marchpane and, in the wet, dim light, he munches as we turn, and, not acknowledging the fevered, hushed voices, we walk calmly toward the boat.

When I reach the gang plank I turn back to wave our thanks but already they have begun to splinter and go their separate ways. We have been as little to them as they have been to us. When I turn back, Captain Langan is waiting on deck, sheltering under an oilskin.

'Captain,' I say and step on board. Although every part of my insides rebel, outwardly it is as if we are kin, my kidnapping a mere trifle amongst friends.

'My lad, come aboard, come aboard.' His embrace is warm and eager.

I embrace him back whilst all underneath recoils in disgust. I am not entirely sure of the rules by which we are playing, yet I'll play anyway. He says nothing more yet holds me at arm's length and takes me in as if I am the lost prodigal son; seemingly satisfied with what he sees he whistles, and the ship comes alive as we prepare to set sail.

Instantly we fall into our old place aboard the ship, assisting the crew in the preparations. As the sun rises, the rain ceases, and we pull out of the port as it begins to come to life. We look back at the land we have no regrets about leaving, we look forward to the open sea, but our destination is full of regret and trepidation.

We take up our place in the rota of the sailors' mess. It is our attempt at keeping a low profile, passing the time and avoiding the captain. We have spoken little since we came on board. I take this as a mutual recognition, a respectful distance. The weather is fair, and we make good progress. I care little for details of our calling; we shall not be told till it is needed so why concern ourselves before? There is little to trouble us, and it is easy to find comfort in the routine. My mind begins to rest and follow the flow; the constant motion creates a sense of stillness. To surrender to the mercy of the winds and the tides is a release we understand.

Despite my feelings for the Society, I had always understood the captain to be a fair man of balance in thought and emotion. He is neither selfless or self-serving and his men offer him respect to his face and that is how I have understood their relationship, yet much is spoken in the bowels of the sailors' mess. I hear stories of his misjudgement, how the sailors feel they carry him as much as he carries them, if not more so. What appears to be fairness is in fact a subtle form of domination and control. We hear stories of men thrown overboard for the mildest of transgressions, men ridiculed and debased for a different view. It is not a side of him we know but it is no surprise either.

At first their conversation is guarded; they are unsure of my loyalties. Mostly we keep ourselves to ourselves but our appreciation of their jokes at his expense reassure them of our allegiances and position. We become known for quiet discretion and gradually, one by one, the sailors confide in us. They each wait for their time and moment, some when they work beside us, some when it is only us awake in the mess, some when we take in the view, the vast nothingness. We hear tales of hardship, escape from brutal masters, from brutal families, tales of heartbreak and love lost. Some have lost all that they have, some have given it away, some drank it away. All, it seems, have made an exchange, the chances and challenges of a life on land for the security and life-threatening danger of a life at sea.

Their trials and tribulations are of little surprise to us, yet it is of interest how the regime that has taken the earth from us all has not served them either. They are as much casualties of the creed that governs us all as we have been. It is not a comfort rather serves only to fuel my anger more. I listen as they struggle with the most elementary of feelings and ideas. It is not long before I am held in a sort of reverence by them. I do not gain privileges exactly, but my opinion is sought to settle disputes or explain a phenomenon that they cannot, such as why being able to swim is a useful skill onboard a ship. Their suspicion of the thing that sustains them is such that they seek only to be on it, never in or of it.

It is a night of doldrums - there is no wind and no tide. We take to the deck of the boat with wine and the stars for entertainment. We sing and play drinking games with the sailors to pass the time, until eventually a companionable silence descends as we all take to gazing at the star-filled sky. In the peace that settles, I call the stars by their names, and tell a story of how they got those names.

> Once, long, long, long ago when there was the earth and the sea and there were no stars in the night sky, the first creator beings in the world huddled together for comfort and warmth and waited for Night God, who had been created by fire and nursed by comet, to join them.
>
> Finally, they arrived, their face masked by charcoal and white paint, seven jewels woven together around their ankles, glittering and blinding. In the middle of their forehead shone a crescent moon, their mouth a full moon. In one hand they held a bag and in the other fire burned in their palm. They walked slowly for, although the earth was young, they had lived for all time. They looked round at the company and were

relieved to see that raven was not present - raven, the shape-shifting trickster. This, thought the Night God, was a good sign.

Without waiting any longer, Night God turned to the East and stamped their feet. All the creator beings gasped for the jewels around their ankles had travelled up to their knees. Night God then turned to the West and stamped their feet and stamped their feet again; this time the jewels jumped to their hip. The creator beings fell silent, such was their wonder. Night God turned to the South and stamped their feet; this time the jewels travelled to their shoulder. This time the creator beings smiled. Then Night God turned to the North and with one stamp of their feet the jewels made their way to their left temple. The creator beings shielded their eyes, so brightly did the jewels shine next to the crescent moon.

Safeguarding her eyes, First Woman asked, 'What do you call these stars?'

Night God smiled and motioned to their temples, 'These,' they said, 'are Pleiades, for the sparkling formation they bring to night.' And they grinned broadly as all the creator beings admired their beauty and power.

Satisfied their gifts would be well received, Night God reached into their bag of jewels and set to work creating the constellations. First, they placed North Star to guide travellers at night. To join North Star they took seven crystals, orbiting them around North Star. They called these the Big Dipper. Next, they threw up Cassiopeia. Once started, they could not stop and soon there was the Huntsman, the Eagle, the Serpent, Big Bear and Dragon. Not content to stop there, they threw up thousands of stars and the stars formed a swirling band called the Milky Way. Night God then paused to consider their work; the creator beings were overwhelmed with joy with all they saw and felt.

Just then trickster Raven swooped down to join them.

'What do you call this?' he cawed disdainfully.

Night God scowled, and all the stars dimmed.

'What is it that displeases you, Grandfather Raven? Can you not see the beauty in my night sky?'

'I saw no fault in the darkness,' Raven replied.

'And what fault can there be when I have given the earth beings stars to guide them, to show them when to plant, when to harvest, when nights will grow cold and when days shall grow warm? North Star shall guide them to safety. People shall not fear the night but look to me for the wise counsel I am.'

Raven shrugged his wings and, exasperated, Night God sat down, crossing their legs.

'What have you ever done, Raven, for earth beings?' they demanded. Raven looked Night God in the eyes, wounded and full of hurt, then he looked away, shrunken, his feathers flattened.

Night God took pity on Raven and put down his bag of jewels, so they could take Raven in their arms. Yet before Night God could reach out, Raven snatched up the bag and, hopping around in circles, threw the jewels up into the night. Jewel after jewel he threw until there were too many to count and too many to name.

Night God leapt to their feet, shrieking and chasing Raven around in circles until there was one last jewel left. Raven took it from the bag, opened his wings and took to the sky.

He circled Night God and the creator beings and said, 'Last but not least, the Morning Star,' and he threw the jewel up into the upper dark and, looking Night God in the eyes, added, 'Now the night sky is beautiful.' And he flew off into the very first starry night.

There is silence once I have finished. I think they are asleep or have long since stopped listening, till I see one or two try to hide the wiping of a tear. There is silent contemplation until the ship's boy speaks up.

'How do you know such things? What sort of magic are you?' he asks, and the others sit up. I can feel the same question from all of them. As I no longer trust in magik as I did, I laugh.

'There is no magic in knowledge,' I say. 'Knowledge is gathered along the way.'

'And so?'

'So, it is a story I read in a book.'

'You can read?' It is both an accusation and a self-flagellation. It is then I realise all that is between me and the sailors is the ability to read. It makes me ashamed for not understanding sooner, for letting myself succumb to their view of me as prophet.

'I can,' I say, 'and so can you.' They all laugh; to them this is a preposterous suggestion. 'But you can. There is magik in reading but it is a magik you all possess.'

This makes them laugh even more.

'Here, let me show you,' I say, and I begin to collect the tankards.

Gradually, curiosity gets the better of them and they quietly watch as I line the tankards in a row. Then I realise I do not know the name of the ship's boy, that it has always been "the ship's boy" that I have known him as.

I turn to him, 'Let me show you your name.'

He looks at me blankly.

'What is it?' I ask.

No one will meet my eye. The boy looks at me quizzically.

'I am Ship's Boy, I know no other name,' he says.

There is an uncomfortable silence.

'He has known only ship life,' says one of the sailors by way of an explanation, a sailor who once had a home and family and knows the value of a name. It is fortunate that we have lived with subterfuge and discretion, for the shock and dismay that I feel remains hidden inside.

'Ship's Boy then is a fitting name,' I say. 'Have you not ever fancied another?'

He takes no pause for consideration, rather his face lights up. 'John,' he says.

'It is a fine choice, very noble,' I say, and he grins from ear to ear.

'Then let us see.' I arrange the tankards accordingly.

'There J-O-H-N – John,' I say.

All look in wonder at the word. Then it occurs to me they have not seen their own names written and a fire rages throughout my body. I cannot fathom how man can keep such a gift from another man, how men can make of themselves fallacious Gods by simply denying access to something that it is not theirs to deny. It is beyond me to worship, at the best of times, but I shall never be able to worship men who have declared themselves deities when they are no better than the next.

'Now you,' I say and sound out the letters with him. We practice a few times till he is confident and comfortable.

'Now you,' and this time I hand him the left-over tankards.

'The letter J is right there before you,' I say.

He looks at me with disbelief, then the rest of the crew, then the tankards. It takes a moment, but with the utmost seriousness and concentration, he picks up the first tankard and places it with some apprehension. I nod encouragement. Then with each tankard his confidence grows. The letter 'J' is soon in place, we are about to applaud his success, but he does not stop there but gathers momentum till there are two copies of his name there on the deck for all to see. The look of joy upon his face will stay forever burned into my consciousness. The sailors are stunned and clap in joy and wonderment.

'See, no magik that is not for you. Who's next?'

That night no one gets to sleep till every one's name has been spelt out and copied.

The next morning as the wind and tides pick up, it is all hands-on deck.

'Boy,' shouts the captain, 'man the rigging.'

'Halt,' I say and all on the ship stop and look, 'Captain, have you not heard? The boy's name is John.'

There is a look of puzzlement and suspicion on the captain's face, not least as it is one of the few times I have addressed him directly this entire voyage. He studies the expectant faces and turns to the boy.

'John, man the rigging,' he shouts and there is happy agreement across the ship whilst John shimmies effortlessly up.

After that there is no stopping them; their hunger is such, they work out a rota to cover each other's shifts. We do not have much time left onboard and it is my aim that all the sailors can write their own names by the time we dock in Leith. It is as if I have unleashed a tsunami of need and enthusiasm. Whatever else this peregrination brings, the lives of these sailors will never be the same again. It is an unexpected discovery, the joy of sharing my knowledge; for once, what I know is better shared than hidden. We have a tacit agreement that our lessons are clandestine.

It is but a day from us docking in Leith. We have discovered a store of chalk hidden amongst the cargo and we have used the side of a tin box to practice on. Although the penmanship is not refined, it is a thing of beauty for me to behold. There has been a change in the men; their heads are a little higher, their footing a little surer, there is assurance in their eyes where once there was shame. Seeing their name in print reflects back to them their existence, something that anchors them to their being and the earth. We have worked covertly; what business is it of the captain's when he has so clearly neglected his duty to his men? So when he calls me to his quarters, I think it is for my instructions.

I knock on his door with a joviality and casualness led by happy expectation. Soon we will be free of this ship and the captain. I shall do what I must to help Grace then I shall slip out of sight. I have learnt a little from Constantine, of how he lives, how he secures the funds he needs for his adventures. It is my plan to find new lands where things are done differently, to seek out and experience what I have read in books. There must be a place in the world where people are not as they have proved to be. I consider myself to be at ease and reconciled with my plan.

'Come,' Captain Langan calls from inside. I open the door; Sabby is hesitant, but I am not, and I enter with confidence.

'You called, Captain,' I say and sit down in my usual seat.

'Did I ask you to take a seat?' he asks. I look at him confused; it is as if I have been summoned for reprimand. His glare is penetrating and slowly I rise to my feet.

'Sit down,' he shouts, and I do not question but drop quickly back into the seat.

'I -'

'Did I ask you to speak?' he asks. I say nothing. Sabby has held back and sits upright by the door, ready to escape. I do not meet the captain's eyes, rather focus on the floor in an attempt at contrition but I cannot think what I have done to cause such fury. He cannot know about my teaching.

'What is this?' he says and throws a piece of driftwood at me. I duck, and it lands on the floor behind me.

'Pick it up.'

Hastily I reach behind me; etched on to the wood is the name "John". It is scratched on and clumsy in execution, yet clear all the same. He has taken it upon himself to practice, with whatever he can find, such is his thirst. I cannot help but brim with pride; at port I shall purchase a primer. John will be able to make sense of it, such is his willingness and aptitude. It will be my parting gift to him.

'You smile?' he asks and slams his hands down on his desk.

His face bears down, close to mine, and the smile falls from my face. He holds my gaze till he is satisfied he has dominion, then sits back down. I have no compunction to speak. If I have transgressed by empowering his crew with a little knowledge and self-respect, then I shall not apologise for it. He studies me from the comfort of his chair; I study the top of the desk, for, if I look at him, I fear the hatred in my eyes shall bore holes in his skin.

'It is my ship, it is my crew.' He pauses to ensure I have understood.

'I shall name them. I shall decide how they live and what they need to know.' Still I do not respond.

'It is not a sailor's place to adopt the ways of the scholar.' At this I cannot help but meet his gaze. How can he believe in such inequality, such injustice? Have the ways of the earth taught him nothing?

'You disagree?' he asks. 'Then come, it is clear you must understand your place.'

He stands. 'I am a kind and patient man, yet I shall not be disrespected.'

He opens the door and signals for me to move. If it were not for Grace, I would gladly slit his throat or raise a mutiny. Instead, I stand and slowly begin to walk towards the door.

'Bring it with you. Bring your insult to my guardianship with you.' I pick up the driftwood and walk out of the room, Sabby close at heel.

We walk on deck to find he has assembled the entire crew; the tin box with our chalk markings and John stand at the helm. He marches us up to meet them; not one of the sailors will meet my eye as we pass their silent, cowed faces. He motions for us to stand in front of the wheel in plain sight of all.

'Raven here has made a mistake and would like to correct it for you all.'

I look at him.

'Make sure and snap the wood cleanly,' he says in a calm gentle tone.

I look at the wood, at John, who cannot look at me for the tears in his eyes, the tears that he does not want any, including himself, to see. I look round the faces of the sailors. I expect their eyes to be downcast, for the shame to be shared, yet now they meet my eyes with accusation. There is not one of them that will acknowledge his part or stand up for his rights. It is as if it is me that has committed an abomination, an abuse of power and not the captain. I do not understand how the gifts we have exchanged have become so tainted, to be so quickly abandoned. How is it that it is I that has done wrong? I am filled with such rage at such betrayal that I turn to the captain and look him straight in the eyes,

'With pleasure, Captain,' I say and snap the piece of wood into as many pieces as I can, and I throw them at the sailors.

'And this, it is an abomination is it not?' And I pick up the tin box, and, with the sleeve of my doublet, pointedly and slowly I wipe clean all their names, one by one, each time seeking out the face that goes with the name, their eyes dropping to the floor as I meet their gaze as one by one their identities are erased. When the last name is no more, I show the box around to the crowd yet there is not an eye that is raised to see it. I hand the box to the captain

'Master, my humble apologies. I did not understand my transgression,' I say, yet there is no apology in my manner. He takes the box and we turn to walk away.

'Where do you go? I have not dismissed you,' he says in a steady tone. We stop and slowly turn back to meet his gaze

'Oh, but you have,' I say. We hold each other's gaze till he turns away, then we walk back towards the hold.

'Boy, take this to its rightful place, then scrub the deck,' are the last words we hear.

In the hold we find the darkest corner we can. Breaking the wood into shards has splintered my soul into as many pieces, such is the betrayal of myself. Every part of me shakes. Yet one thing is steady, one thing certain, one thing that shall direct my actions - a fixed and determined decision to escape. I do not understand why those with power use it to supress rather than liberate but I know that I shall not be contained or controlled by any who use their power such. The ways of the earth do not teach this, yet those that profess to protect the ways of the earth succumb to the ways of man none the less.

I know exactly what I shall do as if the plan was always there, always ready, always waiting for this moment. I feel ashamed for it is a plan that, surely, I could have used before had I but seen it. I do not have time for self-recrimination, my only understanding can be that it is a question of timing. It could not present until it was the solution. In a short while land will be in sight. It will be too far to swim, even for Sabby, but not for all creatures. We search the cargo and it does not take long to find oilskins, some rope and a pistol. I gather a few supplies from the stores and make a handsome pack with luxuries to ease our passage. We hear John shout sighting of land and the scramble of the sailors to see it. Shortly afterwards we hear the key of the hold turn; the captain has locked us in - it is not unexpected.

We wait an appropriate amount of time. We can feel the sun has set. We feast on ship's biscuits, wine and dried meet in readiness for our adventure. We are both now calm and settled in our purpose. It is almost a pleasure. I look round the hold and think of all the times we have spent here. I raise the pot of wine and toast to never being here again. Then we tidy away so there is no trace of us left behind. We shall be guarded but I have no fear. Our purpose has never before aimed to hurt another but if our freedom depends upon it, it is a price I am prepared to pay.

I undress and wrap my clothes in the oilskin. I seal it tightly with rope, so no water shall get in, so it is a tight, firm ball. I make two loops in the rest of the rope. One I fix about Sabby's chest, so she is able to carry the pack with comfort, the other I leave loose but tucked between the pack and her fur. We take one last look around. I take the pistol and we walk over to the door.

I bang on the door with the pistol. 'Quick, quick, open up, there is water in the hold,' I shout.

'Do you take me for a fool,' comes the gruff answer from the other side of the door.

'Only if you do not heed my warning. Quick before the captain finds out,' and with that we hear a grumbling as he gets to his feet. We hear the clatter of a ring of keys and then the lock turns. He flings open the door, confident I cannot be a threat.

I stand in the doorway naked. It has been months since he has seen a woman's body and he is not expecting me to have one. He stops in his tracks and drops the ring of keys. Sabby quietly inches towards the door.

'Do you wish to see the water,' I say and wink.

'What water?' he asks and greedily advances, proceeded by his erection. Sabby picks up the ring of keys and steps into the passageway. He advances his arms wide and, grasping, he is almost upon me when I duck out of his clasp and into the passageway. We slam the door and turn the key. We shall have little time now for the racket he is already making will soon awaken the whole ship.

We speed up the stairs and push open the door to the deck. Another sailor is set as guard, and again my nakedness renders his mind useless. We aim the pistol at him; I have no idea how to shoot a pistol and have never held one before, but its presence is power enough, it keeps him at bay. We make him step down into the stairs, slam the door shut and turn the key. We can hear the shouts of men climbing down the rigging, and banging on the door to the deck. We drop the pistol, run to the bow and climb on to its edge. We take one last look at the ship and, as they break down the door and rush towards us, we turn and jump.

By the time we hit the water I am a large dura whale. It is such a joy to feel the shifting again. How can something that feels so right, that has saved my life, be so wrong? The impact creates a huge wave which sends the ship rocking and the sailors flailing. In seconds I have hold of Sabby in my whale jaws, and we dive deep into the ocean. I shall be Grace's saviour, but I shall do it on my terms.

Chapter Nine

The plan is simple. When the ship docks, Captain Langan shall come ashore. It will not please him to report we have escaped, and I have some satisfaction in that; we shall follow him and gain as much intelligence as we can as we go, making our own way to Grace and Mother Gray. We need little in way of sustenance; the earth shall provide for us, we need little from anyone.

I picture them in a remote cottage, deep within the hills, living a life rich in earth and books away from the prying eyes of our home townsfolk. Mother Gray will have befriended and been welcomed by the locals who protect them from visitors that ask too many questions. I cannot imagine what danger they are in, except for the danger the incompetency of the Society has placed them in. I think of their rural idyll jeopardised and threatened by whatever mockery of leadership and guardianship the Society has enacted this time. Fury fills my being and fires determination to assist, but without interference.

As we reach the shore, I release Sabby from my jaws and shift back to human form. The coast is dark and lit only by the moon that shows itself intermittently between the clouds as they drift along their path. Between the bobbing of the waves we can make out no other people or beasts and we gently approach the shore. The sound of the pebbles is louder than we would like as we clamber to our feet and stand free of the waves.

The air is fresh and cuts through my skin, deep into my bones. We have little time to consider our arrival on the land of Alba, or land of the Scots, as it is now known. In the books in the library, now lost in the fire, the ways of the Picts and Gaels was well documented and, despite my fever to get dressed, I sense a connection with the land that lies beneath my feet, the land that has ways far deeper than the nonsense of our times. It is with some relief I throw on the fine camel-hair cloak Constantine gifted.

The ship shall dock on the south side of the harbour. It's as if we have lived here all our lives so well we know it from the tales of the sailors. It will be easy enough to spot the ship on its arrival. We make our way along the headland, trying to keep to the edge of where the beach meets the land, making our passing silent and giving us places to run if need be.

It is good to feel the earth steady between our steps and smell other than sea water and the sweat of men. Sabby has more energy than she has had since we were shanghaied in London. It is almost possible to see the heat leave her blood, replaced by joy. We are welcomed by oyster catchers, we startle curlews and are serenaded by the gentle lapping of the water. The peace here is active, vibrant and full, not in the least like the emptiness and space we have fled from, yet connected none the less.

As we turn around the headland, the sound of mankind takes over; rigging chimes against masts, drunken laughter spills from the shop fronts, inns and ale houses that mingle amongst the merchant houses. There is only one place they can dock, and it is no hardship for us to find a spot in the shadows to wait. We hide between stacks of wooden barrels whose aroma suggests they are heavy with fire water. It is a slight torment to be unable to drain what's inside, the bite in the air giving deeper understanding to the heat of the drink. We would welcome it now as we shelter in the cool shadows.

My worst fear is that we fall asleep and miss him disembark yet I am occupied by keeping at bay the endless memories of lessons learnt and laughter shared. The taste of marchpane fills my mouth, the smell of Mother Gray fills my nostrils with comfort and the image of Grace and her beloved book is all my eyes can see. It is a struggle to be reminded we are hiding out in a dock, in a strange land in the middle of the night. All around us is still, except for the rats.

First light is upon us soon enough; the wind picks up and we know it will not be long before the ship is in port. Soon all around us awakens. Shop fronts open, street sellers begin their cries, stray dogs begin their morning rounds; as light creeps into every crevice and we lose our shadows I cover my face with my hood, feigning drunken sleep by lying back against a wall encrusted in decaying bits of fish. Sabby is between my legs, hidden by my cloak. It is almost like playing a part and not entirely unpleasant.

We do not wait long, and as the sun begins its assent, a stunning red tints all, and the Black Gladfly pulls into dock. By now all is alive. Sailors from across the world shout and engage in playful badinage. Ships prepare to set sail as others return from a night's fishing. A small army of men arrive to haul on and off, followed by a larger army of women to gut and cut. It is not hard for us to adopt our preferred form of concealment and walk boldly in plain sight.

As soon as the gangplank is lowered, the captain scurries from the ship. He is alert, and we can tell he suspects we have beaten him to shore. He searches the crowd and at one point he looks directly at us, almost meeting my eyes, and still he does not see us. It is good to know we have not lost our touch. After that, it is simple to follow, his nervousness and unease acting like a beacon in darkness; it is easy to pick out his route.

He heads away from the docks almost immediately. I think he shall take us to a carriage waiting for him or a horse which will speed him out of town and I am ready to shift to follow and return later for Sabby. Yet he turns down street after street, it is like we have entered a labyrinth, and with each step we take it gets less clear where we are going and even less clear how we shall return. The streets get darker and our presence more conspicuous. It is a fine balancing act to keep him in sight and us out of sight.

We have long since left behind the three-storey merchant houses, passed the brothels and the ramshackle buildings claimed and occupied by those who have no other choice, when we come to a courtyard with a small dwelling that looks no more than a stable, yet there are no signs of beasts. Smoke rises from a chimney and there is one small window. The captain knocks on the door, his rap urgent but with a clear code to its pattern. He waits for a moment or two and the door is released from inside and he steps through without checking for spying eyes, so confident is he in the remoteness of the location, all be it in the heart of the town.

We pause to ensure no one will leave the dwelling, then approach. The shutters are not fully closed, and it affords us a view of the inside. At first there is just a candle-lit room, the flame dancing on the plain daub walls. We can see little, but I adjust my angle slightly and on a small wooden framed bed, under thick, brittle, woven wool lies Grace, her face pale, her hair lank and unkempt. It is clear there is little life in her. I turn away, my back against the walls and fight the tears that come to my eyes. Of all the possibilities this was not one I had considered. I cannot think how I can assist. There shall be apothecaries here, wise women whose wisdom is deeper and more tested than mine own. What can I do?

I turn back to look again; the captain now sits at her side. She looks expectantly at him, but he shakes his head and she sinks further into the pillow and closes her eyes. Mother Gray wipes her forehead with a wet cloth and signals that that has been enough. Slowly the captain rises to his feet. We duck out of sight round the other side of the dwelling and watch as he leaves, his steps slow and heavy. As soon as he is out of sight we knock on the door. It is as best an imitation of the captain's pattern as I can remember.

Again the door is opened and Sabby runs inside. The squeal of recognition from Mother Gray forces me to enter quickly and close the door behind me. Her squeals soon turn to muffled tears as she holds me close to her. Her usual reserve is abandoned as she tells me how dire the situation is. She holds me at arm's length and considers my appearance, then holds me tight again. It is only the faint cry from Grace as she calls my name that releases me.

I bend down and kiss Grace's forehead and with some effort she brings her hand above the covers and I clasp it. It feels an eternity that we gaze into each other's eyes. What were once deep clear pools that I gladly swam in now are misty, hollow replicas, merely imitations of what once was. It is all I can do to keep the tears from my eyes and the light of love upon my face. After a few moments, I feel Mother Gray's hand upon my shoulder and I release Grace's hand as her eyes close and she falls into what looks like a peaceful slumber.

'Come,' says Mother Gray and she indicates two wooden chairs next to the fire where a pot of pottage bubbles.

Sabby has already taken up residency and pants contentedly. I sit down and let my cloak fall onto the back of the chair, so small the room that the small fire acts as a large furnace.

'I knew you would come,' she says and with great glee and anticipation she hands me a small box. I smile; it is clear what's inside. I open the lid and there is a heart-shaped piece of marchpane. It is as if I have been given back my own heart. I shall never be able to eat it.

'Thank you,' I say. 'My life has been much less without your magik.'

She smiles and hands me a cup of fire water.

'And mine so without your silver tongue.' We clink glasses.

'It is the book of knowledge that ails her,' she says, anticipating my question. 'It has been taken.'

The look on Grace's face when she showed me the book fills my being again.

'That is like her soul has been taken from her,' I say and Mother Gray nods.

'Forgive me but I knew of no one else who could help,' she says, and I feel her love for Grace so that I could hold it in my hands.

'We shall work alone,' I say, indicating Sabby.

'Please forgive me, I knew no other way to reach you.' The desperation in her eyes both recoils me and draws me in.

'Do you know of its whereabouts?'

'Only it is on sacred ground somewhere to the west,' she says, relief in her entire being. I look at Grace, her frailty tears my insides apart. How have they been hidden away so? How has such a treasure been lost to them? Yet there is no time for answers. If it is not returned soon she shall be lost to us for all time.

'Keep her cool with damp cloths and warm with hot poultice. Give her an infusion of hawthorn to drink and whatever fresh clean water you can get. Feed her on rich meat broth, if you can. I shall send word of our progress but do not expect a typical messenger.' I gather my cloak around me.

'You leave without restoration?' she asks.

'We shall have time for pleasantries on my return.' We both turn to look at Grace who murmurs gently in her sleep.

'When she awakens...'

'I shall explain,' Mother Gray says.

I kiss Grace on the forehead. 'Hold on,' I whisper. 'I'll be back as soon as I can.'

Mother Gray nods and we embrace. 'Thank you,' she whispers in my ear.

'Save it till there is something to be thankful for,' I say, and we turn and walk out into the courtyard.

We have little to go on but our intuition. We pause outside, and I close my eyes. We shall feel and sense our way to the book. I stand still in the darkness and it does not take long to get a sense of our first direction. It is as if the book is calling to us, sending out a signal with its location. There is something beautiful about this, to be part of a language that the establishment seek to outlaw and eradicate. For the first time in some while I feel that old pleasure and satisfaction of knowing a truth and being a truth that cannot be seen by all, that could be understood by all but is ignored and denied by most. I want to laugh out loud at the stupidity of its denial.

A power, powers, that can be harnessed for the good of all negated out of existence because those who seek power over other men have seen an enemy in it and not an ally. Those who seek power over other men seek power over the earth. Their need for domination is out of balance with all and at the expense of all they seek to dominate, yet even as I recognise this, I turn away from it, thrown into a confusing internal conflict of emotions and thoughts that tear my insides apart.

I am trapped by a need to rely on this intuition, unable to eradicate it from my being, whilst being full of doubt about it. I have vowed to live the way of normal folk; normal folk live by the ways of those who seek to dominate. How can I be both things? I look down at Sabby, who has none of these concerns. She is alert, tail wagging and ready to go. I know her intuition shall lead us when I shall deny my own, and that, for now, shall be all we need.

'Come, we have little time to waste,' I say to her and she does not hesitate but leads us easily through the web of back streets whilst I ensure we are not being followed.

By the time we reach the merchant's houses the streets are a throng of people, horses, shop fronts full of the silhouettes of customers, the constant to-ing and fro-ing of people, beast and ship. It is easy for us to fall amongst the crowd. Our ears are delighted by the sound of Mother Gray's tongue repeated all around us in different textures and cadences. It is as though we are being serenaded everywhere we go.

We take a loose westward direction following the flow of people towards Edinburgh City. Despite the pressing need of our task we fain nonchalance and at least appear to enjoy the sights and sounds. It's easy to do; after the heat of Morocco it is a pleasure to walk under clouds and fear the threat of rain. Yet all the time underneath the distractions and pleasantries, the burning need to help Grace demands attention, drives and nags at all we do, a constant voice in the background.

It is not long before we are in the depths of Edinburgh town, weaving through the close-packed streets. It's the prettiest town I have ever seen, although the people are reserved, as if the brittle air has formed their spirits so. Still there is much laughter and play in their interactions. I cannot make out all they say but I recognise a generosity of spirit that I have searched for in people and not before found. Despite the urgency of our task we are at ease in these streets.

Our plan is to take the minor roads and head west. I sense the book is surrounded by water, such is the power of the connection; it must be an island close to the mainland. I feel the book captured, hidden under layers; it is in sacred ground but enclosed by what is holy rather than held and protected by what is spiritual. I want to fly directly there, shift right then in the street for all to see. Surely that is what this gift is for? Then I remember every pair of eyes is potential danger. To use my gift so recklessly would bring danger to the very people I am to save, risking Sabby's and mine own life even more. There is a time and a place for all and when I most seek to ignore this truth is when I must adhere to it the most. Instead we purchase some supplies for our journey.

At the foot of the castle gates the market is full of all manner of entertainments - singing, jugglers, acrobats. We take some roast meats and breads from a stall and join a large crowd that has gathered around some players, their bawdy act satisfying the eager audience. We can see little from behind the bobbing heads, catching glimpses of man beating woman, woman scolding man, man taking woman by force. Then we hear it and it is unmistakable, at the height of hilarity, at the very moment of climax, his sweet melodious tone captures every heart and we push to the front. I risk all our freedom to see his face and have his voice hold us. There is no hesitation when we step forward and meet the gaze of Billy Bird. I can see it is all he can do to keep sadness in his song when the light of joyous reunion fills his eyes.

His song is the final act in their show and it is met with rapturous applause, their hat heavy with coin once it has done its rounds. We hold back, choosing a quiet nook in the castle walls, whilst Billy receives acclaim and the rest of the company receive the coffers. It's an arrangement that seems to suit all. I know he works for the Society, I know he could be a plant by the Society, yet falling out of sight of the Society is a skill we are both well versed in. It will be no different than before and maybe we shall gain some insight, some confirmation of our direction. When he is satiated with adoration, he approaches.

'Raven, my friend,' he says, and we embrace; it is heartfelt on both sides. Sabby barks approval and he embraces her too.

'Come, sup with us,' he says. I hesitate; to sit in the comfort of an inn with an old friend and his stories would be a joy, yet each space between thoughts is filled with Grace's ailing face. I know there shall be no rest in my being whilst she is in need. He senses my reserve.

'Surely you have time for one? When it is such good fortune our paths have crossed?' I relent. How could I not?

We join the others in a small inn off the market. The troupe has claimed most of the room, the locals huddled disgruntled in a corner watching with a mix of envy and resentment. The troupe are a welcoming bunch and almost immediately we feel accepted and part of their family. A tankard of wine is presented to both of us on our arrival and even Sabby is given ale in a shallow dish. We all clink tankards.

'Slante,' we all shout and feel ourselves superior for the one word of the local language that we speak.

'Introductions,' says Billy.

'Isabella, acrobat, singer, dancer and mistress of the dramatic arts at your service,' and a woman of medium height and slender build with thick, long blonde hair bends over backwards and offers me her hand. I laugh and shake it accordingly.

'Alasdair Duncan, gentleman, scholar and curator of fine arts,' and he bows regally; it is clear the others humour and ignore his pretentions.

A woman of very short stature jumps up onto the table, jumps up again, flips over and lands in almost exactly the same spot. 'Lizzy Longlegs, all round genius, available for weddings, funerals, birthdays and non-birthdays, reasonable rates.' She downs a full tankard of wine to prove the point.

'Last but by no means least, Avery Gordon, a simple minstrel at your disposal.' He gently bows, a pretty boy. I see him glance towards Billy and I know it is love they share.

By way of mine own introduction, I am tempted to shift to raven there and then and prance proudly across the table, yet I also find myself tongue-tied and a little shy.

To cover this weakness I say, 'A simple adventurer on the voyage of life, known as Raven to my friends, and this my accomplice, Sassaba, or Sabby to friends.' I grin broadly and Sabby barks.

'Then welcome, friends,' cries Alasdair, and we take our place amongst the throng.

We fit comfortably within their mix as they enjoy playful badinage amongst themselves. They are good company, their humour sharp, their wit sharper. It is a wonderment to be surrounded by people and so at ease. I have never felt such kinship before. As the wine flows, so does the conversation and eventually topics of the day surface. I try to keep a low-profile smile and frown appropriately in the hope my opinion is not sought, but Lizzy turns to me directly.

'What say you, Raven, is woman the ruination of man?'

All eyes turn to me, again I feel myself tongue-tied and shy. I would like to turn and run far away, instead I manage a smile,

'It is my experience that man is more than capable, and needs little assistance, from any source, to bring about his own downfall. For is man not the expert in and master of all things?'

There is a short pause whilst this is passed through wine-soaked minds then laughter erupts from all.

'More wine?' I say, but it's clear all have had enough. Isabella and Alasdair have sunk into each other, Avery leans too openly on Billy and Lizzy brings all her focus on to her drink in the hope her eyes will keep her upright.

I turn to Billy. 'Do you have rooms?'

He smiles. 'We have something much better, come,' he says and rises unsteadily to his feet.

'Come, my weary players, lets us adjourn for the evening.' With mixed skill and coordination our brilliant band of minstrels staggers out of the inn and into the dark of the night.

We sway down a narrow alleyway. Isabella and Alasdair intermittently burst into song and are quickly silenced by Lizzy. We reach the bottom of the hill and some stables; parked outside is a large covered cart.

'Home,' says Billy proudly and pulls back the canvas.

One by one they stagger into the cart, which is cleverly packed, the floor laid with blankets; each has a space of their own and despite the lack of privacy it is an inviting place to lay one's head for the night. Within seconds loud snoring is heard from all; it is almost harmonious.

'Will you join us?' Billy asks.

I laugh. 'You know I shall lay with Sabby.'

'Why change the habit of a life time?' he says and sits down on the ground next to Sabby.

'Did they send you?' I ask, still standing.

'Who?'

I look at him wryly.

'Do you not know me by now?' he asks.

I shrug.

'When has Billy Bird danced to anybody's tune but his own?'

It is a good argument that almost has me swayed for it is true his sense of self-preservation exceeds all other vices.

'Why do you think I am here? Have I not tried to get as far away as possible?'

It is an ever-better argument and I relent and sit down next to him. We sit for a while in hesitant silence, not sure who should speak first.

'I'd ask you what brings you here, but I know I'd get no answer,' says Billy eventually and we laugh.

'You know me at least,' I say

'Is it heart or business?'

'Both.'

'You travel alone, I take it?'

'A teaching I picked up from you.'

'It is a lesson I have little taste for teaching.'

I look at him, and for the briefest moment I see his eyes soften into the sweetest expression of love I have ever seen, then it is gone.

'It's a few months since we passed that way but Mary fares well.'

I look at him with open, startled eyes. Mary is a room in my soul that I have closed the door on and fear to ever open again.

'It was hard on her at first, but such was the commotion, such the excitement caused by your exit, rather spectacular I must say. I congratulate you on your sense of occasion.' We exchange smiles. 'Her grief was easily hidden. She is busy with the inn now, the new landlady.'

I cannot help but grin. 'She has triumphed then, it is well, very well,' I say and wish I had another drink to toast her success.

'When I see her next?' he asks.

'When you see her next, say nothing of me. Why offer hope when there is none?'

He looks at me and I can tell he does not agree; I can tell he wants to tell me not to throw this love away, that love like ours only comes along once, that there is nothing else once it has passed, yet he does not. His eyes relent, and he nods his head.

'It is fortunate I have little room in my head for anything but myself; by the time I see her next I shall have forgotten I ever saw you.' And at that we both laugh for it is true enough.

'You have a purpose to your travels?' he asks.

I nod.

'Would the cover of company assist?'

I hesitate.

'We could revive our old act? Shall be a joy, shall it not?'

I look at him in disbelief.

'Our wee troupe has patronage, we are free to roam.'

That is the most sense anyone has spoken all day.

'Alasdair is well acquainted with the routes and roads whereabouts.'

'Congratulations,' I say. 'You have progressed well in your profession.'

'Thank you, I like to think so.'

'Your assistance will be most welcome.' I hold out my hand; despite himself he grins broadly and vigorously shakes it.

'Which direction do we take?' he asks.

'West,' I say. 'Billy, there is urgency in my purpose.' My concern is evident in my tone and intensity.

'Then we must rest; it is not long till first light,' he says and rises to his feet.

He reaches into the cart and throws me down a blanket. 'Sweet dreams, brother,' he says, and climbs into the cart.

I throw the blanket on the ground and pull the cloak around Sabby and myself. That night my dreams are a torment of sweetness as all are for Mary and all laced with the sensation that I should be somewhere else, doing something else, getting where I should be going.

Chapter Ten

He is met with unwelcome groans and bitter grumbles, yet at first light Billy is up and abroad. He instructs Avery to harness up the horse, a beautiful Friesian and I dare not think how Billy has afforded such. The others gather themselves, but it is clear it is temporary, that once we are on the road they shall fall back into slumber.

'Wait here,' Billy says when he sees we have risen, his excitement unexpected and perplexing. I expect a mound of marchpane. Sabby too is expectant, turning in circles, wagging her tail so furiously I fear it shall fall off. I know I should join the anticipation, yet it just makes me suspicious; I fear what may cause such disturbance.

I hear the sound of hooves and think Billy must have acquired another horse, maybe to share the load with the other. I expect him to be at the reins or lead, yet he walks himself around the corner and with utmost seriousness. Then following, he is there, it is like I have seen a spirit walk in broad day light. I look at Sabby who has already approached and been greeted. Billy steps aside, yet still I do not approach, it is such a beautiful gift I never expected to receive, never expected possible. I look at Billy, for I cannot believe my eyes.

'You see your arrival was no surprise. He joined us near Berwick, and we have not been able to shake him since.'

He smiles at me with affection and signals for me to approach him. I walk slowly to savour but also to believe and he walks towards me. Then there is no hesitation and we meet. He nuzzles my shoulder and I step forward and throw my arms around his neck and breathe Jet in. it is a joy I did not know I could feel, a love I did not know I missed, a wonderment that makes total sense. It is as if part of me has been returned. I want to be forever held in this moment, for there to be no future, no past.

'Our budget does not stretch to the finery of a bridle and saddle,' Billy says, joining us. I have been given another gift, to ride with Jet as one without interference of leather and manmade notions of dominance.

'I know you do not need it, but you may have to fashion a rope into a bridle for us to travel without announcing our differences too loudly.' I nod; in this moment, I care little. We three are reunited and I will do anything so that we are never parted again.

Isabella, still blurry with sleep and hangover, approaches and strokes Jet's nose.

'Ah, so this is who my lover has been waiting for,' she says with a wink. I look at her and cannot help but grin.

'He has earnt his keep. Did you teach him all the tricks he has taught me?'

I shake my head. 'It is not I that is the master,' I say, and we understand each other. Alasdair approaches, having finished passing water by the side of the cart.

'This is an ungodly hour. Can we please get moving so I may return to my slumbers, such beauty as mine requires careful maintenance.' We all laugh.

'Do not mock, our coffers shall dip without my looks. Morning, old fella, you understand, don't you?' He pats Jet affectionally on the nose before climbing back into the cart.

Avery has finished harnessing the other horse. I bundle up our few belongings and throw them in the cart. Avery and Billy sit together up front whilst Lizzy and Isabella sit at the back of the cart, facing the way they have come. I clasp the base of Jet's mane and jump easily upon his back, forgetting any use of rope. As the sun rises, we leave the stables behind.

Billy leads us through the Grassmarket; an eerie silence and stillness pervades even though the stall holders are beginning to arrive and set up shop. The bodies of yesterday's executions are still hanging, swaying in the breeze, a reminder to all whose truth is law and that justice is a matter of opinion. Billy stops the cart in front of them and we join him.

'It is a reminder,' he says.

'Of the tyrants that call themselves kings,' I say.

'That you and I live on borrowed time, each day we have should count,' and he pushes the cart on. We linger as his words bring to the surface the urgency of our task. It does everything to deepen my resolve.

We take the main route out of the town, yet before long Alasdair, without moving from his pit, instructs us on the quieter back routes. It's an overcast day but dry and we make steady progress. I think if we were alone we would make much faster progress. Yet still I do not know where in the west we are travelling to so for now it is the best option. The conformation that Jet had joined their company compels me to think it is all part of the plan, that we travel together for a purpose, yet there is not a moment that I do not sense Grace's weakness.

The sun is high when we find a spot with a stunning view of hills and moor. We stop for breakfast under the watchful eyes of a murder of crows nestled in a nearby tree. Then everything springs into action - each has their role and their task. Lizzy sets the fire, Avery prepares the food, Isabella stretches and practices all manner of contortions of her body. Alasdair collects firewood, whilst Billy sees to the horses; their tasks distinct yet they act as one, all certain of each other. We watch in wonderment - it is a thing of beauty to behold, similar yet distinct from the Bedouin tribe. Sabby senses my unease as the shadow of the desert passes over me, so we seek out the burn. Jet drinks, I wash and Sabby fishes; maybe we are our own troupe in our own way. Once Sabby has her catch of pike we join the others who have all gathered around the fire.

Their chatter is of yesterday's performance; they self-critique and support each other to refine their performances. Avery hums a gentle tune throughout, more to himself than the others.

'Sabby, you are my hero,' says Lizzy at the sight of the pike and there is not one of them that does not join in with enthusiastic declarations and congratulations. It is as though they have never seen a pike before. I feel slightly overwhelmed, I do not understand how to receive such behaviour yet Sabby has no hesitation and gladly soaks up all adoration that is laid on her. Alasdair takes to gutting the fish whilst Avery takes up his lute and all join in the fish song.

The Fish Song

Chorus

Fa la la la lie do
Fa la la la do lie day

Oh what do we do with the pike's tail?
Oh what do we do with the pike's tail?
Pike's tail, soul in shoes
Pike's fins, needles and pins
Pikes head, we are fed
And all sorts of things
Oh for all the fish that swim
We are so glad of you

Chorus

Oh what do we do with the pike's eyes?
Oh what do we do with the pike's eyes?
Pike's eyes, pickles and pies
Pike's tail, soul in shoes
Pike's fins, needles and pins
Pike's head, we are fed
And all sorts of things
Oh for all the fish that swim
It is our joy to honour you

Chorus

Oh what do we do with the pike's back?
Oh what do we do with the pike's back?
Pike's back, lad named Alasdair
Pike's eyes, pickles and pies
Pike's tail, soul in shoes
Pike's fins, needles and pins
Pike's head, loaves of bread
And all sorts of things

Oh for all the fish that swim
We leave out none of you

Chorus

Oh what do we do with the pike's belly?
Oh what do we do with the pike's belly?
Pike's belly, lass named Isabella
Pike's eyes, pickles and pies
Pike's tail, soul in shoes
Pike's fins, needles and pins
Pike's head, we are fed
And all sorts of things
Oh for all the fish that swim
We love but all of you.

By the time the song has finished the fish is perfectly cooked and we feast, all quietly contemplating flavour and satisfaction. Alasdair is the first to break the silence.

'In which direction shall we venture next?' he asks the company. All eyes turn to Billy.

'If it so please the company, our good friend here Raven is heading west. Our company shall be enriched by his for a short while.'

'Excellent,' says Alasdair. 'Is there a destination in mind?'

'For this I seek your guidance, if I may,' I reply.

'How splendid, please, my extensive knowledge of the central lowlands is at your service.' The others groan - it is clear they expect a lecture. I look at Billy. I am not sure if I can trust anyone.

'Master Raven is on a quest,' he says, and everyone pays attention.

'Of love or war?' asks Isabella.

I laugh. 'Of love, of course,' I say and blush a little, they think because I am shy to declare my heart, yet it is more a shame that I have forgotten how to dissemble.

'A forbidden love?' asks Isabella

'Forbidden, indeed,' I say, reluctant to elaborate too deeply.

'Does your heart yearn? Do you wither without yon love?' she asks.

'There is urgency in my quest. I fear my love is in great danger,' I say, to foster support, yet all but Billy and Isabella withdraw.

Isabella wipes away a tear. 'Then we shall do all we can to assist. Shall we not? Is not ours a life lived for the heart and not the head?' she asks her companions, so that they cannot deny her and reluctantly mumble agreement.

'Do you have a location?' asks Alasdair, on being prompted by a shove in the ribs from Isabella.

'This is the guidance I seek. I know only that my love has been taken west, somewhere surrounded by water.' He thinks for a moment and I can see him run through options in his mind.

To help I say, 'It is most likely my love is in the hands of the church.' There is a shift in all present, no longer unwilling recruits in another's battle,

'Eileen MoLaise,' they declare in unison.

'It's a holy isle just off the coast of Arran. Between the main land and Arran,' says Alasdair. 'The monastery there is well known as a "retreat".'

Lizzy scoffs. 'I know of such retreats,' she says and pulls at her back, loosening her dress so all can see the scars that crisscross down it.

'The church decreed my size the Devil's work and made sure I was exorcized.'

I cannot help but reach out and touch the scars, tracing my fingers lightly over the web of pain. She pulls down her dress with a snap.

'There shall be no doubt in my support,' she says and offers me her hand. I clasp it with gratitude but also distress. How well my grandmother protected me.

'I have not spoken or written to my family in three years. For them I do not exist. I am no longer part of the family,' says Avery, in a tone so soft we all have to strain to hear.

'His father is a priest,' says Billy.

'With aspirations to be a bishop,' adds Alasdair

'I have chosen love,' says Avery, looking at Billy. 'It will be a divine duty to assist you.' He clasps my hand.

Alasdair slaps me on the back. 'The church takes what it has no rights to claim. My innocence shall be forever forsaken by a priest's desires. My fists and my gifts are at your disposal.' We shake hands.

I turn to Isabella; for one so vocal before she has fallen silent, her head dropped.

I kneel down to her. 'May I dry your tears?' I say and offer her a kerchief.

She looks up, tears falling silently from her eyes. 'It is not the Lord, this wrong doing, it is not the Lord but the corruption of man,' she says.

Alasdair comes and encloses her in his arms. She turns and falls into his embrace, releasing her sobs into his shoulders.

He looks at us. 'She is of our mind, Raven, and will do all she can.' I nod, and he leads her away.

'Her father was a priest but of the liberal kind, happy for the ways of the Earth to co-exist with the ways of Rome,' says Billy.

'Till the new regime thought to teach all a lesson,' adds Lizzy, 'hung, drawn and quartered with his head suspended outside his own church for the crows and magpies to feast upon.'

'We found her singing to the head. The locals said she had not left its side since it was placed,' says Billy.

'She had a good voice,' says Lizzy.

'And Alasdair fell as soon as he saw her,' adds Avery.

'He is a buffoon in most ways but there is not a thing he will not do for her,' says Lizzy.

'We shall find and release your love, Raven, for we know what it is to live with a different view,' says Avery and we begin to pack up, our resolve certain.

I glance at Billy and he greets my eye with a proud twinkle; the family he has created may not be conventional, may be shunned by all "decent" folk, but they know the truth in their hearts and have not denied it. My credentials are not worthy of theirs, so confused am I about my truth, so I receive their generosity with humble gratitude. Yet a seed has been planted inside me - maybe there is a way for my truth to be for it is clear to me now no matter the laws and rulings, those that do not match them shall never be eradicated.

Their routine is such that it is minutes and we are on the road again.

'To Strathaven,' says Alasdair and the cart begins to rumble.

I pull up Jet beside Billy. 'Strathaven?' I ask

'It's en route, a market town where you shall earn your keep,' and he winks at me. 'Besides which, it shall afford us an opportunity to agree our stratagem for the following day.'

I smile. This is good news indeed. If we can secure the book tomorrow, I could ride through the night and, with Sabby setting the pace, we shall travel fast and sure. Grace's health could be restored by the third sunset. It seems so near and so far away at the same time. I sit in the quiet rhythm of Jet's steps and try to feel Grace, to sense if she is still with us. Again, I see the memory of her face when she showed me the book. It is a confirmation and sets my resolve deeper.

I feel her need and it brings certainty to everything. I hold Jet back a little and, whilst no one is looking, I take my knife and cut a lock of my hair. I call Crow to me and she perches boldly on the base of Jet's neck. I offer my hair and, as she takes to the skies, she grasps it in her claws. I hope this message shall encourage Grace and Mother Gray.

Our pace is good and, as the sun begins to fall from the sky, we reach the top of a hill. Below us we can see the town of Strathaven. We take a pause to let the view sink in and let our limbs rest. It is a mistake, for we have but caught our breath when out of the trees that line the route, four men, whose garb has seen better days and whose weapons are at hand, block our path.

'A fine day for it, is it not, master?' asks Billy, as our company prepares for whatever may befall.

'It is that,' says a man of experienced years and unkempt appearance. 'It is an unusual route you travel.'

Alasdair steps forward. 'It's a short cut for those who know it.'

'For those who have something to hide perhaps.' The man draws a pistol from under his coat, sending a ripple of tension amongst all.

'What have we to hide, sir? We are simple players. We have but two groats between us.'

'And a stolen horse which suggests otherwise.' The man indicates Jet with his pistol, the lack of rope or bridle evidence of deception not deprivation.

I laugh and leap from Jet's back. 'Sir, we are too poor for bridle and saddle. It is a testament to our poverty not a denial of it.' He laughs in disbelief, followed by his fellows.

'Besides which he is not a riding horse but a valued member of the troupe,' says Isabella, stepping up to Jet and stroking his nose whilst smiling sweetly at the him.

'Let us show you,' and she steps away from Jet and clicks her fingers.

Jet rises up, instantly, onto his hind legs. She clicks again, and he takes three steps towards the man, casting a shadow over him and his crew. The man cowers, unable to move his feet as his body trembles. She clicks her fingers again and Jet whinnies a high piercing whinny, circles his front hooves and drops to the ground, his nose but an inch from the man's face. I am impressed, yet full of jealousy that she is so intimate with Jet. It seems that Jet and I are alike in our weakness for a pretty woman. Later I shall appreciate this as another indication of our deep connection.

'It is customary to reward such a display,' says Isabella and hands the man an apple from our supplies. He looks at her, looks at Jet, takes the apple and, with a reserved touch, offers it to Jet. Jet happily receives and happily chomps, nudging the man for more. The man cannot help but be charmed.

'Did you see that?' he says, turning to his companions. 'What a magnificent beast.' He turns back to Jet, patting him confidently on the neck. 'Bob, run ahead, tell them to prepare the market square. Tell them the sheriff announces entertainment for all.' The youngest one turns and hurries away.

He turns back to us. 'Let us escort you into town; never have we been blessed so before.'

'The honour shall be all ours,' says Billy, offering the man a hand up to sit beside him. The sheriff hesitates to take Billy's hand; I go to mount Jet, but Isabella stops me.

'Will you not ride in style?' says Isabella, offering him Jet.

What was once mild jealousy is now simple humiliation; I see her sense but the thought of his fat behind on Jet's back breaks me inside. The sheriff's eyes light up, but he is hesitant. Isabella stares at me and with great, hidden, reluctance, I turn to the sheriff,

'Let me assist, once on board you shall wonder at the need for saddle,' and I cup my hands, so he can step up.

'He shall not perform further tricks?' he asks.

'Sir, a more well-mannered beast you shall not find,' I say, and Sabby barks approval.

'Then what better way to introduce you to our town,' he says.

His stature is such that he can hardly raise his foot to meet my hands. Alasdair sees the predicament and steps in to further assist. It takes some muscle and some amount of puffing but eventually he is secured on top of Jet. I scowl at Isabella as I turn Jet towards the town; she smiles innocently back. Alasdair chuckles quietly to himself as he re-joins Isabella and I, at Jet's head, lead our caravan toward Strathaven.

By the time we reach the town there is a welcoming committee lining the streets. All our troupe, except for Billy driving the cart and I leading Jet, have changed into brightly coloured costumes and have hung ribbons all across the cart. Avery has begun a merry tune on his lute. Isabella punctuates her steps with cartwheels and backflips whilst Lizzy balances on Alasdair's head, throwing dried flowers and petals at the crowd in a shower of colour. The sheriff waves graciously and proudly. He is greeted with knowing and affectionate cheers by the crowd.

We drive into the square and, whilst I help the sheriff dismount and Alasdair entertains with wit and ceremony on current affairs, the company prepare the cart. Within minutes the everyday has been stored away under the cart. One of the sides has been raised, props have been set and a stage erected. It is a magical transformation. The sheriff and his deputies have been given prime seats above the heads of the other people and they have been joined by the laird and his family. The inn is taking orders and delivers amongst the crowd. It is an impromptu festival of pleasure and I can see no one who does not wear a smile. It is a gift to bring such joy into the mundane of the everyday.

I stand at the side with Jet and Sabby, as much spectator as support. At his designated cue, Jet takes his place on the stage. He is well rehearsed, and I am humbled and proud at the same time. I have little time for gloating as Billy drags me backstage behind the cart and throws a fool's costume at me. I am barely dressed when he drags me on stage. This time I am more prepared, and we fall into our old routine. By the time we have finished, and Billy has sung his final number, we are faced by a crowd of tears. The applause is deafening, and we are showered in coin and gifts.

We are still gathering them up as the crowd disperse and a servant boy approaches Billy. They converse, and the boy stands aside, waiting.

'Hurry into your glad rags, we have been invited to take supper at the castle,' says Billy.

I glance round me for reaction. I am nervous of such connection and such visibility. The others seem to receive the offer with anticipated reluctance.

'Remember, enjoy the food, smile sweetly and graciously refuse all and any offers of a bed for the night,' says Billy and there are resigned looks all around.

Sabby and Jet are at peace, but it is clear all any of us really want is to sup a little ale between ourselves and let sleep claim us. Yet the cart is packed up again, so it would be unimaginable that its transformation is so easily achieved, and we travel in satisfied silence towards the castle.

Lizzy is counting the takings in the back. I walk with Jet and Sabby, our bond growing deeper all the time. Isabella, Avery and Billy ride at the front of the cart whilst Alasdair lies flat out, whistling a tune.

'It was a good crowd,' says Billy, breaking the quiet.

'A crowd that reminds me of the purpose of our path,' says Isabella.

'A crowd to hold up to all those that call us wicked,' says Avery, and we fall back into our sense of peace.

Our cart is given a prime, sheltered spot in the grounds. Jet and our carthorse, Harry, are fed and watered with the finest oats and freshest water. We smarten our appearance as best we can and walk as one into the great hall.

It is a grand but simple design; oak beams high above create a lattice that is both decorative and functional. There is a top table, but the guests are not ordered as in the halls of my birthplace. Those of different status mingle and sit bedside each other with an informality that is inspiring but also terrifying. Half of me expects the Devil, whose existence I do not even recognise, to rise out of the earth there and then to claim all who so flagrantly disregard the social order as decreed by their God. For it is they that say the status of people is the Lord's work. Inside me though there is a deep understanding of this social mingling, for it is the way of the earth for all to be seen, all to be heard.

The laird sees us enter and at once approaches us with open arms.

'Welcome, welcome, come away in,' he cries and begins to applaud once more.

He is joined by the other guests as we are ushered to the top table. Our tankards are filled with wine and our plates piled high. We eat, drink and take in the sights. There is much badinage amongst the guests; it is clear a sharp wit and a sharper tongue are respected qualities to possess, yet there is ease and acceptance between people, conflicts and difference of opinions, but all have a space, it is as if we have been invited to large happy family gathering, not an official burgh function. I have travelled across the world but never had I considered this a possibility.

After all have taken their fill, the tables and benches are moved to the side and it is our turn to be entertained as each presents their act. Our approval is of much importance and our faces hide a million pains as heartfelt renderings of local songs are yelled tonelessly from eager, expectant faces. I see Billy court the laird, a robust man of solid structure with a fire of red hair and beard, with a laugh that shakes the roots in the trees. I know, by now, if the laird knows, by morning we will have all the information we need about the monastery on Eileen MoLaise.

At the end of the turns, the music begins, and the floor erupts with dancing. We are already deep into the night and now our company takes to the dance floor with unbounded joy. This Bacchic spirit is one that speaks to me. I have a sense of being found and for a short while it is as if every care that has ever weighted me or torn at my soul is lifted and I feel fluid and free as if I am shifting as I twirl around the hall. Then it is like I have dropped from a great height; my spirit plummets, crashing and falling. How can I idle away the hours when Grace feels the touch of death upon her skin, her being? Suddenly all around me are hostile, the earth itself set against my task, myself. I sink unseen to the back of the crowd and quietly seek fresh cool air.

The grounds are less kempt, less ordered than at Lady Bamford's house, yet it has a majesty, a handsome beauty of its own, a balance between man and earth rather than the enforced order of man. It is much easier to breathe and release, yet to some it would look like neglect. I find a spot in the moonlight where we can still hear the music and sit on a fallen tree, beautifully shaped into a seat, and sip on my wine. The peace soon seeps into my being. All the colour, all the sparkle of the day begins to fade, and I am left with my feelings of love for Grace, the sense of powerlessness and need for agency. It is not enough; I do all I can for her, yet all I can is not enough. Her life rests in my hands. I have never felt so alone.

'She is a lucky woman.' Lizzy's voice catches me unawares.

She steps out of the shadows and looks expectantly at the seat next to me. I offer my hand and pull her up beside me. We sit quietly for a while, caressed by the moon.

'When it gets to the dancing it is my cue. I have been trampled underfoot once too often in my life.' I turn and look at her.

Her eyes catch the moonlight and I am ashamed that I have never considered her beauty before now.

She smiles. 'I am a secret not all can see.'

I nod. 'It is a loss for those with poor eyesight.'

'Thank you, if only your heart was not spoken for.'

I look away. I am not sure if I even have a heart anymore.

'It is not a woman you seek at the Holy Isle.' I am afeard to look at her and do not respond.

'Yet you travel for love for it is only love that would inspire such measures.' She waits for my answer.

A sour bitter taste fills my mouth and spreads throughout my body. Love is a word which has lost all meaning for me.

'It is for a woman.' I spit out the words as if they are poison.

'It is more than love then.'

I look at her, her words a comfort I need to believe.

She smiles kindly. 'If ever I am in such need, I hope I have a Raven to call upon.'

I smile. 'To serve you would be an honour too great for such a simple bird.'

'That's what they all say.' And she laughs. 'It's getting late and we shall need an early start if we are to storm the monastery tomorrow night.'

She goes to jump down from the seat. I stay her hand with mine and she stops and looks at me.

'It is not what you think, she is dying, I have no choice.'

'You have no need of explanation.'

I look into her eyes and see a wisdom and compassion born of pain and suffering, of one who has seen the bleakest depths of themselves, of others, and walked through to the other side. Yet there is a yearning, a gift no one has bestowed and one she cannot make for herself. A desire yet unfulfilled. It is a gift I know I can give. It is not much but it is the least I can do. It is not a gesture of pity but of genuine affection and desire. I lean in and our lips meet. At first our kiss if soft, almost perfunctory, but with a little gentle persuasion she relents, and we kiss deep and sweet and long. It is a reminder to me of what an honest exchange is. I thought I offered her a gift, yet it is I that have received the greater prize.

Our lips part but our eyes linger. Eventually she smiles.

'I knew it, I was not sure, so well is your disguise but only a woman knows a woman so.'

I cannot help myself but grin. I am flattered in every way. It would be easy to kiss her again, but our intimacy is broken by the others who tumble along, wrapped in each other, wine and merriment. Lizzy stands on the seat.

'To bed!' she cries, and they sway towards our cart. I stand and hold out my hand; she accepts and jumps down from the seat.

'Shall we?' she asks, and we walk side by side.

I know a deep bond has been formed between us, yet I also I know nothing more shall be sought of us either.

At the cart, Isabella and Alasdair fall into each other's arms and slumber instantly. Avery meticulously but clumsily prepares Billy's and his bed whilst Lizzy curls up in her spot, complete without another. Billy drops unsteadily to the ground where Sabby and I have created our comfort under the cart.

'Turns out the laird has an affection for the old ways. Considers Christianity an affectation of the English and the Irish. Claims the Picts as his ancestors.'

I smile and nod. 'Then we are well met,' I say as Billy begins to draw the layout of the island and monastery in the soft earth.

'Pay attention, for tomorrow this shall not be in my mind, so it needs to be in yours.'

He names the rooms he has drawn, the routes through the isle, where the vulnerabilities are and where the strengths.

'How does he know so much?' I ask.

'Seems he needed some persuasion to convert,' says Billy and he falls into a slumber sitting up with his eyes open.

'Come,' I say and heave him to his feet.

I guide him to the back of the cart where he falls head first into the delicate arrangement of Avery's blankets, already snoring. Moonlight illuminates the map and I study it till my eyes can only close and a plan has taken shape in my mind.

Chapter Eleven

Despite my expectations, it is Billy that is first to his feet at first light. Avery joins him to harness the horse and, whilst the others sleep, I make sure we leave no trace of our habitation. In the early morning mist before the castle or the town awake, we set off for Ayr, the nearest port to Eilean MoLaise.

We are almost at the gates when, charging down the drive way is the laird, dressed only in his nightshift, puffing and panting, as if his life depended on it. Billy pulls to a stop and I turn Jet to greet him. He stops, hands on his knees gasping for breath.

Eventually he waves a sealed letter at us. 'It will gain you entrance.'

I reach down and take it. 'Thank you, your hospitality knows no bounds.'

'I know what it is to lose a loved one to the church, fi kindred spirits there are no limits.'

I reach down and clasp his hands. There is hope in this meeting; it seems you do not need to be part of a Society to resist domination, it is a choice that all can take.

'Speed you well,' he says as we set off again, 'this door is always open.' And he watches us leave.

I feel his presence imprinted on my back. Wherever we roam, we shall have a friend in Strathaven. It is an odd sensation, a sense of connection to someone and something I expect never to see again. It is as if we are not leaving, rather letting distance fall between us. It is a pleasant sensation, yet it causes great disturbance inside, as all pleasant sensations do, so that I dismiss it from my mind instantly and focus on the plan.

We should reach Ayr by late afternoon. Billy shall secure us a boat, Isabella shall gain all the intelligence she can of the state of play at the monastery, Lizzy shall secure us a crew whilst Avery, Alasdair, Jet and I secure our reputations as players and minstrels of a king.

The sun has well risen by the time Billy selects a spot for breakfast. I help Lizzy down from the cart; she does not need it and we both know that, but it is a tacit agreement to respect the intimacy between us without expecting more. Avery, in search of feed for the horses, squeals with delight as, when he uncovers the oats, he reveals a basket laden with dried roasted venison and grouse, oatmeal bread and sweet meats. We shall feast for days, or rather the troupe shall, for if the plan works, this time tomorrow Jet, Sabby and I shall be speeding through the backwaters towards Grace.

I swing between sensations of peace and relief, for now our journey has a focus and an end in sight. It feels our success is not in doubt, for I do not allow myself to consider failure and quickly deny its presence in my mind by focusing on the image of Grace's face. To consider Grace's death is a weight too much to bear. I cannot consider what I carry, to do so would render me powerless to the dense mass that would engulf me. I vow to ignore all the voices in my head that wage war on my purpose. I shall listen only to the purpose and do whatever it takes, pay whatever the price, to fulfil it.

After a breakfast of hair of the dog and a selection from our gift basket, I lay down the bones of our plan. 'Once we have secured the boat and night has fallen, we shall set sail for the island.'

'Do we arrive as pilgrims or players?' asks Billy.

'As players; it is my plan that whilst you have the attention of the monks I shall secure my prize, take the boat and return to the mainland.'

'And what of our show? How shall the monks receive it?'

'Our show shall be the show we offer every religious house we visit, a heavy dose of smut and lewd enterprises with a slight sprinkling of sacred masses and motets,' says Lizzy, and we all laugh in recognition.

'How do you leave the isle? A night in a monastery is not restorative,' says Avery with a degree of concern. It is clear a monastery is a place that throws up pain for him.

'I shall send it back,' I say

'It is best you don't,' says Billy 'for it shall confirm our innocence if you have stolen a boat from us.'

'I am with Avery; to be stranded with monks all night, I shall not sleep,' says Alasdair and it is clear he fears for Isabella and Lizzy's safety.

'They shall have a boat. We shall guide them to use it to pursue you,' says Billy.

'Be sure I have a healthy advantage,' I say

'You shall go unnoticed until we have filled our coffers, drank our fill and laden our stomachs. Then when we insist that we return to the mainland, we shall discover your trespass,' says Billy.

It is a complication to the plan I had not anticipated. I had thought I would have until first light, at least, to gain a start and gather my distance, yet it is clear none of the company consider a Holy Isle inhabited by those devoted to their Lord a safe haven for anyone and I cannot further endanger their lives.

'It's a plan then,' I say. I place my hand in the centre and each joins me.

'A plan,' we say together, our resolve certain. I think for them this is somewhat a game. I think it is best they think that.

We pack up and set off again; a quiet focus settles over us, each lost to their own thoughts and worlds. It is a pleasant route and easy to forget that we are on a quest that risks our lives. Eventually Isabella takes up a refrain, an ancient song of betrayal and love lost. It is one we all know and soon we are singing away miles and doubt.

It is late afternoon when we reach the main road into Ayr. There is a gentle but steady flow of traffic; carts carrying cargo to and from the ships, well-dressed dignitaries and empty-bellied beggars pass before us. It would be common for the troupe to set the cart now, hide the everyday with the promise of a story, announce our arrival with ribbons, colour and song, yet there is a tacit understanding that today shall be different and we slip unnoticed into the throng that heads towards the port. A silence has fallen upon us, a focused resolve. We each know the parts we are to play and to what end, each focused on our task.

We take our time to reach the port at the mouth of the River Ayr. It is a small port; there is but one ale house and what feels like a vast army of people with nothing to do but wait for their boat to come in. It is not what I expected; it is as if we have walked into a wall of eyes with nothing else to gaze upon but us. We pull the cart up next to the livery.

Nothing has been said but we all feel the tension and the threat it possesses. We are all that they have been taught to despise, to consider evil. I think this has gone far enough, that this is not a quest I should embroil others in. There is an urgency now to my task. The stale hostility that lingers in the indolent eyes of the bystanders confirms the need of my actions but do others need to suffer, to pay this price too? I am about to speak, to release my companions, when a look is exchanged between us all. It is a look of commitment and I know that whatever I say I am no longer alone. Then we break, each to their own role. Avery takes the cart and horses to settle in the livery, Isabella to the ale house and Lizzy to the idle captains with heavy anchors for their idle boats.

I follow Billy and it is as if he has grown in size and stature. He seems to fill the port walkway with colour and light. It is impossible not to notice him, not to be drawn to him, to be charmed by the force he exudes. All eyes now follow him as I trot behind, his eager fool. He comes to a stop, claiming the best position to be seen by all. He opens his arms wide and smiles and it is as if a million candles shine from him.

'Fellow travellers. We come to banish your cares, fill yon hearts with joy and your souls with light.'

No one moves, although the desire to can be felt. Billy is undeterred and, from seemingly nowhere, produces a sea of ribbons that billow in the sharp cutting wind, a blaze of colour splitting apart the sombre grey sky. A small child stands transfixed; it is clear they have never seen anything of the like before. It is not just I that have noticed her for before I can argue, Billy has 'magicked' up a single red rose. He throws it to me, and I feign clumsiness, catching and not catching, ducking and rolling in order to catch it. I hear laughter and sense smiles in the blank empty eyes of those who look on. I make a final grand pretence of missing the rose, so it is thrown high into the air; I twirl round, catching the rose as it falls and land on one knee, rose in hand, in front of the girl. Bashfully I present it to her. She smiles a broad, confident smile and does not hesitate to snatch the rose from my hand and the crowd erupts.

Then it is easy - as they step closer, so our antics increase. I try my best to hinder Billy in his serious business, trickster to his honest everyman. It is not long before we are prompted by excited, eager heckling and cheers. What was once a solemn screen of unrelenting hardship has become a carnival of life. Then, bursting out of the ale house comes a priest, a thin, slight man of sombre manners. He strides purposefully and with enraged indignation towards us. It is a black cloud falling over a sunlight sky. At first, I do not notice; I am low to the ground engaged in tumbles and falls, yet I sense the chill spread, ice over a still lake.

Billy sees instantly and before I can follow, he has dropped all foolery and struck up the most beautiful motet that I have ever heard. The priest stops in his tracks, the crowd fall silent and step aside as Billy approaches, singing directly to him, and the priest swoons. Soon the crowd has followed, and Billy holds them all in his palm. I wonder what it is to have such power over those who scorn you and who you scorn in return. I do not know if this is a thing of beauty or of poison.

I see Isabella and Avery make their way to the dock and know Lizzy has secured us a boat. As the crowd swoon and weep in spiritual ecstasy, I collect all that is ours and signal to Billy. The crowd have largely closed their eyes and those that have not are full of tears and, as he sings the last notes to his song, Billy begins to silently step away. He throws his voice, so none are the wiser. We are out of sight as the last note fills their ears. We follow Avery into a dinghy with sails. The sun is approaching the horizon and we set off towards the deep red sky and ocean.

Lizzy has command of the boat and it seems we are the crew. The owner of the dinghy, far wetter than the sea for the ale in his belly, sleeps contentedly at the bow, his slumped head almost resting on a full belly. Sabby takes position just below the swing of the sail and lets the air ripple through her fur. There is little room. Lizzy instructs Avery and Alasdair who demonstrate some experience of seamanship whilst Isabella and I compensate, balancing out the boat as Billy leans over the side and empties the contents of his stomach into the darkening waters.

'The wind is with us,' cries Lizzy, clearly in her element at the stern of the boat and in charge of direction.

It is not a large boat, good for our purposes, but I shall not manage it on my own and, as much as Sabby is loving the sensation of the sea, she shall be of little assistance. A fraction of doubt creeps into my consciousness. Will the plan I have visualised begin to unravel?

'How long?' I ask.

'At this speed we shall arrive on cue, in time to be the after-dinner entertainment,' says Lizzy. Billy groans and I fear our star attraction shall have no stomach to enrapture the pious men of Eilean MoLaise.

'They say we shall not have much of an audience,' says Isabella. 'Seems there is no thirst for religious rigor on the isle. The numbers dwindle with no fresh recruits.'

'Why hide away when the dominion of the church claims more and more of our land and people?' says Avery.

No one answers but we all feel the pinch as if there is a little less air for us all to breathe, even less room for us in the world.

I see the reasoning. Bury the Book of Knowledge in a forgotten place, that in time shall be forgotten and in time no one shall seek its wisdom. How easy to lead a flock that know no different, that does not think there is difference, does not know of the possibility of different voices joined in one song.

I wonder if it shall be easier or harder with few people. Easier in some ways, harder in others, I think, as I quickly revise my expectations. Billy tries to speak but his stomach has another idea.

'Still should be an easy audience,' says Isabella. 'Maybe no more than ten folk who live a life of solitude away from their fellow men. How eager they shall be for company and song.'

'We shall say we seek retreat from the clamour of the world of man. Say we seek only to live simply for a while and in return we will bless their ears with sacred song,' says Lizzy and there is agreement from all.

I shall wear my cap low, sink into the shadows, play my part as support and skivvy so they do not expect to see me join the song. For I am sure the words would stick in my throat so alien to the ways of the earth these sacred songs have become.

Night has fallen by the time we see the outline of the isle, rugged and unapologetic against the skyline. I do not sense a welcome, instead fear flutters in my belly as I approach this unchosen destiny of mine.

'We approach from the Arran side - there is landing opposite Lamlash,' says Lizzy and we fall again into our separate silences.

For days, urgency has eaten away at my senses, Grace's need and her gasping breath driving all I have done. Yet now, as we slip smoothly through the waves and the dark unforgiving sea, I want nothing more than for the wind to drop, for us to hover forever in the dull space between action and inaction. I feel every part of my body resist what it knows is inevitable. Yet how hard can this be, a few aged monks and a book? What real harm can befall us? I think myself hysterical under a veil of calm and certainty. Maybe I have prepared us for a mighty purpose when in fact it shall be a simple night of song and quiet slumber. Maybe this all-consuming, inexplicable fear is fear of humiliation, fear to be exposed as the fool I so clearly am.

The wind begins to bite through, a chill enters my bones. I call Sabby to me for warmth, yet her presence does not still my heart but rather confirms my fear for I can sense her unease, sense her shrinking into herself as she expands her coat, so she appears twice her actual size. Everything begins to feel hostile, the water threatening, the darkness suffocating, the wind a trickster that plays with our hopes and fears. My face wears a comfortable smile, yet I am so lost in nervous anticipation I cannot tell if others feel the same.

It is hard to get a sense of distance in the dark, but we turn around the isle and we can see lights at Lamlash to our left. Then I look to the isle and the reason for my fears looks back at me. The Black Gladfly is moored and anchored at the landing of the isle. I cannot fathom it. Is it they that have stolen the book from Grace? Have they come to retrieve it also? Who else has taken up residence on the isle? For just behind the Gladfly we see the mast of another ship. Panic surges through my entire being. This is not part of the plan.

Billy has seen the ship too and it has stilled his stomach. We look at each other, both questioning, both accusing. Did the other know? Yet our accusations confirm our innocence; this is unwelcome, for both of us.

'Seems we shall have an audience after all,' he says. Lizzy has seen our look and understands this ship is unwelcome news.

'An audience appreciative of the fine arts?' she asks. Billy and I laugh.

'Since when has there been anything fine about us?' he says, although that is not why either of us laugh. Sabby is resolutely calm but with the focus of a hunt. The others too consider the ship.

'You know this ship?' asks Isabella. I look at Billy; our nod is our answer.

'Friend or foe?' asks Alasdair. We both shrug our shoulders, we do not know.

'Is the plan the same?' asks Avery, seeking Billy's eyes for reassurance.

I do not know how to answer. A million thoughts, a million scenarios, run rapidly through my mind whilst the whole time I hear the rasping of Grace's breath and the weight of her life upon my shoulders. It would make the most sense to turn and go back but I cannot do that.

'Let me disembark,' I say, 'you turn back. There is no sense for you to risk life and limb.' I look Billy in the eyes.

Lizzy laughs, 'You think we are not up to it?'

'I think it is my fight and should not cost you.'

'My, how big you are to think we fight for you,' she says. I am confused; is this an accusation or a vote of confidence?

'We fight so all can have the right to be who they are,' says Avery in a certain but gentle tone. Billy smiles and I can see his pride in his lover. All eyes turn to me - it is clear all are of the same mind. Then it is certain what we are to do.

'Set Billy and I down out of sight but not too far from the landing. You go on as planned, present the letter of introduction if questioned. Stick to the story of retreat and offer your services for this evening. Billy and I shall gather what information we can and meet you in the monastery.'

'How shall you find us, reach us?' asks Avery, his eyes imploring Billy.

'Never fear, we shall find you, no matter what,' says Billy, and Avery is calmed by Billy's open show of love. The moment is broken by a loud snore from the boat owner, still deep in slumber. We all laugh.

'It is a plan then,' says Alasdair and Lizzy steers the boat on.

'What did you give the boatman?' asks Isabella.

Lizzy taps her nose. 'It's best you do not know,' she says, and they smile. There is something in her way that reminds me of Grandmother and all the things I did not know for my own safety; it is a comfort and a warning.

Our spirits uplifted, it takes little time before Billy and I feel solid earth beneath our feet. With whispered farewells, the others set sail for the main landing. There is no moon and the ground is uneven and shifting, sometimes sand, sometimes knotted grasses and rocks. We make slow and silent progress towards the monastery.

As we approach, we see armed guards patrolling. Two approach the boat as it pulls in to the landing. We cannot hear but we see Lizzy wave the letter in their faces. Reluctantly the guards escort them towards the main gates of the monastery. It is hard to see in the darkness, but their helmets bear a rose that in daylight would be red and white. The isle is under the control of the English army, troops that must have been sent from Berwick Upon Tweed. In whose hands does the book lie? Does the Society and the army work in cahoots or are they at war? A look to Billy confirms he has the same questions. Either way there is more that rests on this book than Grace's life.

I look at Sabby. She has a clear intention and I know we are to follow her lead. She picks a gentle, quiet path taking us well around the back of the landing, slipping through the shadows as is our way. The monastery seems to be crumbling, almost in ruin, patched up with canvas and wood. No wonder their numbers dwindle. All around its parameters are guards, cold and bored-looking, easy to distract. We drop down deep into a dip of the earth as the rest of our party are escorted inside. They maintain a cheerful outlook, but the guards are unimpressed. The sense of the guards' boredom is strong; they have been here too long without entertainment. I fear for our comrades' safety amongst the unfulfilled lusts and cravings of an army. I grasp hold of the intention to be off the island before first light; maybe they shall be protected that long.

We scan the geography and there is no obvious way into the monastery. I think to shift as Raven; I could easily slip in between the canvases but to what end? A naked woman roaming the walls of a monastery. Again, my gift is more hindrance than use. To have such a powerful skill and no obvious need for it, yet Sabby is clear on her part and leads through burns and ditches to the back of the friary, to the kitchens.

The door is open, and we have a good spot to observe, inside a furnace. We are some good feet away and we can feel the heat of it. If my nerves where not so altered the smells carried on the still damp air would have my taste buds turning somersaults in glorious anticipation. We watch for a short while; there is little coming and going but the guard by the door is easily distracted. He watches with greedy eyes the preparations inside far more than he watches for approach from the outside.

We think Sabby has led us far enough that now we are to continue a plan of our own, yet she has simply paused and, when she senses the guard's distraction, she approaches further. She is in plain sight; even in the moonless night the spill of light from the kitchen is enough to catch the silver in her fur and illuminate it, so it is as if the stars have landed to shine from her. Still she goes unnoticed, dropping down into what looks like some sort of moat or ditch surrounding the monastery walls.

We wait until we see her face above cover then run as lightly as we can to join her. We drop into the shadows as the guard stands, but a few paces away from us, turns and relieves himself, his water splashing against the stone walls. We all squeeze out of the way as it trickles past us. I follow its flow as it falls through some bars into the monastery, a window into the cellars.

Inside the cellar I can see a dimly-lit corridor, water seeping through the walls and up through the ground. There is a thud as a heavy wooden door is heaved open. Two guards drag a slumped body between them, followed behind by the key holder. In the dim light I begin to make out the outline and shape of the body, bruised and swollen from thumb screws, his limbs rendered loose and without elasticity from being stretched for so long, his head hung and roped. The key holder opens a heavy-set door and stands aside to let them throw him in. Before they do, the key holder holds back the head by its hair and spits in his face; as the torchlight catches his skin I see it is Captain Langan.

I am transfixed; for a moment it seems as if everything has slowed down, as I watch them laugh at his degradation and throw him casually, as if discarding peelings for the pigs, into the dark room. They reach into the room and pull out the first body to hand. Time speeds up with a jolt when I see the ship's boy wriggle and squirm and beg for mercy as they drag him nonchalantly away, already tired and uninterested in their new task. The key holder heaves the door closed and turns the key with a satisfied finality.

I lean back against the monastery walls. At least it is not the Society we need to fear, yet what does either party know of the book or its whereabouts? It is but a matter of time before the torture takes affect and what is known shall be spoken. Billy signals to me to join him and we three crouch together, low to the ground.

‘I shall distract the guard, claim I have been sent for supplies to welcome the players. Time enough for you to slip down to the cellars and discover our predicament. Join me at the great hall, where we shall find the others; it is clear tonight they feast.’

I nod approval and follow as he approaches the door. He waits until the guard is in conversation and slips behind him, only to approach him from inside as if he has been inside the whole time. I wait until they are in conversation and, despite our agreement, turn back the way we came. It will be quicker and safer for me to finally use the gift that has brought us all here and I know exactly what shape to choose.

I meet Sabby’s eyes and know she understands. In amongst the danger and rawest human behaviour, and despite the urgency, I cannot help but surrender and enjoy the softening, the melting of my flesh to take on a new form. The beautiful sensation of fluidity is over too soon, and I am left with the eternal question of why this is no longer permitted, how something that feels so completely authentic should be viewed so wrongly. It is such a joy to discover my eight legs work perfectly.

Despite the dampness of the walls, I climb quickly down and there is a healthy gap under the door. Inside it is pitch black yet I see clearly. Tentatively I creep into the room. It’s a small square of thick set stone, no windows, and with the entire ship’s crew squeezed inside. There is no room to sit or lie, barely room to stand. The dirt floor is thick with urine and faeces. The smell of fear and shame fills very available space between bodies. The air is so stale I wonder if a slow death by suffocation is the intent or if they have simply not considered the consequences of caging men so close together. It is a torture either way. The captain is propped up against the wall, the only way to gain any respite.

Their eyes have become accustomed to what little light there is; it takes a moment or two till I am noticed, then they clamour to the edges of the room, body pressed against body. There should be something reassuring about grown men in the direst of situations crawling over each other to be out of a spider's way, to wield such power, yet although anticipated, it is mostly just disappointing.

Despite his fragility, the captain understands; it is almost as if he expects me. From somewhere he finds the strength to stand and, with his arms, gestures for all to turn away. The crew are reluctant to turn their backs on the object of their terror, but the threat of his anger even here holds sway and even the most defiant turn their backs. Whatever my feelings about him, the captain's protection of my modesty and gift, even here, stands in his favour.

The shift is delicious but fleeting and I stand before him naked, yet I have no shame, no sense of anything to be ashamed of. His mouth is caked in blood and swollen, yet he prises it open and I see the gaps where they have torn out his teeth. I go to reach out to him to comfort him, but he signals for me to keep a distance. I feel him a fragile tower that, with the slightest touch, will crumble to pieces. Summoning all the effort he has, he breathes out words. I have to lean closer to hear but take care not to touch. He tries again and this time the word 'cave' escapes on his breath, the next breath 'MoLaise'. It is all we have before we hear the turn off the key.

I shift back to spider almost instantly. The door opens and all turn to face it and all shriek at the sight of spider. I have shifted to such a beautiful spider too, firm round body with long slender legs, beautiful tender springs to hold my frame. A guard's boot descends towards me, but I have advantage of form and leap up on to his leg. He squeals, dropping his torch and runs around, screeching as I dance up his body, dodging the frantic and wild swipes of his hands. I reach his face and he freezes in abject terror. I take my time to tread very slowly around his chin; all gaze on, gripped in anticipation, wallowing in someone else's horror. I take my time stepping over his lips, making sure he feels the weight of my tiny feet. I tickle his nose as I advance towards the space between his eye brows and before the slap that comes from his colleague, I throw out my web and swing out of the way and back up through the bars as the guard falls to the floor from the force of his rescuer's blow.

'Hey!' he shouts as all prisoners and guards collapse in laughter. It took all my resolve not to bite and inject a deadly poison; still his humiliation is more effective and shall last much longer.

I watch the guards relishing regaining order with bitter, angry blows. The captain flounders away from the support of the wall. I am not sure how long he has left or if he will survive. I am surprised that I feel nothing about this. I do not even feel the compassion I would grant a stranger. All that has passed between us has come to naught, yet there is little time for reflection. They toss the ship's boy into a heap on the floor, his bones broken and unable to sustain his weight. That at least stirs some sort of emotion in me, though I have no name for what it is. They drag another sailor out, cowering and squirming, and I wonder if this is what they think it is to be a God. I wait until they are out of sight and shift back.

Sensing Sabby's urgency, I dress quickly. I do not know how we shall pass the guard but when we get to the door, Sabby does not hesitate but marches boldly in and along the passage. So startled am I that I chase after, only then to find the guard has found a pretty wench to "protect". I fight the desire to rip his genitals from his being and make him eat them, and hope, instead, she has the experience and sense to protect herself from his protection. Sabby growls in a low voice, pressing me to follow and not intervene.

We slip between shadows, just about keeping out of sight of the "staff" the English have ensconced here. From the plates and platters that pass us by, they have come well supplied. It is not hard to find the great hall for all the traffic to-ing and fro-ing from it. Keeping outside of the hall, we work our way around the walls until we come to where the wall has decayed and a crack splinters from top to bottom; someone before us has created a larger space where they have sought to observe, and we appreciate their toil. From the laughter in the room the players are deep into their act. Making sure I cannot be seen, I peer in.

It is a scene of debauchery; the monks, who have chosen to live a simple, pure life, have taken little time to be corrupted by wine, food and pleasures of the flesh. The monks throw themselves upon the whores that the English have brought with them. Isabella and Alasdair perform a complex routine of balances and planned falls viewed by all through blurred and lascivious eyes. The usual social order is abandoned, and all mingle with each other. By twisting, I can just about make out the top table. I blink, unable to comprehend what I see. Sitting in stony silence, with a gaze that takes him far way, is Stephen the castle keeper, by his side is Ben Lovell, more engaged with the antics than Stephen, but with an air of superiority, of the observing of mere mortals behaving as the lowly beasts he considers them to be.

I pull back and lean against the wall, hardly able to catch my breath. It is a horror I had not imagined. To see them again was something I hadn't anticipated. I had buried them in a past that no longer exists. I am paralysed, I cannot think, cannot act, cannot feel. Sabby paws and whines but I am unable to respond. It's as if everything is happening far away from me. I do not know how long I stay like this, but it is Billy's breath in my ear that brings me back, from where I do not know, only that there is a black hole in my memory.

'What says the captain?' Billy asks. His voice has pulled a lever in my mind and I can now see and think and behave with clarity devoid of humour or emotion.

'My prize is held in the hermit cave of St MoLaise. Sabby and I will go. Collect the others and meet us at the boat. We must leave as soon as we can - there is nothing safe here.'

'And what of the captain, the crew?' he asks.

'What of them?' I say.

Our eyes meet. I can see he thinks me heartless, yet my focus is clear and specific. We shall collect the Book of Knowledge and return it to Grace as quickly as possible. It is our only obligation. He can tell there is no discussion to be had and does not question but simply nods his head and slips back into the hall.

Sabby leads us on our way back to the kitchens. The cave is a short distance from the monastery and it is clear we have little time, when we hear a shriek. The great hall falls silent, there is a moment of pause, then Lizzy runs out carrying a large set of keys.

'One of the guards was too free with Isabella and Alasdair…' she says.

Billy follows her out, 'Go!' he yells at her.

He looks at me. 'We need reinforcements,' he says, almost as an apology, then, 'Go, we shall not be able to hold them for long.'

Sabby barks and bites at my clothes; without speaking I turn on my heels and run. We do not care who sees or who knows of our intent. We simply run as fast as space and time allow us, barging all and any out of our way as we go.

The cold air hits us as a wave of resistance as we run past the kitchens and into the night, yet it has no impact on our trajectory. We hear the sailors burst out of their dungeon, their cry a mix of war and release. There shall be nothing left of the monastery but fragments by first light. I let Sabby lead; I know she is following scent and instinct and know hers to be far more accurate than mine. I trip constantly whilst she bounds effortlessly over obstacles I cannot see till is too late. The clouds have thickened and thunder rumbles in the distance. I fear my next fall shall prove fatal, yet I cannot stop my legs from moving. I am driven by another force; something inside me has taken agency and I am powerless to resist my own direction and momentum.

Sabby leads us to the shore; the waves grow and swell, fierce and hostile in their inky blackness. I feel the sand give under my feet and I am filled with a sensation that the closer we get the further away our prize, that no matter what we do the book shall always be one step away, one step out of reach no matter how many steps we take. But, as the first flash of lightning strikes, we dive into the cave, out of the rain as the clouds split open.

Inside the cave it is as if we are a million miles away from the chaos and fury that rages outside. We can hear gun shots, the battle in full flow, lightning flashes again filling the cave with light. There is nothing there, just some old rotting fishing nets, and the remains of a fire long since spent. There is no sign of digging or searching by others. The English do not know of this cave - at least the captain has some degree of integrity, to withstand the torture he has so far and not yet disclosed secrets. Is this the right cave?

Yet I know the Society too well; I have inhabited their stratagem and understand exactly what to do. It will be at the far corner of the cave. I run my hands along, the walls damp and unforgiving. I reach up and disturb the bats who momentarily halt my search as I am engulfed in their number. Then it is clear; where else would you hide it? And I reach up to where the bats have their roost. Then I feel it, a short gentle pull and the door slides open; it has the Society's hallmark all over it.

Yet it is not a door to another chamber but to a safe embedded into the wall. Lightning strikes again, followed by a loud thunder clap directly overhead. I can hear that the fight has escaped the monastery walls, hear thumps and bodies falling into the waves. Sabby is impatient, anxious; we have little time before we need to be aboard the boat. Grace's face flashes before me, yet my focus is crystal clear and undistracted by the pressures that threaten everything. I have no time for what ifs. I feel the edges and the surface of the safe; an intricate and complex relief has been built into the surface, a spiral labyrinth that leads to the centre. Lightning flashes again, revealing a round hole in the centre, the keyhole.

'To the boat,' I hear Billy shout and it is a signal for me as much as for the others.

I drop to my knees, feel amongst the sand for an anchor, stone or crystal, run my fingers along the walls seeking a shelf with hidden gems, yet there is nothing. Panic is about to engulf me when Sabby jumps up at me, tearing at my doublet. Then it is as if every candle and every sun and every moon in every world and dimension is ablaze. I take my knife and rip open the hidden corner of my doublet. There, as it has been all along, is the coin, the coin my grandmother made me sew into my doublet for safe keeping. The coin Grace gave me, the coin my grandmother said I would know when to use and, despite being penniless and destitute, we never have. Even in the cave of no light it seems to shine. I hold it in my hands and feel its glory.

Sabby barks her urgency, snapping me out of my reverie. I take time to kiss the coin and then place it in the centre of the spiral. A small gentle clicking sound is heard and the door swings easily ajar. I push it open, surprised by its weight and thickness. Inside is the book, wrapped and sealed with love and care in oilskins. I am almost too humbled to touch it, but the sound of a pistol shot but feet away from the cave sheds me of any pretence. I lift the book with the utmost care I can and hug it to my chest. I swing shut the safe door. The coin stays in place and I know it is shut for all time now. I resist the pull to run and instead search for the lever. A gentle pull and the door closes, and we leave no trace behind, nothing but our footprints in the sand that the waves soon wash away.

I pull my doublet over the book and tuck it in as best I can as we hit the lashing rain. The waves crash as we stumble past a guard and sailor locked in mortal combat. Lightning flashes again, illuminating the shoreline and we see Billy standing at the boat, ready to set sail as the others make their way to him.

Isabella drags Alasdair away from the punches he would like to throw. Avery ducks and dives, avoiding as best he can all blows, all attempts at violence, his slight agile frame intact but only just. Lizzy is running up behind; she avoids all grasping hands and stamping feet but cannot make the speed of the others. Still I see her pleasure in staging avoidance with bites to the knees, by lying in wait unseen in the dark, making an obstacle that causes the guards to fall. It is a pleasure to see her work. I am filled with pride that she is on my side.

Sabby speeds ahead and I follow in her steps; the book is heavy and awkward to run with, yet I feel light and we fly along the shore with wings on our feet. Ducking pistol shots we dive into the boat with Avery, Isabella and Alasdair.

'Lie flat,' says Billy, who is raising the anchor.

We shall need oars and set about placing them as the others pant and laugh, happy in their safety. Lighting and thunder strike again and I see Lizzy speeding along the sand, pursued by two men - Stephen and Ben.

'Run!' I scream. 'Lizzy, run!'

She hears my cry and from somewhere finds a little more power. They are almost upon her and I go to help her, but Billy holds me back

'There is no time,' he says, and she leaps towards the boat as Billy begins to push away. I reach out to catch her, standing in full view, caring little if I live or die. I hear the sound of a pistol shot as Lizzy jumps into my arms. I hold her so I can see her face and she smiles her warm cheeky grin.

'You're welcome,' she says

'You're safe now,' I say, and she closes her eyes. 'It is not the time for sleep; we are escaping,' I say, but there is no response.

'Lizzy,' I say. Still nothing. I go to lie her down to make her comfortable and find I am drenched in her blood.

'Lizzy,' I cry but know it is too late. I can feel all life has dropped away from her.

I would howl with the grief that engulfs me but something else takes charge and without any consciousness I hand her to Avery as fury fills every part of my being. I am about to leap from the boat and end it with Stephen and Ben once and for all when suddenly there is only blackness.

Chapter Twelve

I awake in the hull of the boat and can hear Billy cuss and Avery moan. I sit up slowly, rubbing the bump on my head. Sabby is at the stern of the boat barking direction. Alasdair and Avery, each with an oar one side, Billy and Isabella the other. Lizzy lies stiff and motionless beside me in the bow.

'Don't just sit there,' yells Billy, 'do something.'

In the distance we can see the monastery in flame, the Black Gladfly raising its sails. The thunder and lightning have abated but the lashing rain continues.

'I'll push from behind,' I say, and I slip out of my clothes and into the water. As the cold water hits and I feel my blubber take shape Billy positions himself between his crew and the stern, so none may see me or rather not see me but a large bull seal in charge of his hareem.

I cry out with the loudest seal call I can muster. Soon we are joined by a team of seals all with only one intention in mind. I push from behind joined by the others at the side. All on the boat are transfixed. Billy signals for them to hold their tongues and I can see how it pains them to do so.

Despite the rain it takes no time at all to reach the harbour in Ayr. I thank our friends and release them from their calling. As I shift back they hold the attention of Billy's crew with a display of diving, bobbing and dancing through the waves. The water is biting cold and by the time Billy has pulled me on board again I am almost seized up. He takes a cloak from his pack and wraps it around me before the others see my modesty, yet I do not really understand why my naked body should be so hidden as if we do not all share what lies beneath our clothes. If my friends can lose their life for me why can they not see my body?

They have wrapped Lizzy's body in anything they have to hand, scarfs and coats, silk and ribbons - she is wrapped in a rainbow of love. I can barely look at her. I must move lightly, swiftly now and the weight of her death is too heavy for me to hold. I know somewhere inside me one day her death will make a sense, have a reasoning and a purpose, shall become clear, but now there is a mass confusion, of conflicting emotions that threaten to disable me completely if I give it them any time and credence.

As the boat comes to dock, I dress as quickly as possible. I take the book, still perfectly protected in its oilskins, and slip it under my doublet. It is heavy and too big to sit comfortably but to have it any further away from my heart creates a pain in every part of my being. Billy and Avery lift Lizzy from the boat and hand her to Alasdair and Isabella. I follow them on to the dock.

Sabby has gone ahead and is leading Jet out of the livery. The first light creeps over the harbour and we see the Black Gladfly breaking the line between sea and sky. It is heading our way and it will not take long, yet how can I leave? How can I set off into the distance and leave such devastation behind? How can I abandon the friends that have given me so much? Trusted me so when all I have done is bring them to danger to satisfy mine own ends? It is as if I am two parts, one already mounted and heading in the direction of Leith, the other travelling in the opposite direction, leaving behind a book that has cost too many lives.

When we are all gathered there is an awkward silence. I know not what to say, what to do. Then it is as if we have one mind and in unison we say, 'Sorry.' Yet for what are they apologising? We are all confused

'How say you?' I blurt out, more from shock than sense.

'We have not secured your love. How will you be?' asks Isabella. Then I remember we were to save a life not a book.

'She was not there, but I now know where she is,' I say and can barely believe my subterfuge.

I cannot believe I am capable of giving voice to such deceit and so easily. All my life I have lived with secrecy, mastered its shadows and walked side by side with the knowledge that to lie is a necessity of life. It has been more game than anything else, a tool that has served us well, yet this feels so different to cheat those that have trusted me so, it is as if I am cheating myself, that I find myself capable of the same depths of betrayal that others have shown me. The lie is necessary, yet I feel it has no integrity. It is as if a stable pillar in my life is taking a new form that I do not understand. It is not pleasant.

'You must go fast then,' says Billy and glances towards the Black Gladfly. I look at him and know I am forgiven and understood yet I do not really understand why or how. I have cost him a companion and a healthy contribution to their troupe.

'Lizzy?' I ask.

'Lizzy died a hero, as she lived,' says Avery and there is not one of us that can deny that.

'We shall make sure she gets a good send off,' says Billy

'She will live on in our hearts and souls,' says Isabella.

'Her funeral shall be the finest,' says Alasdair and he empties his pockets of coins, jewellery and candlesticks stolen from the monastery.

'I wish she were alive to celebrate in the flesh but that was living,' says Alasdair and we all begin to laugh, a deep, heartfelt release. I do not understand it or understand why but I know this shall connect us for all time.

'Here, you shall need supplies,' says Alasdair and pulls out a roasted leg of lamb from under his doublet and we laugh some more. Then the first fishing boats begin to return to harbour.

'I must make haste,' I say and mount Jet without thoughts of farewells such I am jolted back to my purpose.

'You travel alone?' asks Isabella, ready with protestations.

'He has little time and shall be faster without us,' says Billy.

I reach down and claps hands with Alasdair, and Avery, I kiss Isabella on the forehead. I clasp hands with Billy, and we share a look that speaks more and with more depth than any conversation can.

He leans in close. 'We shall distract and delay.'

'Till we meet again,' I say, to all.

'Till we are meet again,' they echo. I look at Sabby and we set off, her pace steady but swift.

As they fall out of sight, so they fall out of my mind as I return to my purpose; all I can see, all I can think of is Grace. Will I be too late? I would feel heartless that so quickly I can leave friends that have served me so well so easily behind. Have I used them or served them? Yet there is no room then in my mind for such consideration. I do not even take pause to reflect upon my success of finding and securing the book. I do not even take time to consider Captain Langan's role. Was he protector? Was he there to return the book to Grace? I know I was not about to take the chance either way.

Sabby leads us across a mix of back routes, tracks and carefully chosen wild land. We rest often for short periods of time, so we may continue through the night. Alasdair served us well with his gift of roasted lamb. We make sure and certain progress, each of us coming together forming one single focus, one single intention. We become one body, three separate, distinct beings shaping one focus. Despite the constant and nagging urgency we are at peace and in full flow with the earth.

As we travel further east the weather eases, the rain ceases, and a crispness fills the air, yet we do not stop but continue on, traveling through the night. It is easy for me to take this partnership for granted, yet our mutual collaboration is a beautiful thing. Survival, yet so much more. By late afternoon the next day we stop on a hill overlooking Edinburgh and beyond to the docks of Leith.

We have worked so hard to get here, to get to this point, we are but a short hour away from our goal and yet we do not push on, do not speed the last few miles. Rather we pause and take the longest break we have taken so far. It is as if we sense this is the ending of something. As if the delivery of the book shall cause a change that we all can sense but do not know what shall befall or where the change shall take us, other than together, for our bond now is unbreakable.

It would be kind and wise and responsible for me to release Jet. I know not what is to befall, if I shall be able to protect and care for him, yet I know he shall not go, know that he has made his choice and whatever befalls us, befalls all of us. Sabby and I share the last of the meat whilst Jet feeds on the heather and sorrel that grows in abundance. We are held by each other in companionable peace. For the first time I let myself consider Lizzy. I expect to feel shame, to feel guilt, to feel the hatred of myself which is so familiar, yet all I feel is a resolve, a deep certainty that her gift to me shall somehow be honoured. We shall do what we must to respect her memory and all that she has given me. I know then that whatever the future holds, we were and are beloved by her and by Grandmother. We shall do what needs to be done. I gather our things and we set off again, refreshed, revived and ready.

Chapter Thirteen

It is night fall by the time we reach Leith. Jet cannot travel with us to Grace's so we leave him at the nearest livery and slip through the lanes and alleyways, Sabby leading the way, for without her I could not fathom this labyrinth. The book burns my chest; it is a throbbing, beating heart of its own that knows it shall soon be home. We resist the temptation to run, keeping in our mind our needs for secrecy. Our senses are sharp for anyone who may be following us, yet we sense no one.

We reach the door and for some reason I do not burst in full of the joy that fills my heart. What if we are too late? What if they have already fled and it is a stranger that opens the door. What if she is fine and lives have been lost for no purpose? Sabby grows impatient at my hesitation and to stop her bark I rap softly on the door. I hear Mother Gray putting pots down, her step more of a heavy shuffle towards the door. My apprehension grows - whatever is behind the door is not well.

She opens the door a crack and I see a drawn and withered face that once was round and full and confident. Sabby pushes the door open and hurtles inside; normally I would chide her for her manners but the light it brings to Mother Gray's face excuses all; it is as if the sun has decided to shine out of her eyes. She abandons care and discretion and falls upon me. I hold her as close as I can. She feels frail and a fraction of the size she was before. Once to be held by her was to be engulfed in soft, comforting flesh supported by a robust structure, now it feels if I let her go she will collapse in a heap. If I squeeze too hard she shall break.

'You have it,' she says, feeling the book against my chest, on her face a look of wonderment and disbelief.

'Did you think I was not good for my word?' I ask with lightness in my tone. She smiles, and I see a glimmer of the woman I know.

'Still with yon cheek, I see,' she says, releasing her hold and standing aside to usher me in. I step inside but can go no further; if Mother Gray has diminished, Grace holds on to life with the thinnest of threads.

'Come, you must need rest and refreshment,' and she indicates for us to take the seat next to the bed.

'We can wait,' I say, as I watch Sabby pace anxiously up and down the side of the bed.

'You know what to do?' asks Mother Gray and, despite my expectations that she shall lead, I find I do know exactly what to do.

'Have you wine and cloves and cinnamon?' I ask.

'We do.'

'Then heat them together. If you have crab apple, add that too,' and Mother Gray gets busy. I undo the buttons on my doublet and ease out the book. It has been so pressed to my skin it is as if I am peeling away a piece of myself. I lay it on the chair and gently unwrap the oilskins.

The inlay on the cover is as beautiful as I remember it; it is as if the book is a beating heart and not tree in the form of pages and cow in the form of leather. It is impossible not to fall in love with it. I consider asking it for instruction on how to heal Grace but fear a blank page will tell us there is no healing to be had. Gently I pull back the covers from Grace. She is skeletal, her skin loose around brittle, tender bones.

'Mother, I need your help,' I say and together we remove Grace's linens. Our touch is gentle for fear one heavy handed gesture shall shatter and splinter her to pieces. Her breath is so slight I think she does not have any, until she omits a sigh and gentle cough.

'Have you lavender?' I ask. Mother Gray looks at me as if I have asked the most insulting thing possible and out of the small cupboard by the bed produces a dried sprig and a bottle of essence. I smile. Of course they have lavender.

'Some essence in warm water?' she asks

'Do not be sparing,' I say, as Mother Gray warms the water. I run my hands up and down Grace's body, not touching but skimming her outline. I gather as much of the stale, putrid energy as I can, and flick it away.

Soon the air is heady with mulling wine and lavender steam. We tear a little of Grace's linens and soak them in lavender water. Together we wash and cleanse her from head to toe. A little colour returns to her skin but there are still no real signs of life. We place the dried lavender around her body. I pick up the book and stand at the foot of the bed.

'Spirit of the Book of Knowledge, we call on you to guide our beloved Grace to health or afterlife, whichever is her calling.'

Mother Gray does not look best pleased with the latter and would protest but my look is firm but kind. She knows it is not for us to ask for what we want but our love for Grace demands we want what is for her.

I skim the book over Grace's feet and along her legs. I place it momentarily on her pubic bone and let the energies connect. I place the book on her belly, then her heart and her forehead, laying it to rest finally on her heart. We fold her hands over the book to keep it in place and create a circuit of energy. Then we cover her in blankets.

I sink down into the chair; there is nothing more we can do now but wait to see which is her path - life or afterlife. I feel the weight of the last few days fall away from me. If it were left to my body I would fall into a deep motionless sleep for days, yet my mind and spirit are alert, waiting on every breath Grace takes. Mother Gray hands me a tankard of mulled wine

'For us, I take it,' she says.

'And for when...' but I do not finish, the book shall revive her if it is called upon.

Mother Gray takes her tankard and sits on the opposite side of the fire from me. Sabby has taken a place on the bed, lying at Grace's feet; her snores are reassuring. I take her peaceful slumber as a good omen or at least reassurance that we have done all that we can and all that we should. I ignore that I have without consciousness returned, at least temporarily, to the ways of the earth.

We sit in companionable silence for a while and then both speak at the same time.

'Are we safe here?' And we laugh a gentle laugh.

'Do they know you have the book?'

'The Society or the crown?' I ask.

'Both.'

'I do not know. I think both are in pursuit.' I tell her as succinctly as I can of the events of the last few days.

'Billy and the troupe shall divert the Society and the royalty I cannot speak for. Now it is time for you to speak,' I say.

'You want to know how we are here?' she asks. I nod. 'It's a long story.'

'We have all night,' I say, indicating Grace.

She takes a moment to compose herself and then begins.

'I had always known her, long before we met in person. She had always been a presence in my life. Unnamed, unidentified, till we met, she has always lived inside me. I am not possessed rather inhabited as if everything I am is shared. I knew it, felt it and accepted it. Yet back then these things were not feared but understood, not explained; who needs explanations when there is understanding?

'Some folk would say we lived simply, my family and I, our remote location a privation. Yet we were able to keep to the old ways, mostly. We had time and space to listen, to work in partnership with the earth. Some would look at how we lived and consider it deprivation yet to us there was no end to the abundance offered to us by the earth. We knew nothing of scriptures but everything about what they call God. We were foolish though, for all our wisdom, we did not heed the warnings. Did not believe the stories our neighbours told of the way of things, the way things were changing. How could such stories be true? Why would they be true when we had all we could ever need or want?

'When they came, they destroyed everything. It took them minutes to dismantle our entire lives. Everything we had created was eradicated. My father and brothers did what they could. I was but a slip of a girl, hidden for safety, hidden because I could be, and the others couldn't. Hidden in the hope that I was forgotten, and I was. Yet through the slats in the basket I watched as they beat my father to death, sliced open my brothers' innards, raped my sisters and mother until their bodies lay motionless and debased. They set fire to the remains of our dwelling and rode off, content and satisfied with their domination, their good day's work.

'As soon as the last horse was out of sight, I leapt from my basket and raced flames to my safety. I stood shivering, despite the heat, till the flames consumed all that had been my life. I could hear someone crying but did not know then it was my own voice that wailed.

I must have surrendered to darkness for I do not remember what happened next, just that I awoke in a bed, in a room made of stone, a first for both. I think then that I must have been captured by the murderers of my family. I am dressed in linens and a fancy dress is laid by the side of the bed. I decide it is best I make my escape when I hear light eager footsteps clattering down the corridor. I jump back into the bed and pull the covers over, try to remember how I was when I awoke.

'She flings open the door, runs and jumps onto the bed, on top of me. I freeze.

"Do not pretend," she says, "I know you are awake," and she kisses me, and I cannot help my eyes from snapping open.

'She grins broadly. "I see you are a tease." I try to speak but no words come.

"I am Grace and I shall call you Bunmi," and she kisses me again. "I've been waiting for you for so long, but I shall not chide you for it. You got here as quick as you could." Before I can respond we are interrupted by a frantic nurse who bursts, panting, into the room.

'Later the nurse tells me they found me in the gardens sitting amongst the herbs, with a tearstained face and clothes darkened by smoke. Neither conscious nor unconscious. It wasn't hard for them to put events together; her parents had more eyes for each other than for God, Grace simply had to claim me as a friend for them to open their home to me. Grace always says she called me to her and that is how I found my way to the herb garden, and maybe that is so, for there has never been another explanation.

'After that we were inseparable, for I recognised her instantly, the other part of me. For all my advance on years it is Grace that teaches me. She that helps me to read so we may take lessons together. We sleep in the same bed, share our clothes, our food. Her parents are loving but otherwise engaged, our lessons take but a fraction of the day and we have a whole manor house and grounds for our adventures. We have quarrels, sometimes petty squabbles over who had the biggest share, sometimes because something in the present takes me to the past and I am lost in a sea of emotion. Yet there is not a time when she loses her love and her compassion. She holds me even when I do not think I want to be held.

'It is not one way though. When her mother dies in childbirth to her stillborn brother, I know only the earth can heal and I teach her the ways of Mother Earth. Then the earth begins to teach us, to share her wisdom, to guide us in our endeavours. After her mother's death we are left more or less to our own devices. We stop going to church and when the vicar complains her father banishes him from the house, such is his grief, he has lost all faith in God. We try to reach him, to teach him how the earth can heal the deepest wound, yet he has chosen another poison to soothe his injury and has even less time for us than before.

'We grow entwined together. We mature into womanhood with the guidance of the earth. We each have our suitors and champions. None that are a match, of course. Grace's beauty far outshines my own, it is well, I have my own beauty, but Grace's was always more to popular tastes than mine own. Anyway, we both knew, without even thinking or speaking about it, that marriage was not our destiny even if love was.'

She pauses, lost in remembered romances. Grace lets out what sounds like a sigh and we both turn to look. But there is no further movement, no further sound. It is as if even now they travel in harmony and the remembrance of a lover has passed over Grace as it has passed over Mother Gray.

'One night after the refusal of yet another eager, yet unsuitable suitor we decide to discover our purpose.'

'But -' I say, for surely they are their own suitors?

'But never you mind,' says Mother Gray and I do not understand why she will not confide in another such as herself for surely their love is more than sister or companion? Then I am ashamed - maybe I am supposed to know, to understand and know not to speak of it. I do not press further.

'We wait until the midnight hour, gather our offerings to the spirits and guides. We are given our purpose instantly; it is so clear we are almost ashamed we had not seen it before. Our house has a library with empty shelves, and we have a duty to gather all the teachings we can, so that, when humankind remembers it is not the master of the earth but its guest, the wisdom to live differently shall be at hand. We shall rescue, protect and defend the ancient wisdoms. To the world we become collectors.

'Her father rarely ventures far from his whiskey or his study. He does not notice our absences. We leave the charge of the house and grounds to the housekeeper, who has really been the one to raise us, and set off on our adventures. Even then women had their freedom curtailed. Turned from warriors into skivvies. It was not fit for two women to travel alone and it is then the adventures begin. We concocted all manner of ways to hide in plain sight, disguises and personas. One time I am an aged aunty traveling for her health accompanied by her doting niece, another time Grace is a chivalrous, dashing hero of the seas.

'There was not a part of the known world we did not travel to. We sought out forgotten tribes, hidden in inhospitable mountains, and wrote down their secrets and wisdom. Bargained with dealers of stolen antiquities in back street dens of capital cities to secure ancient texts.

'We knew little of what we were doing, yet learnt as we went, our ignorance our protection. When I think back now, knowing what I now know, I would never do even half of what we did, yet they were times of great joy that I would not exchange for all time.

'It was then we discovered the Book of Knowledge and Alfredo, Grace's husband, it was then everything changed. We had, by then, acquired quite a mass of books, most of the library,'

And she pauses, as I do, the fire that destroyed the library still a raw and open wound for us both. I watch her fight back tears, her life's work, her youth literally up in smoke at the hands of an angry mob.

'It is the loss of wisdom that devastates the most. Things that shall take us centuries to re-discover lost in one night. Whole cultures and peoples lost for all eternity as if they never were. Leaving huge gaps in our consciousness; it is a tragedy that most shall be ignorant of or not even recognise as such.'

Grace lets out another sigh and Mother Gray rises and goes to her side, her gaze a complete manifestation of love. She takes a silk cloth, dabs it with some lavender oil, and with utmost tenderness strokes Grace's forehead with it, then sits down on the bed next to her.

'Theirs was a unique love, unquestioned devotion on both sides, almost instantly. He himself was unique, the only man I have ever met not interested in domination in any way. Oh, he was not weak, not passive, but he expected negotiation and if you could negotiate all was well.

'We had heard tell of the Book of Knowledge, it was almost mythical in status, likened to the oracle stolen from Gaea, mother of the earth, by Apollo God of war. It was said it was a book so powerful that in the wrong hands it could end all that we know. Yet it was said that it would only travel with those that it chose, said for those it did not that it would appear as nothing, be overlooked and so it was with us.

'It was in a house sale in Paris, an aged spinster of some wealth. We often found great treasures hidden and unrecognised amongst the other "more valuable" items. Yet it was not hidden or buried in a box in the attic or cellar but in plain sight. Left open on a table in the withdrawing chamber. The sale was well attended with many people glancing at the book and seeing empty pages. Yet as soon as we arrived, we could feel it, feel its energy. We knew it was special, in all our adventures nothing had shone forth as this did. Trying to look nonchalant, we approached the table. It was Grace who opened the cover, the pages bursting forth with colour and welcome.

'We fell instantly and when we finally managed to tear our eyes away from the pages we noticed Alfredo and we knew he too had seen. From that point on we were bound by an unspeakable, unbreakable bond. Later we discovered we had all seen something different on the pages.'

She squeezes Grace's hand, gets up and refills our tankards with mulled wine and warms herself by the fire.

'Their marriage was an obvious destiny and within a year we had sold up the estate in Scotland - her father was long since passed by then - and set up the home in middle England. We thought it afforded us the most protection. A small neglected backwater away from the endless battles between Scotland and England with easy access to the sea and the rest of the world. It was heart-breaking to leave Scotland and the home that had afforded us such freedom, but by then we spent so little time at home we thought we just needed a base, and so it was for a time.

'There was not a soul who was not charmed by them. They were a beautiful couple. We entertained the right people the right way which afforded us privileges to travel that would not be tolerated for others.'

She sits back down by the fire.

'But we became careless, forgot to read the signs, forgot to be aware, so secure we were in the world we had created, we lost sight that whilst we grew closer to the earth, others grew further away. It was on a trip to Germany that Alfredo was lost to us.' She cannot speak more.

I reach out my hand to take hers, but she snatches it away for the fear of the tears my touch would release. I do not press further, thinking I will have the opportunity another time for further detail.

'After that Grace started the Society -' I cannot help but interject.

'Grace, the Society is under Grace's leadership?' I ask, incredulous in my disbelief that she is at the heart of all that has betrayed me.

'If that were so would we be here now?' asks Mother Gray, affronted at such an allegation.

We lock eyes for as long as it takes for understanding to flow between us. She has been betrayed by her own creation, the creation that was supposed to offer protection. It is clear they are as much on the run as we. It is well we did not trust the captain, did not turn to him for assistance. To my horror it means we have little time and confirms we are fleeing two foes. It is but a matter of time before they arrive at our door.

'We must move fast,' I say. 'At first light we must leave. I'll service a carriage so Grace...'

'We must wait first,' Mother Gray says and I know she is right.

We must wait to see if Grace makes it through the night, knowing that by daybreak someone, be it the captain or Stephen, shall be at our door. I am pinned to my chair, overwhelmed by a sense of dread and anticipation of a fearful end, sitting like inanimate targets awaiting our own annihilation.

I want to run, to take arms, to do something. To do nothing but wait is the cruellest torture. There must be something to be done? To have come so far, to have been granted life whilst others have fallen. For the ways of the earth to be lost or corrupted for all time by ignorance of those that think they know. The weight of this responsibility pins me to my seat. None of this is of my choosing. I do not understand how it is my shoulders that must carry such burden.

'And the book? How are we here?' I ask.

She nods acknowledgement, she seems pleased, as if I have passed some sort of test. This simply adds anger to the myriad of emotions that swamp me.

'When we fled the fire, it was not just Stephen and the forces of the new regime we fled. We took only the Book of Knowledge, for over the years we have learnt something of its power, in the wrong hands...' She pauses, the consequences unimaginable for limited consciousnesses.

'At first they did not know. It was never anything we spoke about, rather we both just knew not to tell anyone in the Society. The book is world-renowned, all be it more rumour than fact. It is a sought-after prize more valued for its power than its teachings. You were the first person that we ever shared the Book of Knowledge with. Our entire house had been designed around the protection of that book. The secret escape, a secret entrance too and it was through it that the book arrived in the dead of night.'

'Yet it is a different book for all who view it. What is its power?'

'Therein lies its power. What do you know?'

I laugh. 'Very little it seems.'

'It is so, what can any of us really know? Yet ask the book and it shall tell you. It is both a reflection and a direction. It is what is done with the knowledge wherein lies the danger. The book is but a gateway to all that is known, all that can be known and all that cannot.'

'And in the wrong hands...'

'It takes great strength and wisdom to wield such knowledge, for it is a heady, greedy sensation that is too easy to be lost to.'

'And Grace is it's guardian?'

'It is so; everything in our lives led us to the book, from the first instruction to build a library, from before even.'

'And yet you did not trust the Society?'

'We knew its power because we had lived its power.'

'Alfredo?'

'Alfredo. At first it was almost a game. We could ask anything, and it gave the answer. What boat we should take, what port at which to dock. Yet his hunger grew with each question, his thirst becoming need till he thought himself the book, thought himself knowledge, thought he knew. We ceased to exist for him, in the end all things ceased to exist for him until he ceased to exist for himself. Then it was just a matter of time. He had been long dead to the earth by the time his body passed.

'Still the end hit us both hard, a shock even though we expected it. The morning we found him, it was like he was but a shell, there was flesh and bones, but they were hollow and empty. I could pick him up, easily, so empty was he. The book lay on the table next to him open, as if it was just a book. The pages were blank to me but not to Grace. Her connection with the book had always been strong.

'None of us ever said anything but we all knew it was to her the book belonged, to her the book spoke. I think that's one of the reasons it took Alfredo. He wanted access in the same way as Grace and never understood that Grace was the custodian and not he. Had he been a different man it is Grace who would have been found dead and not he. For her bond with the book is unbreakable; after she finished reading the pages, her face expressionless, the pages closed of their own accord, the cover snapped shut and the book leapt off the table and to her chest. Her face was as full of shock as mine.'

'And? What had the pages said?'

'I have not asked, nor shall I.'

'And the book?'

'We kept it safe and never looked at it again. It was never far from Grace, but she did not seek its wisdom again. It was the first time, the day she introduced you to the book, it was the first time, since that day, she had looked at it.'

'Such is her bond with the book?'

'When the Society found out, the night we fled the fire. When they saw we had had the book all along they were furious. They could not understand why we had not told them. Why we had not used the book to stop our demise. That itself reason enough, their ignorance of their own weaknesses, reason enough.

'Lord Affrington, as he was the public face of the Society, had for some time sought to challenge Grace's leadership, as much enamoured by the story of male dominance as any of his god-fearing counterparts, despite it being against all teachings of the earth. Yet knowledge can blind as well as illuminate and so it is with them.

'We knew it would not be easy once we had lost our base and the library. At first their approach was to ingratiate. We were treated with respect, our comfort a prior consideration. Just as it should be though, nothing in excess of our seniority.

At first, we were taken to a safe house in Berwick. It was there that the trouble began.

'They wanted answers, wanted the book to give them answers. They thought with the book they could claim the power they believe themselves entitled to. It was as if all their talk of equanimity, of living as one with the earth and understanding our humility, our place as guests not hosts had evaporated into thin air or had never really been true for them. The change was so sudden, if I had not witnessed it I would not have believed it.'

'Maybe Alfredo was stronger than you thought,' I say.

'Maybe so, for each and every one of them - Lord Affrington, Astral, Captain Langan, Philip, Squire Farthingale, the Tanner - all became strangers overnight. They made all sorts of offers, promised us all manner of things, things not within in their gift to give, not within anyone's gift. Grace gave instruction, she ordered Captain Langan to dispatch his best men to engineer your escape. We were told he had. We awaited your arrival and then planned a midnight flit, planned to take the captain's ship from him right under his nose.'

'Good plan,' I say and how I wish that had come to pass.

'After a week we knew we were being lied to, that whilst they pretended Grace was still in charge a mutiny had taken place and we were prisoners. I was furious, strode briskly to the front door to "take the air" and was gently but firmly guided back indoors, the weather being far to "inclement for my constitution". Have you ever heard such stuff and nonsense?' I cannot help but laugh, a tempest wouldn't take on Mother Gray.

'Grace had a job that day. It took her the best part of the day to talk me down. I was ready to burn all down, whether we survived or not, at the very least. If I'd had my way I would have taken the heads off all of them with a blunt sword until one of them killed me. Which I would not have minded, but how could I do that to Grace? Her strength is unrivalled but there is not an ounce of violence in her which is her strength and her weakness.'

At that Grace sighs as if she is tired of hearing this argument again. The look in Mother Gray's eyes is heartbreaking, I have never seen such devotion, except maybe when I have caught myself gazing at Sabby.

'We could not believe they intended you to die at the hands of Stephen and Ben, but we could not find a way to help you. It matters little perhaps but we did spend our days thinking of plans we could not execute to rescue you. Please, you must understand we were as much prisoner as you?'

Then she takes my hands, searching my face for forgiveness. I know I should grant it, know I should be able to have compassion with their plight but whilst I know it I do not feel it. Why did they not do more no matter the sacrifice to themselves? In the end I say,

'Go on,' and for the time being she leaves it at that.

'The night we heard of your escape was the end of the pretence. I cannot tell you how proud we were though. So spectacular, you shall be a legend. A true warrior of the earth.' She beams at me full of a pride that I do not think she should claim. Still, I cannot help but blush.

'It was all in the timing,' I say. 'The rope was around my neck, the whole town, the whole shire gathered waiting to see the she-devil destroyed. And it was so simple, so obvious. I just remembered who I was, and the shift began. I had forgotten who I was, but the ravens had not. I was so proud and grateful to them. It was joyous the way they dived at the crowd.' We share a naughty giggle that settles into a moment of intimacy that both of us quickly dismiss.

'That night they demanded we use the book to give them guidance, said that surely now the situation warranted it. I did not expect it, but Grace agreed, said she would consult, said she was the only one that could. For a time they believed her for when we let them view the book all they saw was empty pages. We thought if we could get you to safety the deceit would be forgiven. We knew Stephen and Ben would be in pursuit. We had already dispatched of several of their spies who had been in search of us. For a while it brought us time, appearing to take instruction from the book. We were able to regain some control and even had aspirations that we would be able to restore the Society to its former purpose.

'Then the crown in the shape of Stephen and Ben took Berwick. I do not know if they suspected we were there or if it was part of a larger stratagem, but our safe house was no longer safe. It all happened so fast, that night, the king's men arriving, the preparations for us to leave. They wanted to take the book, to secure it, to ensure Stephen and Ben never knew of it, but I think they knew all along. I think that is what drew them to our town in the first place. Why else target that town out of the many forgotten backwaters?'

'And so?'

'And so Stephens and Ben's men were ransacking all the houses. We had but minutes. We wanted to keep hold of the book, needed to keep hold of the book - our lives depended on it. Everybody's life depended on it.' She stops and looks down, unable to meet my gaze.

'Go on,' I say, but I am not sure I want her to.

'Forgive us, we told them only custodians of the book knew its secrets.' She looks at me with wide and hopeful eyes.

'They think me a custodian?' She nods her head, her eyes to the floor.

'That night we both dispatched homing pigeons. Ours to Constantine, theirs to Captain Langan.' The sound of the rock pigeon cooing in my tiny room at the inn in the docks of London echoes eerily around my being.

'They did not hear her soul scream when they took the book from her. They did not see the devastation at their fingertips, so certain were they that they knew best. She held a protective charm over the book, but it was only makeshift. It is that, in part, that endangers her so.' We both turn to Grace and her frail empty frame.

'Our lives were spared only so in the direst of need they could call upon us to advise and rescue them, the separation from the book making us prisoners of ourselves. At first it was manageable, she could maintain connection with the book. But then we knew they had taken the book to a powerful place to test it out, to master its ways, for the connection was severed. That's when she got really weak.'

'And they thought I would do their bidding?'

'Thought we would be ransom, our lives for your knowledge.'

'Do they learn nothing? When have I ever been compliant?'

She laughs. 'They thought you eaten by a whale not to have become a whale.' At that we cannot help but laugh again, long and hard, at which point Sabby wakes from her slumbers as if there is not a care in the world to be had.

She stretches and jumps down from the bed. I am at once reassured by her nonchalance and also infuriated. Can she not see our predicament? Yet I pat her and pour her some ale, none the less. As she drinks, I see first light begin to creep under the door and through the cracks in the shutters.

'And is there no wine for me?' asks a quiet but recognisable voice and we all turn to face Grace. She has awoken, her face turned towards us, a gentle, teasing smile on her lips. Mother Gray rushes to her side and begins to fuss over her. Relief and love surge through my being; I am at once exhausted and exhilarated. It is as if Grace herself has brought light back into the world. I approach her, and clasp hold of her hand. She smiles at me; she is weak but full of love and even now she is grace personified.

'Thank you,' she says.

'It is an honour to be of service,' I reply. I would take her in my arms and hold her tight, yet I fear she will break into pieces if I do. The love we exchange through looks shall have to suffice for the time being. We are held for a moment by deep peace. She unclenches her fist and I see the hair I cut and sent with crow. It is such comfort to know she knew all along we were on our way.

It is then I feel it. Sabby has dropped her ease; she hunkers down and slinks towards the window. Despite the joy and relief that soars through my being, I sense an eerie stillness in the quiet pause. I hear the sound of a horse snorting. My first thought is that Jet has come to our aid, and I almost throw open the door to welcome him to our happy union, yet caution and Sabby guide my actions otherwise.

Making sure my shadow is out of sight, I peer through the cracks in the shutters. I glance one way and see Captain Langan, propped up on sticks, with a face so swollen it is hard to identify him, his bones held together with bandages. He resembles more mummy than living being, yet he stands determinedly with his men. This must be of greater importance than life and death for him to summon such will. I glance the other way and see Stephen and his men. We are surrounded on all sides. Whilst we have reminisced, they have taken up position. How long have they been there?

Chapter Fourteen

I step away from the shutter. I have half a mind to step outside and let them fight it out between themselves, let them slaughter each other for the prize of me. Maybe the battle would take my life, and everyone would be safe once more. Yet to my surprise I feel the thought as a betrayal of myself, that somehow I negate the pain I have eased in favour of the pain I have caused. It does not help me form a plan, yet it does encourage a commitment to a plan that saves us all and not one at my expense.

Mother Gray is pouring some wine for Grace. I take the tankard from her and with a subtle nod of my head indicate for her to look out of the shutters.

'It is well you have decided to return to us,' I say, turning to Grace with a wink in my voice whilst Mother Gray finds an excuse to approach the window.

Mother Gray has helped Grace sit up and I hold the wine to her lips. She raises her hands and places them over mine. She holds my gaze and with honest simplicity says, 'I shall be forever grateful for you,' it is one of the most treasured moments of my life, to have been of service to one who has given me so much. It is all the accolade I shall ever need. I try not to think that a moment ago I was prepared to throw myself away. I cannot speak in return, but nod my head briefly as if she has said that the weather is fine today. I let her take the tankard from me and sit down next to her; she drinks slowly but with intention.

Mother Gray comes and sits down on the other side of the bed and we exchange a glance. Grace finishes the wine and Mother Gray takes the tankard; such is the synergy between them I wonder if, when alone together, they ever have cause for speech. Grace leans back and closes her eyes. I indicate for Mother Gray to join me at the fire, so we may speak, but, without opening her eyes, Grace says,

'There is no secret passage; this time our escape calls for a different approach.' Both Mother Gray and I laugh - it is good that Grace is back. She opens her eyes and looks at us both.

'We are under siege,' I say. 'Maybe we can last longer than them?'

I know this is not true before I say it, yet I do not see another way. To move is certain death, to stay put is certain death. We are trapped, yet it cannot end so. Lizzy gave her life, so Grace could live, so we all could live. We cannot betray her sacrifice. I look at Grace; has she the strength, even if, somehow, we find an escape route?

'How long will our supplies last?' I ask and Mother Gray shakes her head as tears begin to fight for release from her being. I reach out to comfort her, but she snatches her hand away and takes herself off to a corner, the only hope of privacy in our close quarters. Already the room feels half the size, as if we have all been in each other's company far too long and the walls have begun to move in on us.

I look at Grace; she is reviving but there is still some way to go before she will be on her feet. I go to the fire and ladle pottage into a bowl and take it to her. She holds my hand as she takes the bowl.

'I'm sorry,' she says. I look at her, bemused. What has she to be sorry for?

'We should not have left you, you should have come with us. It was up to us to protect you and we did not. I'm sorry.'

It is as if a damn has broken inside me and I am flooded with all the emotions, all the loss I have been trying to deny. If this were water it would be our way out, our escape. We could simply wash away our captors with a tsunami of emotions.

I too turn away, unable to respond. I want to absolve her, receive her apology, yet all I feel is anger and confusion. By her own admission she betrayed me, yet she still asked for my help when at death's door. Further, I gave it without question and at great cost to all. I have no sense for any of it, no rhyme or reason, how one moment her gratitude is all the validation I need and how now I feel she has done nothing but betray us. There is no need for battle when such war rages inside me.

Sabby growls deep and menacing, bringing clarity to my thoughts. I am brought back into the present and there is a simplicity in it.

'Do you have a place to go? Have you a place of safety we can aim for?' I ask Mother Gray, who has composed herself and begun to aid Grace in dressing.

'We were en route to the woods of my birth,' says Mother Gray. 'People who live there, live there to be alone. We shall be undisturbed and unquestioned there.'

'Further north?' I ask.

'Two, maybe three days, with good weather.'

'The book must be protected at all costs,' says Grace. 'It cannot fall into the wrong hands.'

Then it is clear it is not us they are interested in, it is the book. The book is our downfall and our redemption. Part of me seeks to hand over the book - just give it to them and let them fight it out. Let them destroy each other for its ownership. But even I can tell this would be the start of a war with no end. I think of all the shifting I can yet there is nothing that secures the safety of all five of us, not when all armoury known to man is pointed at us. I think to call upon fire yet to do so when in such close quarters to others would be to start a massacre that would risk ourselves as soon as others. We are defenceless and, in my panic, I come to detest the book, to detest all and everything that has brought us to this point - the benign ways of the earth, the malignant ways of mankind, love, greed, compassion and heartlessness. What difference does any of it make when all comes to this, our lives spent for the ignorance of others? Fury fills every part of my being, so I no longer see what is before me, so I no longer care for reason or strategy. I seize the book and it is my intention to throw it in the fire.

'Wait,' says Grace and despite all I would like to think about myself, I stop dead in my tracks. Mother Gray takes a log from the woodpile and alights it in the fire like a torch. I think it is she who seeks to set fire to the book and what was a moment ago my resolute intention is now the opposite. I hold the book close to my chest. If she wants it, she shall have to take me first.

'If we go, we go together,' says Grace and she holds out her hand for the book. 'We shall not leave you again, Raven.'

'We have all had lessons to learn,' says Mother Gray and reluctantly I hand over the book.

'What takes you so long?' shouts Captain Langan from outside.

'Wolf got your tongue?' asks Ben and we hear at least twenty men laugh and snigger, confident in the triumph they think they already have.

'Are we as one?' asks Grace, finding strength in her steps as she walks towards the door where Sabby is already waiting. I know not what to do. I want with every part of me to trust, to feel this connection, to be one with them, yet do not know how to, how to make that leap. Then a rifle butt bangs against the door to the pattern of Captain Langan's knock.

'We know you are home,' he shouts.

'Pretty wenches, surrender, and we shall leave your pretty faces intact,' says Stephen. It's all I need - without hesitation I stride over to the door and fling it open.

The guard scatters in surprise and fear as I walk boldly into the centre of the courtyard, followed by Sabby, Mother Gray and Grace. We take position, forming a tight small circle. To our left are Stephen, Ben and their men, to our right Captain Langan and his men. We are surrounded on all sides. I know I should be frightened, know I should feel defeated, yet I am consumed by a brilliant, bold and glowing defiance. I care little for what happens, but everything for this rebellion.

A look of satisfaction passes between Stephen, Ben and Captain Langan and it takes me all my will to stay in my spot and not rush to wipe the supercilious pride from their faces.

'Gentlemen, we are well met, how can we help you?' asks Grace in the sweetest, softest voice she can.

'Grace, we seek you no harm,' says Captain Langan and I almost believe him. 'Ye know what it is we seek.'

'Captain Langan is right, we only offer our protection to such a valuable treasure,' says Stephen.

The tension between them is palpable. I have a small sense of gratification they are such uneasy bedfellows. It has cost them both dearly to join forces. Yet it is mitigated; such is their conviction that the Book of Knowledge cannot be in the care of a woman that they sacrifice all else. A vile, bitter, stale taste fills my mouth, such is my disgust. I should pity them but why should I afford such generosity when generosity is not part of their vocabulary.

'Gentleman, your concern is noted, your chivalry applauded, yet we do not require such attention. We are at peace and wish to remain so. If you will excuse us,' Grace says, and she motions for us to walk way.

Instantly all are on guard; Stephen and Ben cock their pistols. I stand before Grace, ready to defend with all and anything, including my life. In my mind I run through all the beasts I could be, but cannot settle on one and conclude I must have faith that my intuition shall know.

'We shall grant you access, we shall just be the keepers,' says Captain Langan, yet a glance between Stephen and Ben tells otherwise.

I want to smash their skulls together – how stupid do they think we are? Grace merely smiles and begins to walk again. The troops step closer, tightening the circle that encloses us and firmly blocking all escape routes.

'You waste all our time, madam, the book shall be ours. You can leave with your lives intact or not, it is up to you. It matters little to us,' says Ben, taking aim at Mother Gray.

He means to pick us off one by one and enjoy every minute. One day it shall be just him and me and I shall chop off his hands and gouge out his eyes and leave him to wander the wilderness alone.

'Gentlemen, the book is not my gift to give. I cannot give you what you cannot have. I'm sorry but we really must be on our way.'

We follow Grace as she takes another step, as do they.

'Woman, I grow tired of this nonsense. This, gentleman, is the Devil's work.' He points to us.

I laugh, for if there is such a thing then surely it is he that is the Devil, surely it is he that defiles his own God. Sabby hunches down and snarls as Ben pushes his horse closer.

'Silence, wench.' Yet his horse will not advance.

'Grace, please,' pleads Captain Langan; he thinks he shall have a say in the book's future, but his naivety is evidence that he shall not.

I consider again the bloodbath that would ensure if we just gave them the book and think it a shame it is not a reasonable stratagem.

'Enough,' snaps Stephen. 'Guards,' and his right-hand men approach; we are pushed tighter together.

Grace holds up the book and Mother Gray the torch. Everything stops. Then it is Stephen's turn to laugh, his guffaws splitting the stillness, tearing apart my soul. Why have we no power to stop them? Gradually all the men follow his lead, his hilarity infectious. We are surrounded by a wall of mockery. I have never felt so useless in all my life. Grace and Mother Gray hold fast but I see their resolve is weakening. Grace does not have the strength to hold on much longer. I know it is I that must do something but cannot see what I can do.

With a flick of his hand, Stephen silences the men. All that can be heard is the flame of the torch dancing and biting in the fresh morning air. Stephen, Ben and Captain Langan raise their pistols, one pointed at each of us. Sabby is frantic, ready to pounce, but who should she pounce at?

'This is your last warning, lay down the book,' commands Stephen and Captain Langan cocks his pistol, yet what point is there, they shall kill us all anyway.

I glance at Grace and Mother Gray, resolute in their defiance. If we go down, we shall go down together. We may have lost, and we shall most certainly lose our lives, yet we shall go with dignity, integrity and honour. True to ourselves. Others shall see us as victims or fools or both, yet I am filled with a sense of glory. They may be the victors, but it is us that are the champions.

I turn back to Stephen, Ben and Captain Langan and smile, free of all fear, let them do what they will. I cannot explain why but I have a strong sensation that they do not matter at all; it is as if it is they that are nothing. I have no prior warning of my actions, yet my mouth opens and out of it comes the most beautiful, ethereal sound I have ever heard, it is as if all the heavens speak through me. I have become a vessel for this song and gladly I open up to it, surrender to it and as I do I feel the heat of the desert and the smell of sun-drenched sand.

At first, they are a little startled and shift uncomfortably in their seats, swapping nervous glances. Yet my song just grows louder and stronger, the notes and cadences shifting and undulating. I make sounds I did not know existed. Mother Gray and Grace join me, becoming one sound, rich and full, beautiful and also slightly comic. Stephen and his men do not hold back and let themselves succumb to laughter, this time felt and not forced. They think we just humiliate ourselves further, yet Captain Langan does not. He tries to hide a look of deep fear and as quietly and subtly as he can, he and his men begin to retreat.

Our voices grow, invigorating and energising as we open ourselves to the song of the earth, yet there is no sand to shift, no tribe to multiply this force. I do not know what this shall do, but I cannot and do not stop. It is not that I carry the song but that the song carries me. It is so loud and so free it feels like the whole world must hear it.

Then it begins, at first a tremble underfoot, getting louder and stronger. The buildings begin to shake, and we sing on. Then the thunder of a multitude of horses' hooves pounding the earth approaches. Then the horses before us begin to rear and scatter, shaking loose their riders and trampling them under foot. It is as if years of servitude are released and every whip, every beating, every humiliation they have received is now being returned, three-fold. Windows splinter, shattering glass in all directions. Parts of buildings begin to fall.

Captain Langan has given the signal and his men flee in all and any direction as storming into the courtyard is Jet, joined by every horse in the livery and others who have heard our song and joined along the way. Chaos swirls around us as men scatter, as men fall, as men trample over each other in search of safety. Dust billows around us and still we sing untouched and unharmed, our voices loud and strong, forming one sound with the earth. Each breath, each sound, an eternity, each breath, each sound, a fleeting moment. All is as it is.

I have no sensation of time, but it must take just minutes for the courtyard to clear. I do not see Stephen and Ben go but they must have for there is not a man in sight once the dust begins to settle. Gradually the buildings come to rest in their destruction, gradually all the horses leave bar Jet and a Shetland pony, free to form their own herd and find their own paths. Gradually our song comes to a close, softening in cadence and volume till we are brought back into our own bodies, our voices still and at peace. I stand with my eyes closed, drinking in the peace and sensation. Gradually I turn to face the others as they turn to face me. Our eyes meet and we cannot help it, at first it is just a twitch from deep inside me, then a rumble that grows in force, and before I can question it we all burst into laughter, a long deep, belly-holding, floor-rolling laughter. It is at once a release and a joyous recognition of triumph. The earth's song sung to serve us.

I hear the cry of a raven overhead and know that from above they shall see three women turned toward each other lost in hilarity, lost in each other as the circle of dust that surrounds them settles and a wolf, a horse and a pony look calmly and patiently on. There are some that would call them witches but I know raven knows of no such word.

Rachel McJury

Rachel has worked for many years within the arts environment initiating, leading and managing a wide range of projects but with specific experience of cross-artform events that have brought together poetry, dance, theatre, music and film. To date, she has written, directed and produced ten theatre and musical productions. She has performed her poetry at a variety of locations across Britain and Europe from Brighton to Dundee to Dublin. Her poems and short stories have been published in: Chameleon, Nomad, Cutting Teeth, Citizen 32, Poetry Scotland, The Gay Read, Hidden City, Mookychick and her collection of poetry *Laughin' Lesbians Vol 1*. In 2006 she received the Jackie Forster Memorial Pride Award for outstanding contribution to culture in Scotland.

Printed in Great Britain
by Amazon

46546402R00116